Y0-CBG-203

PRAISE FOR STEPHEN GREENLEAF AND *DEATH BED*

"AS GOOD A PRIVATE-EYE NOVEL AS ANYONE IS GOING TO ENCOUNTER."
Newgate Callendar
The New York Times Book Review

"ALL THE RIGHT COMPONENTS ARE HERE—VIOLENCE AND SEX, INTELLECTUAL DEDUCTION AND GOOD GUESSES, WIT AND CYNICISM—PLUS LOTS OF SURPRISES!"
New York Magazine

"MR. GREENLEAF IS A REAL WRITER WITH REAL TALENT!"
The New Yorker

Also by Stephen Greenleaf
Published by Ballantine Books:

FATAL OBSESSION

GRAVE ERROR

STATE'S EVIDENCE

DEATH BED

A DETECTIVE STORY

Stephen Greenleaf

BALLANTINE BOOKS • NEW YORK

Copyright © 1980 by Stephen H. Greenleaf

All rights reserved. No part of this book may be reproduced or transmitted in any form or by any means, electronic or mechanical, including photocopying, recording or by any information storage and retrieval system, without the written permission of the Publisher, except where permitted by law. Published in the United States by Ballantine Books, a division of Random House, Inc., New York, and simultaneously in Canada by Random House of Canada Limited, Toronto.

Library of Congress Catalog Card Number: 80-15437

ISBN: 0-345-32742-X

This edition published by arrangement with
Doubleday & Co., Inc.

Printed in Canada

First Ballantine Books Edition: June 1982
Third Printing: April 1985

To my mother and,
in memoriam,
my father

One

We had been sitting in the room for close to an hour, talking about this and that—the Warriors, the Democrats, Mozart, Montaigne. I was a nondescript private eye who could stuff all of his assets into some carry-on luggage if he owned any carry-on luggage, and he was one of the ten wealthiest men in the city if you didn't count the Chinese. He had everything money could buy and most of the things it could rent. In a while he would be renting me.

The room had once been a den, comfortable and masculine, the repository of riches gathered during a lifetime of commercial conquest. From where I sat I could see a pre-Columbian torso and a post-Impressionist landscape and a harpsichord worthy of Landowska. But the riches had been shoved into the corners to make room for a bed because in spite of all the prizes, or just maybe because of them, Maximilian Kottle was dying. When he realized I knew it he told me why.

"Cancer," he said crisply, with cocky defiance.

I had guessed as much, but even so I had nothing to say worth saying. The word lay in the center of the room, the way it always does, like a dead rat that everyone sees but no one wants to pick up and carry out to the trash.

"I'm sorry," I mumbled finally, embarrassed because I was embarrassed.

Kottle shrugged. "Don't be. Poor Belinda, my wife, is sorry enough for both of us. I tried to spare her all this, to send her away until it's finished, but she will have none of it. I love her very much," he added unnecessarily.

He shifted position slightly, making me wonder if he had bedsores, and what bedsores were. "Do you contemplate death much, Mr. Tanner?" he asked when he got comfortable. "I mean, do you attempt to truly engage it, intellectually?"

"I'm afraid these days the only thing that engages me intellectually is my tax return."

He laughed and I was glad. "Come now," he said. "The subject is ubiquitous. I myself have confronted the concept in earnest for several years, ever since I realized I was the only male in my family still alive."

1

"Have you reached any conclusion?"

"Two of them. One, I don't want to die. That's not as silly as it sounds. There have been times when I wasn't certain of that. Do you know what I mean?"

"Everyone with a brain knows what you mean."

He nodded in agreement. "Second, I decided, somewhat paradoxically, that whatever comes next must be better than what has gone before. I'm not sure what form it will take—I tend toward a belief in spiritual reincarnation, although an amalgam of the Mormon and Zuñi concepts of an eternal journey is also attractive—but I think at bottom it gets better. I think perhaps that's what salvation is—our successive and progressive approximation of the good."

"That doesn't sound so bad."

"No, but getting there is no picnic. This cancer. There are no choirs of angels, let me tell you. As the most notorious of modern afflictions, I of course often imagined cancer as the eventual cause of my demise. To tell you the truth, I fully expected that, should I in fact contract the disease, it would prove mildly disappointing, as so many notorious things are upon close encounter. Unhappily, I was wrong. Cancer is truly evil, Mr. Tanner. With the exception of certain misguided religious and political movements, it is perhaps the only unmitigated evil that still exists in statistically significant quantities."

Kottle chuckled dryly, then seemed to wince. The wrinkles in his face broadened briefly, then returned to their original expanse. I asked if I could get him anything and he shook his head.

"The insidious thing, of course," he went on, "is that with cancer it's not a matter of ill fate or accidental exposure to a source of contagion or a slow and natural debilitation. No. Thanks to modern biology we learn that cancer is an entirely self-inflicted wound. The grotesque result is that millions of us must endure not only the pain of the disease and the humiliation of a host of sincere but ineffective treatments, we must also live with the thought that we brought all of it, our own suffering and that of the people we love, completely upon ourselves. It's so simple, really. According to the scientists the cause of cancer is stupidity."

His closing smile was ironic, but then for a man in his position everything must seem ironic. I tried to show I understood what he was saying, but he didn't see me do it.

There were mirrors in front of his eyes, and he was looking at the reduced and reflected image of his past. When he spoke again it was an incantation.

"Cigarettes and Scotch, bacon and ham, smog and saccharin. Stress. Too much sunshine. My God, sir, my whole life has been calculated to put me in this bed." He chuckled again and enjoyed it, then coughed and didn't. "Shall I tell you something else amusing?" he asked.

"Sure."

"Do you ever feel that if something good happens to you, then something bad must surely follow?"

"With me it's more than a feeling, it's a law."

"Yes. Well, my business has many facets, but the one I have been concerned with most intimately over the last five years is a complex chemical and engineering problem. I've poured millions into it. For years there was no progress at all. Now my people tell me we are almost there. Finally. A few more months, at most. And I know as surely as I'm lying here that I won't live to see it happen."

"Is it the shale?" I asked.

He peered at me with interest. "You know about that?"

"Some," I said. "I know your company and others are spending money like drunken sailors trying to get oil out of all that rock in Colorado. I know that the first outfit to do it commercially will have a license to print money."

Kottle nodded with sudden vigor. "There's over a trillion barrels of oil out there, Tanner. We're going after it. Others are too, but I've given my people a blank check. Now they tell me they're on the track. By the twenty-first century we'll be pulling four hundred thousand barrels a day out of those mountains. Maybe more."

"Sounds good."

"It is good. It's good for everyone, but the people it's best for are the poor people, the ones being knocked silly by OPEC and their prices, the ones whose livelihood depends on what an increasingly penurious government doles out to them. And it's going to keep this country from being held hostage by a lot of camel jockeys who don't give a damn about anything but making money and humiliating us."

The exegesis had tired him. He paused to catch his breath, then waved a hand as if to brush the words from the air above his bed. "Forgive the monologue," he sighed.

"One of the less attractive aspects of my predicament is that I've become obsessed. But then, obsession has had a lot to do with getting me where I am, or at least where I was before I became metastatic. I should probably be thankful that I retain the capacity for it, however perverted it might have become. Which brings us to the purpose of my calling you, Mr. Tanner."

The telephone on the stand beside him suddenly buzzed and he picked up the receiver and listened wordlessly. I got up and went over to the window that stretched from floor to ceiling and looked out at the city and the rain that fell on it.

We were on top of a twenty-story stack of apartments occupied by people who hadn't had to look at a price tag in years, high above Sacramento Street, sharing the top of Nob Hill with the Fairmont and the Mark Hopkins the way a five-year-old shares a beach towel with his older brothers. The building was called the Phoenix. Like the Dakota in New York, it was one of the truly prestigious addresses in town. Max Kottle owned every brick of it.

Over on California Street a cable car clanged to a halt. The people who clung to its sides like barnacles wouldn't let any other barnacles on. Down by the bay the car lights strung along the freeway stopped moving, as though the commuters had all paused to take a collective breath. Six inches from my nose raindrops beat against the window in a hundred jealous slaps.

Max Kottle was still talking on the phone so I quickly thought over what I knew about him. He was one of those men who seem born with the ability to make the economic system jump through hoops of their own design. Kottle operated impulsively, almost like a kid, but he collected companies, not baseball cards. Big companies, small ones, solvent ones and insolvent ones—companies with nothing in common except that they all fit neatly into the conglomerate Kottle had begun putting together shortly after the Second World War and which now ranked comfortably somewhere just below the Fortune 500.

I could remember when Kottle had gone public back in the days when I was a Montgomery Street lawyer instead of a Jackson Square private investigator. For a long time before that Max had run a close corporation, owning his enterprises entirely, but when he needed a big hunk of capital to buy a fleet of tankers from an aging Greek he had offered shares to the public, retaining just enough of the stock to exercise practical, if not mathematically certain, control. At the time, the corporate types I knew were guessing that, given the price the stock had climbed to a month after it hit the market, Kottle's net worth must have been close to fifty million dollars.

I didn't know where things stood now—I stopped following the stock quotations when they took them out of the sports section—but I had vague memories of oil discoveries off Yugoslavia and real-estate ventures in Venezuela and a Justice Department injunction against some merger proposal a few years back. Kottle's holding company was called Collected Industries. It had hundreds of millions in assets and its holdings spattered the globe the way Pollock spattered a canvas. And Max Kottle ran it all from this room.

Lately Max himself had become more legend than real, more phantom than fact, appearing in print only among the periodic lists of California's wealthiest residents or when one of his sorties into the currency exchanges or the art markets resulted in a particularly brilliant coup. I could recall pictures of him sitting on the decks of private yachts and strolling on the shores of private islands, usually alone, looking as hard and brown as a buckeye.

But that was a different man from the one I had just been watching. The man I was talking to—the man lying naked under a thin white sheet, the man cranked up at the waist by a steel-framed hospital bed, the man whose hair was white and tufted, whose skin was loose and mottled, whose eyes were gray and dull—that was a man I had never seeen before.

"Sorry," Kottle called out as he replaced the phone. I went back and sat down in the chair beside his bed. For some reason, we said nothing to each other. Over at the window the raindrops seemed to mock us, tittering.

"Doctor Hazen is here by now," Kottle began finally, glancing at his watch. "He comes by daily to chart the progress of my disease. He's my friend as well as my doctor, so I don't want to keep him waiting." Kottle smiled at a memory. "Three weeks ago Clifford estimated that I had two months to live, absent divine intervention. I think the only reason he comes by is to assure himself that he can remain comfortably atheistic."

"I'm sure he's concerned about you," I said inanely.

"Oh, of course he is. I'm only joking. Now let's turn to something that is almost as painful to me as my sarcoma. I mention my projected life span only because it has some bearing on the reason I asked you here today."

"Which is?"

"I want you to find my son, Mr. Tanner. I want to see him before I die."

Two

As though the reference to his son had purloined his store of strength, Max Kottle fell silent, his face slack, his eyes closed. His chest, unclothed and furred with gray, rose and fell mechanically, forcing whistling streams of air through his nostrils. Soon even the whistling ceased.

Empty of sound, the room seemed empty of all else as well. Dark, draped only in folds of shadow, lit only by the lamp beside the bed, it was a ghostly still life of modern illness. At the edge of light there were suggestions of bookshelves and floor lamps, tables and chairs, but there was nothing vivid, nothing real. Somewhere, something clattered briefly, then was silent.

Kottle opened his eyes and sighed. Without thinking, I reached for a cigarette, until I remembered the disease that shared the room. I dropped my hand to my lap. Kottle smiled weakly. "Stupidity," he said. I kept my hand where it was.

With some effort Kottle looked over at the small digital clock on the nightstand, then asked if I wanted a drink. I said I'd have what he was having. He pressed a button and a door opened and a young black woman wearing a stiff white dress and crepe-soled shoes entered the room.

"My nurse, Miss Durkin," Kottle said to me.

I nodded a greeting and the woman nodded back with careful insouciance. The thin gold bracelets at the wrist of her long brown arm chimed gently. As she moved, her white stockings scraped against each other like brushes across a snare.

Kottle asked his nurse to have someone named Ethel make some drinks and bring them up. Miss Durkin nodded and left the room without saying a word. Nothing she left behind was intemperate enough to melt. "I suspect she despises me," Kottle said with a grin.

"Nurses usually despise the disease more than the patient," I said, "but she could be an exception."

Kottle shrugged absently. He seemed a camera without a lens, unable to sustain a focus. For the next few moments he searched the room, seeming to seek something bright and cheery. I considered suggesting that he read *Leaves of Grass*, that its optimism might be helpful, that it had helped me more than once. But I didn't. I'm not that brave. "What's your son's name?" I asked instead.

"Karl. Inexcusably alliterative, isn't it?"

"How old?"

"Thirty. His birthday was last week."

"How long since you've seen him?"

"Ten years."

"A long time."

"A lifetime, as it turns out."

"Any communication from him at all in that time?"

"None. That is, there were letters, but nothing important."

"May I see them?"

"No. They would not be helpful."

"I might be a better judge of that."

"Perhaps. But I am the judge of which of my affairs shall remain private. I won't disclose them. I'm sorry."

I shrugged, making the mental check marks I always make when the client starts being elusive. "Where did you see Karl last?"

"Right here. He paid me one of his increasingly infrequent visits. It was my birthday. I thought perhaps some of our problems might have evaporated with age, but Karl was obviously on drugs that evening and we soon quarreled. I threw him out. He never returned."

"Have you any reason to think he's not alive?"

Kottle started, his head lifting briefly off the pillow. I shouldn't have asked the question.

"What?" Kottle sputtered. "Of course not. Why would I think that?"

I shrugged. "Just asking. What were those problems you and Karl were having?"

Kottle sighed heavily. "This was 1969. Karl had just finished four years at Berkeley. I was already monstrously wealthy. Karl embraced left-wing politics as though it were a long-lost panda bear. We quarreled about just what you would expect—our values, our pasts, our futures. Karl decided my life was indefensible and I decided to defend it. It seemed important, then. It seems ridiculous now." Kottle shook his head in puzzlement.

"What was Karl doing back then?" I asked.

"Nothing. He'd finished college with a degree in philosophy, but he didn't have a job. He was drifting, as so many of them were in those days. Drugs. Sex. Politics. I don't know. None of it seems so wretched, in retrospect. But at the time, well, those were difficult days."

"Where was he living?"

"In Berkeley, I assume. I can't be sure."

"Did you know any of his friends?"

"Not really. Oh, he brought various revolutionary types around from time to time, and I would endure their calumny for an hour or so before ordering them out. It was all very predictable. And very boring." Kottle smiled. "Of course I'd give a thousand shares of CI stock if I could relive those moments today."

"What about high school friends?"

"I don't think he had any. We sent him to boarding school back East. Another mistake."

"Do you know of any particular reason he might have for dropping out of sight?"

"No, I . . . no. Nothing."

Suddenly nervous, Kottle reached for one of the pill bottles that littered the nightstand. In his haste he knocked one of them to the floor. It rolled across the carpet and came to rest against my shoe. I bent down and picked it up and put it back on the table. The name on the bottle was sesquipedalian; the capsules inside it as blue as liquid sky. As I sat back down I noticed one of the capsules lying on the floor, like a frozen tear, just next to the leg of my chair. I picked it up before I could step on it. Then I repeated my question about why Karl might have dropped out of sight.

"I don't know," Kottle answered after washing down his pill. "Perhaps he just needed time alone. I may have given you the wrong impression, Mr. Tanner. Karl was not stupid and he was not a drug addict. He was brilliant, as a matter of fact. When I say he used drugs I mean mild forms. But of course, for someone of my generation, there *were* no mild forms. Every drug called for maximum denunciation. A pharmacological domino theory prevailed." Kottle chuckled. "Likewise his opposition to the war. Certainly his vision in that regard was much more farsighted than mine. He was eloquent on the subject. In fact I suspect that part of our difficulties arose out of my own jealousy over that eloquence, and the serenity he seemed to possess at such an early age. Perhaps, afterwards, Karl simply became disillusioned, Mr. Tanner. Cynicism lurks beneath every bed."

"Have you made any effort to find Karl before now?" I asked.

"None."

"Why not?"

"I don't know, actually. I suppose I thought he would eventually come back on his own. And I always had something that seemed more important to do. And I always thought I had time. Christ. We never have time."

I got some more details about the boy, but they were all coated with dust. Young Karl had endured the things the sons of rich men always endure—private boys' schools, French tutors, 'cello lessons—but the war protests and the related turmoil that raged through Berkeley in the sixties had eaten away the underside of Karl's early conditioning and the boy had ultimately rejected his father and everything he stood for. It was a common pattern, and when the numbers were all filled in it spelled Heartache. I knew parents who had turned their sons in to the cops to get them out of their lives and I knew girls who had turned whore for reasons that had nothing to do with sex or money and everything to do with mom and dad. A tough time, the sixties.

Kottle went on, reciting the details in a formal, clipped style, even more Teutonic than before, as though he were forecasting the exchange rate of the yen. By the time he was finished I was wondering whether Max Kottle had any genuine emotional attachment to his son, or whether he was just lining up good deeds to trade on that great stock exchange in the sky.

As though he had read my mind, Max spoke. "I'm not trying to pretend I currently love Karl in any meaningful sense of the word," he said gravely. "I never have been able to love anything I couldn't touch or see. But I feel I could love him again, and I would like to. And besides, there are arrangements to be made, assets to dispose of, wills to write, all that. I can make Karl a rich man or I can disinherit him. I would prefer to make an informed choice." He paused. "He is my son. It didn't mean anything to me while I was alive. Perhaps I can make it mean something once I am not."

The thin lids slipped down over the eyes again and the wizened face fell forward until the chin reached the chest. The discussion had clearly exhausted Max Kottle, but there were a few more things I needed to know so I plunged ahead. In this business you get real good at plunging ahead. "Any suggestions where I should start looking?"

Kottle stirred awake, but barely. "Only one," he said thickly.

"Where?"

"His mother."

"Who's she?"

"Shelley Withers, she calls herself now . . . lives in Sausalito. Any gigolo can tell you where. She's a famous writer, I'm told. I married her when she was nineteen and I was thirty-seven. She gave me a son and I gave her a million dollars plus the plots for her first three novels."

"Is she likely to cooperate with me?"

"Maybe. She likes men."

"Anyone else I should see?"

"Not that I know of. Karl was artistic as a child, that might help. I still have a silver bracelet he made for me around here someplace. He liked peppermint ice cream. He hated to wear shoes. And in time he hated me." He shook his head. "Karl is a complete stranger. I know more about the doorman in this building."

Kottle pinched the bridge of his nose, then looked at me blankly, as though suddenly lost in a place that frightened him. It was time to wind it up. "Have you got a picture of Karl?"

He reached into the drawer of the nightstand and took out two squares of paper. "Here's Karl's high school graduation picture and a check for five thousand dollars. I hope both prove sufficient."

I looked briefly at the picture. The face was purposely sullen and flabby from self-indulgence, the jaw hidden by a lot of flesh and a little beard. His hair was long and greasy, masking his face like a cowl. Abandoned and confused. Spontaneous combustion a certainty. I had a feeling it was a face that had changed a lot over the next four years, after it got to Berkeley.

As if to confirm my assessment Kottle spoke. "Karl lost all of the flab and most of the petulance when he went to college, Mr. Tanner. Whatever he found there made him a man. A man I couldn't accept at the time, but nevertheless a man."

I nodded and looked at the check. "You've bought a hundred hours of my time, Mr. Kottle," I said. "Sometimes a hundred is enough; sometimes a thousand isn't."

"Time is of the essence, as you can see," Kottle said wearily. "If you need anything further you can reach me here. I won't be going anywhere."

"One last thing. Your illness. I haven't read anything about it in the papers. Doesn't the Securities and Exchange Commission like heads of big companies to tell folks when they get sick?"

Max Kottle managed one last grin. "My lawyers are drafting a statement now. I assume they will release it in a few days, as soon as they've driven up the fee to a level commensurate with my ability to pay."

"So I don't have to keep it secret?"

"No, but use discretion. It should not under any circumstance appear that you are trying to elicit sympathy for me."

"Don't worry. I use discretion once a day whether I need to or not."

"And that reminds me," Kottle said heavily. "The police should not be brought into this. Not in any capacity."

"Why not?"

"Because those are my instructions. Am I clear?"

"Sure. Just so you know that your five grand doesn't include my helping young Karl commit a crime. If that's what he's into, then the cops may have to be brought in."

"I'm certain that's not the case."

"I hope that's enough."

Kottle's phone buzzed again. He listened to it for a moment, then said, "All right," and put down the receiver. "Doctor Hazen can't wait any longer," he told me. "I'd better see him."

"I've taken too much of your time anyway."

Kottle shook his head. "I assure you I have nothing better to do with it. If I think of anything further that might help, I'll call you. Please keep me informed."

I told him I would and then stood up. I wished him luck and reached for his hand. It was as malleable as a bag of beans.

As I bent over, Kottle drew me even further toward him. "There's no one who can do anything for me now except you, Tanner," he whispered urgently. "When Karl was young he was a seeker. He was always searching for something—meaning, purpose, truth, call it what you will. Now I'm seeking something, too. I think if we could come together, Karl and I, even for a brief time, each of us might find at least part of what we're looking for. What do you think?"

"I think maybe you're right."

"It's worth a try, isn't it?"

"It's worth a try."

I left the room the way I came in, through a private entrance to a private elevator. I walked out of the Phoenix and crossed to the little park on the other side of the street and sat on a bench beneath my umbrella. On the swings and slides there were raindrops where the kids should have been. On the other side of the street three businessmen got out of a black limousine and hurried inside the Pacific Union Club, eager to confirm their blessedness.

I looked back at the Phoenix. A man was shouldering his way outside, a man stout and smug and in too much of a hurry to let the doorman do his job. There was a broad smile across his face, not an attractive smile, but one that reassured me not everything was dying, not every cause was lost.

When I remembered Ethel had never shown up with the drinks I walked downhill, in search of a suitable door.

Three

We cherish the myth that we are private people, free to pursue our pains, our passions and our perversions out of the view of others. Unlike most myths, this one has no basis in fact. We have no secrets. The garbage men and meter readers acquire their insights unavoidably, without design, but other organizations, from the Internal Revenue Service to the Credit Bureau, strive mightily, indiscriminately and often illegally to acquire raw data about each and every one of us, to sate their insatiable computers. The insurance companies know more about us than anyone, but they talk only to each other. The federal agencies know a lot, too, but they talk only to the FBI and the White House staff. So when I need information I'm stuck with the next best alternative—the Public Library and the City Hall.

The morning after I talked with Max Kottle I did what I always do when I get a new case: I ran a check on the client. It saves a lot of time and per diem money when the client turns out to be who and what he says he is, and luckily that happens about sixty percent of the time. The other forty, well, that's why I run the checks. When I retire from the business and establish an Academy for Detectives, the motto over the door will read "Know Thy Client."

This time it was easy. After flipping through *Personalities of the West and Midwest, Current Biography* and *Who's Who in Finance and Industry*, I knew that Maximilian Kottle had been born in Kokomo, Indiana, in 1911 to Ludwig and Rachael Kottle; that he had a degree in Mechanical Engineering from Iowa State University and a Ph.D. in Economics from Harvard; that he had been married three times and had one child, Karl, born in 1949; that he was on the boards of directors of sixteen companies, including Pacific Gas and Electric, and that he was a member of the Bohemian, Pacific Union, Commonwealth and Olympic clubs in San Francisco alone, and about five times that many national and international business organizations. He had been appointed to the Board of Regents by the first Governor Brown and had served in the Kennedy Administration on the international trade and tariff negotiating team. He had even written a book, *Microeconomics and the Multinational Enterprise*. He wasn't as powerful as Geneen at ITT or Bludhorn at Gulf & Western, but Max Kottle was quite a fellow.

I didn't have time to go back more than a couple of years in the *New York Times Index*, but it brought me up to date. First, it was clear that, despite being a publicly held company, Collected Industries was still Max Kottle's baby. Max was the spokesman for the company, and obviously the architect of its business policies. On the few occasions when Max wasn't quoted about the company, his assistant Walter Hedgestone was. One article noted that no senior Vice President was hired or promoted until after he and his family had spent a weekend with Max at his ranch near Santa Barbara and passed the unwritten but nonetheless stringent test that Max imposed. Another article described the company's massive entry into the energy field—the establishment of a multimillion-dollar oil shale processing plant near Grand Junction, Colorado. The article concluded that it was too soon to tell whether the gamble would be successful, but it was not too soon to tell that Max Kottle was one of the most farsighted industrialists in America.

There were two other pieces of interest. One, about three years old, noted that Max had donated five million dollars to San Francisco Bay University for a new wing at their medical center. The second reported that an unknown buyer had tried to take over Collected Industries several months back, by buying up its stock gradually over a period of almost a year. Kottle had finally realized what was going on and had gone to the SEC for an injunction against the takeover, and the buyer had been scared off.

It was getting close to lunchtime so I stopped collecting information on Max and started trying to find some on his son. The Periodical Room of the library has all the San Francisco city directories and telephone books back to before the turn of the century, and I looked for Karl in each of them for the past ten years. I didn't find him. Which meant I had to move on to City Hall.

City Hall lies on the other side of the Civic Center Plaza from the library, its granite dome looking down like an imperious doyen on the derelicts and the destitute who squat in the plaza. I walked across the plaza by way of the reflecting pools, dodging pigeons and panhandlers, and went inside the main doors and stood in line for the metal detector.

They check for guns at City Hall now—the Mayor and a Councilman were murdered in the building not long ago. I'd known the Mayor pretty well and the Councilman a little and this was where they laid in state, in the rotunda. I don't suppose I'll ever not think of that when I walk into the place.

I pulled open a door marked "Registrar" and talked to a man who finally agreed to find out whether Karl Kottle was registered to vote. He wasn't. I went through a door marked "Assessor" and pulled out the Alphabetical Index and looked to see whether Karl owned any property in the city. He didn't. After I threatened to see her boss, a woman in the Hall of Records checked to see if Karl had been issued a marriage license anytime during the past ten years. He hadn't. The Tax Collector didn't have any record of him, either. And he wasn't in the Plaintiff or Defendant indexes in the Clerk's office.

I had run out of easy places to look and was standing next to a bust of General Funston, looking absently at the building directory, when I got an idea. Max had told me that Karl had tried crafts as a youth—silver. In this city craftsmen often try to sell their work on the streets, but they need a license to do it. The licenses are given out by the Art Commission, which has an office on Grove, right next to City Hall. Before heading over there I turned and thanked the General for his inspiration. He was a pretty stern guy, but he looked as though he would enjoy a good joke.

The Art Commission is wedged into a narrow two-story building in the shadow of the new Performing Arts Center. A woman in the office just inside the door told me the street licenses were given out on the second floor. I climbed a dark stairway that rose between walls that seemed to move closer together with each step I took.

At the top were a large loft off in one direction and some smaller offices off in the other. Nothing was happening in the loft. There were a lot of pictures on the walls, and a few were pretty good, but they had been put there to prove something, not to be enjoyed. I turned toward the smaller offices.

No one was sitting behind the reception desk, and the offices I could see into were all unoccupied. Then I spotted a door marked "Street Artists Program." I knocked. When I thought I heard something, I went inside.

A man who was older than he wanted to be looked up at me from beneath a mop of unnatural curls. There was a gold loop in his ear and a silver medallion on his chest. He had no eyebrows at all. "What do you need?" he asked flatly.

"I need to know if a boy named Karl Kottle ever had a street license issued to him."

"What you need to know that for?"

"Does it matter?"

"It matters to me. I got work to do."

"It won't matter to the person who runs this place. Those are public records. I'm entitled to know what's in them."

"You ain't entitled to nothing I don't entitle you to, man. You want a license, fill out this form. Otherwise, I got shit to do."

"Are those the licenses in that cabinet?"

"No, man, those are fucking toothbrushes. What do you think they are?"

I could have scooped up the sarcasm and filled a rain barrel. I could also have applied some knuckles to his jaw.

"Can I look for Kottle's name myself?" I asked between teeth that wanted badly to clench.

He looked at me a second, ready to order me out, then backed away from the cabinet. "Help yourself," he allowed grandly.

I went behind the desk and thumbed through the files. They had been maintained by a spastic steam shovel operator, but I finally found the *K*'s and thumbed through them. Kottle wasn't there. I asked if there were any other files.

"Some stuff down the basement," the man said casually.

"Can you show me?"

He shook his head. "Filthy down there, man."

"Who else knows what's down there?"

"Who knows who knows, man. Now, I got stuff to do. I don't know what you are, but you ain't no artist."

"That your stuff on the wall?"

"Yeah."

"Then neither are you."

He swore but decided to let it go at that, and I gave it up. I probably shouldn't have—there might have been something down there I could use—but I can only root around in the barn lot of bureaucracy for so long.

I walked back outside and found a phone booth and got the number of Shelly Withers, Max Kottle's first wife and Karl Kottle's mother, and called it. The voice that answered was male and laconic.

I was immediately informed that Mrs Withers could not possibly be disturbed, for any reason. I listened to a lot of "absolutely not's" and "out of the question's" before I got a chance to mention Karl Kottle's name. Even at that I had to identify him as Mrs. Withers' son before the voice reluctantly speculated that if I came by the house about four I might share a few seconds of her majesty's life, but only a few seconds, of course, because some theater people were coming for cocktails at five thirty and Mrs. Withers always allowed an hour to prepare herself. When I asked if I were speaking to Mr. Withers the voice said, "You are no longer speaking to anyone," and hung up.

I shoved my way out of the booth and started down the street toward the BART station to wait for a ride downtown, but as I was about to step into Larkin Street I got another idea so I headed back to the library. The woman behind the counter at the place where they give out the library cards was young and eager to please. I told her how important the library was to me—for the wonderful movies and lectures as well as the books—and then I told her I had lost my wallet last week and the first thing I was trying to replace was my library card, even before my driver's license. I also told her I had moved recently and needed to report a change of address. When she asked me my name I used Karl's.

The woman excused herself and came back a minute later with a paper in her hand. "You don't live on Twenty-sixth Street anymore?" she asked brightly.

I smiled. "I do, you see, but I moved up the street. Less than a block. But maybe my wife already called in the change. What number do you have there?"

"Three seven two seven."

I nodded several times, my palms upturned in mute worship. "She did, all right. Sally's amazing. That's the new number, so all I need is a new card."

The woman gave me a form to take with me and I did.

Four

The address wasn't quite as good as it looked. After I left the library card lady I checked it out in the city directory, and the name beside 3727 Twenty-sixth Street was someone named Jefferson. I'd go out there sooner or later, but since I'd already been granted an audience I decided to start with Shelley Withers. If Karl was still living on Twenty-sixth Street he'd keep, and Mrs. Withers might be able to tell me, accidentally or on purpose, whether there was more to this case than met the eye. When a man as prominent as Max Kottle finds his way down to my level, that's often the case. By three thirty I was watching the whitecaps cavort like Easter bunnies beneath the span of the Golden Gate.

I took the Alexander Avenue exit to Sausalito and wound my way down toward the town. The sun had broken through the gray for the first time in days. Its rays lingered on the mist-covered hills, sparkling here, twinkling there, enjoying themselves. I felt rather sparkling myself.

I turned left onto Sausalito Boulevard and left again onto Third and then turned onto Edwards, the street I wanted. It was narrow and winding, barely wide enough for two cars to slip by each other even if both drivers were being careful. The hillside rose sharply on my right and dropped away just as sharply to my left. Other than shrubbery, the only things I could see were the tops of trees and the roofs of houses. I parked in the first wide spot in the road.

I spotted the number I was looking for after walking about thirty yards. It was painted on the face of the bottom step of a flight that led up from the street to a gap in a six-foot hedge. From where I stood I couldn't tell what was on the other side. I climbed two steps and looked back over my shoulder. Belvedere and Angel Island rose up at me, heaps of green liquefied by the late-afternoon light.

There was a house behind the hedge, a house anchored to the hillside only by a brace of foot-square beams and four concrete pilings. It was literally overhead, its cantilevered deck reaching toward the bay like the beckoning arm of a red-skinned siren. I felt small and helpless standing beneath it, but I would have felt even less secure if I'd lived in it. There was nothing between the house and the bay that a seven-point quake wouldn't eliminate. But I kept climbing, up the stairs and through a well in the deck, and walked over to the door.

They had chimes. People who own houses like that always have chimes. This particular set pealed a phrase from Rachmaninoff after I pressed the button. The tones were flat. If anyone within earshot could identify the work I'd give up Scotch for a week.

I pressed the button again and waited. The door was a slab of frosted glass, eight feet high, four feet wide. The knob in the center of it was silver. For a couple of minutes the only thing I could see was a hazy and vague reflection of myself that made me seem senile and boneless. Then, for a minute after that, a shadow stood behind the door, waiting for something. Finally the door opened.

The man had black hair flecked with gray and black eyes flecked with red and features that had been designed with a T-square and a protractor rather than a compass and a French curve. The cleft in his chin could have lodged a tribe of Hopis.

"I'm John Marshal Tanner," I said.

The man didn't answer, but he did step to the side after my name worked its way through his neglected synapses. I accepted his invitation, but not graciously.

The foyer floor was a path of pebbles that had been set in concrete, then covered with a clear plastic coat so they would shine brightly while they were bruising your feet. We clomped over them to a long, dark hallway and followed it past several closed doors until it opened onto a two-tiered room, large and airy, a brilliant blur of white-on-white.

The very indistinctness of the room kept me from focusing on anything but the woman. She was sitting on the white leather couch in the exact center of the lower tier. Her gown was red and silk and so were her shoes and so was her hair. They set her off the way a cherry sets off a marshmallow surprise.

The wall beyond the woman was all glass, curtained except for a narrow slit by a drape of white muslin. A white wall hanging usurped another wall with ropes and wires and shredded yarn. All the furniture I could see had been made to be viewed rather than occupied.

My escort strode forward and sauntered down the two steps leading to the lower level and walked to the woman's side. I followed suit. He muttered something that I couldn't catch but didn't have to and gestured back at me with theatrical contempt.

The woman had been watching me all the while, smiling serenely if vacantly, and when the man quit talking her right arm lapped toward me like a mastiff's tongue. I stepped forward smartly and clutched her fingers. They were too warm and too dry and too limp. The lumps that felt like warts were really diamonds. "Mr. Tanner," she crooned throatily.

I did half of what Emily Post says you're supposed to in that situation, then released the fingers. They glided to her thigh and lay there like bright-eyed worms. "Mrs. Withers, I presume," I said.

Her precisely painted lips pursed tolerantly. She nodded once and turned to the man. So did I.

The eyes that jumped from her face to me and back to her again were round and small, the kind of eyes that look down at you from the end of the dice table when you crap out. Everything he wore was shiny. None of the buttons above his waist were being used. "You may leave us, Randy," the woman said to him.

"I better stay, Shel," Randy protested.

"No." The word was solid, reinforced with something known best to Randy. "This is family business," she added. "You won't be needed."

Randy stayed put for a moment, but what he saw in her eyes made him back off. He glanced quickly at something out on the deck, then walked away. As he climbed the steps the hole in his sock winked at me.

While I waited for Randy to disappear I glanced through the slit in the drape. The portion of the deck I could see through the curtain was red and canopied, and the city beyond the deck was on the far side of two miles of blue-green water.

Then I noticed something I had skipped. There on the deck, lying prone on a yellow chaise, was the body of a girl, young, firm, tan. I could only see from her knees to her waist, but the part I could see was naked.

Mrs. Withers' gesture kept me from lingering over the view. I sat beside her on the couch, my back to the deck. "Your husband seems to believe I'm some sort of threat to you, Mrs. Withers," I said as I sat down. "I'm not sure what caused it, but I'm just here to get some information about your son Karl."

She laughed heavily, the tops of her ample breasts ballooning at the neck of her gown. "Randy helps ward off my pursuers," she said happily. "At times he's overprotective. I'm sorry. And Randy is not my husband. Mr. Withers is at our home in Palm Springs, where he spends each winter. The dampness up here makes his joints swell."

Another laugh swirled up out of her throat, hissing merrily. She reclined more comfortably against the couch,

striking a pose, her bare arm trailing across the back of
the brocade like an albino python on a padded limb. I
could have licked her thumb by moving four inches.

"What does Randy do?" I asked.

"He does me, Mr. Tanner. I suppose you might call him
my researcher."

"What kind of research?"

The makeup made room for another smile. "Do you
know what I do for a living, Mr. Tanner?"

I shrugged, feigning ignorance. "I guess not."

"Over there."

She gestured with one of her fingers and two of her diamonds. Along one wall, stretching six feet or more, was a
glass showcase, the kind you see in museums with something old and small inside them. In this one there were
twelve miniature easels, and on each easel was a paperback book, thick and squat, with a cover photo displaying
a young woman in one stage or another of sexual jeopardy. The titles of the books used words like "savage" and
"flame" and "desire."

I said the first thing that came to mind. "You must be
rich as hell."

"Not quite," she said with amusement. "I'm not even as
rich as dear old Max. But I'm getting there."

"And you owe it all to Randy and his research."

"Well, let's say that Randy does what he can. What he
can't, I get from someone else. Interested?"

"Not this month."

"I thought not. But you may show up in my next book
anyway. My imagination simply soars at times."

"I can imagine."

"I doubt it. Have you ever read one of my books?"

"Not yet."

"Oh, don't be embarrassed. Men aren't interested in
what I write. Only women. And certain kinds of women at
that."

"What kinds?"

"Women who aren't what they always thought they
would be."

"None of us are what we always thought we would be."

"But some are closer than others. My readers are the
ones who missed the boat completely, either because their
dreams were too grand or their accomplishments too
feeble. Men with the same problem jog or race cars."

The woman fascinated me, in spite of myself. Her cheeks were geological treasures of foundation and base and blush and rouge and powder and God knows what else, and her eyes seemed sculpted from blocks of black crust, possibly coal. The effect should have been ghastly, but it wasn't. Quite. If not for the stalks of wrinkles that sprouted above her lips and the flesh that dripped below her bicep, she could still pass for what she was struggling so mightily to be. "How do Randy and your husband get along?" I asked.

"They've never met. They never will."

"Anyone else live here?"

"My daughter, Rosemary. Six cats. One watchdog. Not that it's any of your business." The arm came off the brocade. "You said you were here about Karl."

I nodded. The fun and games had ended and in her eyes I saw a glimpse of the resolve that had gotten her into Max Kottle's bed at the age of nineteen. "I'm trying to find him," I said.

"What's he done now?" She eyed me carefully, her lips pursed once again, extending the wrinkles.

"Nothing I'm aware of."

"Then why do you want him?"

"I'd prefer not to say."

"Then you may leave. I'm too old for guessing games."

She had called my bluff with the confidence of the inventor of the game. I decided there wasn't much point in fencing over Max Kottle's identity, at least not with her. "His father wants to see him," I said.

"Max?"

I nodded.

"Why? After all these years?"

"Do you have to know?"

"I most certainly do."

"Max is dying."

The words plucked a nerve. Her hand began to vibrate. It drifted to her throat where it clutched at her flesh, as though to remove it from bone. "How?"

"Cancer."

"The poor man."

She stood and walked to the glass wall and looked out. She seemed held erect only by the folds of her gown. "Max has always been like an insurance policy for me, Mr. Tanner," she said, still facing the window. "I always felt that, whatever might happen, I could rely on Max to see that I had enough to get by on." She laughed dryly. "I imagine, in light of what he must have told you about me, you find my confidence somewhat naive."

"Somewhat."

"Well, whatever he says now, Max was very much in love with me at one time. The past is never erased completely from the memory. But you tell me my insurance policy is being canceled. Well, luckily, with the books, I no longer need it."

"Max needs you," I said quickly. "If you know anything at all about Karl's whereabouts."

"Max needs you," she repeated dreamily. "That's a first." She turned to face me. "Would you like a drink?"

It was close enough to five not to be an issue. "Scotch."

She walked to a glass cupboard at the far side of the room and took out a crystal decanter and two glasses and filled them both. I nodded to show I'd take it neat. As she walked over to hand me the glass her gown rustled like a gonfalon in a zephyr.

"I was not originally inclined to give you any information," she said as she retook her seat. "But I've changed my mind. A woman's prerogative. Unfortunately, I have little information to give you."

"I'll take what I can get."

She nodded. "I haven't seen or heard from Karl in more than four years. He clearly desires privacy. I was not a very good mother, Mr. Tanner, as I'm sure you've guessed. Until now I thought the least I could do was respect my son's wish to stay incommunicado. But things have changed."

"Because of Max?"

"Yes. It's not public knowledge, is it, that he's dying?"

"Not yet."

"Karl should know. Also, I believe it might be in my best interest to help Max gratify his last wish, so to speak. Do you think so?"

"I don't know." I assumed she was talking about the will.

"Will you tell Max I was cooperative?"

"If that's the way I see it. Tell me about Karl."

"Since the time he went to prep school we've seen each other only briefly. During his last years at Berkeley, when he began to despise his father so, he began to sympathize more with me, and he came to see me a few times. But then he got into that trouble and went to Canada, and when he came back I couldn't tell *what* he was thinking, about me or about anything else."

"Then you've seen him since he came back?"

"Yes. He stayed here for a few days when he first returned. I gave him some money and the next day he left without a word."

"When was that?"

"Let me see. Six or seven years ago, I believe."

"And since then?"

"He has been here, oh, maybe three times. Always at night. Always alone. He was frequently high on drugs."

"What was he doing for a living?"

"Nothing that I could see. I'm not sure why he came here, I gave him no more money. He would sit and stare out this window for hours, then fall asleep on the couch and be gone by the time I woke up the next morning. We barely exchanged a word."

"What was the trouble he got into?"

"I don't remember the details. Something to do with all those war demonstrations. The police were here once. A building was burned, I think. Something like that. Someone was hurt."

"Is Karl wanted by the cops?"

"I suppose so. I'm not sure. They wanted me to call them if I saw him again. Of course I wouldn't."

I couldn't tell whether her indifference was calculated or real. It could easily have been either, she was that kind of woman. "Can you give me any lead at all?" I asked.

She frowned. "How do I know you're really working for Max? How do I know you're not someone else?"

"Call him up."

She paused. "No. You wouldn't lie about something like that. You wouldn't dare. If Max found out, you'd be finished in this town. In this world."

"How about that lead?"

She thought for a minute. "Just one. I said Karl always came here alone, but once he brought a girl. This was the last time I saw him, about four years ago. She was even more silent than Karl, if that was possible. Lovely, but disturbed."

"Who was she?"

"I remember her first name. Amber. I used the name in one of my books."

"Anything else?"

"Not really. She was blond, thin, blue eyes as big as robin's eggs. She appeared to worship Karl."

"Any idea where I can reach her?"

"As a matter of fact, I do. She telephoned me last week and left a number. She's looking for Karl, too."

Mrs. Withers went off to get the number for me. I glanced back at the deck but the naked body was gone. When she came back, Mrs. Withers handed me a piece of paper. "I must ask you to leave now," she said at the same time. "I have guests."

I told her I would let myself out. On the way down the hall I heard voices. I paused in front of one of the doors. "Who is he?" It sounded like Randy, but I couldn't be sure.

"None of your business." A girl. Young. Recently naked, I guessed.

"Everything in this place is my business."

"Like hell. You're nothing but the hired hand, and the only tool you're hired to use is the one between your legs."

"You bitch. He's old enough to be your father."

"That makes him just about as old as you, doesn't it, Randy?"

"You're like animals. I can hear everything the two of you do in here, you know. So can your mother."

"I doubt that. If she heard she'd probably come in and join us."

"Whore!"

"Get out of here, Randy. I'm warning you. If you take another step I'll see to it Shelley makes you pack your bags by the end of the day. Think of it. You might have to start earning your living with something besides your cock."

The sound of steps came toward me. I hurried across the pebbles and out the door.

Five

I wanted to talk to Amber that night but I couldn't; I had a dinner appointment with a friend.

To say Chet Herk is a newspaperman is to say William Faulkner wrote books. More can be added. Chet got a journalism degree at Missouri back before journalism students were more common than colds and before all official pronouncements of propriety were taken with a dash of sodium chloride. After a brief stint with UPI, Chet came West and latched onto the Oakland *Tribune*. When we first got together I was a young lawyer and he was a cub reporter and we were both grasping at straws any sane person would have shunned, trying to make both names and dollars for ourselves.

Less than a year after we met I got a client who was charged with multiple homicide—the chain garroting of his girl friend's parents and younger sister at their home in Hayward. Just before he was killed the girl's father had forbidden her to see my client anymore, mostly because of his oddly cut hair, and that was more than enough motive to suit the Hayward cops. The case was considered closed. I pleaded my client not guilty because that's what you always do, but sometime after that he convinced me he really wasn't, and for some reason Chet Herk decided he wasn't, either.

So Chet began to dig. And after three weeks he broke it. He spent every free moment hanging around the neighborhood where it all happened, and one night in the bar nearest the scene of the crime he'd noticed some red scar marks on the hands of a kid at the next table, marks that could have been made by a motorcycle chain tugged tight around a father's throat. The kid in the bar turned out to be a biker the girl friend had jilted three years earlier and within a few days Chet wrapped it up in a bow and gave it to the cops in such a tidy package even they couldn't resist opening it. My man walked, and today he's a top investigator for the Oakland District Attorney. I've never paid Chet back for that one, although I've come close a time or two.

A year or so later Chet began to feel uncomfortable

with Bill Knowland's editorial policy at the *Trib*, and after a short stay at the *Chronicle* he made another switch, to a newly established sheet that swore to tell San Franciscans, allegedly for the first time, the truth about their city and the people who ran it.

Now Chet was managing editor of the paper. It was owned by an heir to a sugar fortune and its offices were in a converted processing plant down on Battery and, contrary to all expectations but Chet's, it was making muckraking respectable again. Chet and his troops had caused a cell door to slam behind more than one civil servant and had blown the whistle on a couple of Ponzi schemes and pyramid scams along the way. The paper was called *The Investigator*. Rumor had it that an *Investigator* reporter named Covington had a good chance for a Pulitzer for his series on a Contra Costa County cult that slaughtered livestock with power saws and used the entrails and reproductive organs in their initiation rites.

Chet was early and I was late and he was a drink ahead and I was a drink behind and that was the way things usually went with us. We had dinner together twice a year whether we were hungry or not—no more, no less—and we ate well. Chet said he only kept in touch with me so there would be at least two meals a year when he didn't have to pretend to enjoy the greasy spoons that all newspaper people seemed to frequent.

"Marsh."

"Chet."

We shook hands and I sat down and we looked each other over. If you're fond of the notion that you're not looking older you should see your friends every day or not at all, or find some way to convince yourself that what's happening to them isn't happening to you.

"This isn't too rich for your blood is it, Marsh?" Chet joked, gesturing around the room. It was a private nook on the second floor of a place laid out to look like an English inn, darkly paneled, dimly lit: rich.

"Probably," I said, "but at our age the blood can use a little thickening. You may have to co-sign a note to get me out of here, though."

"If I do, my friend, it will be the most succulent surety you've ever engaged."

" 'Succulent surety.' My, my, my. Such a wordsmith."

Chet laughed and so did I and we just left it that way

for a minute. The thought that we will one day be without
friends is never among our youthful nightmares, but as the
years go by, friends become both rare and crucial. Chet
Herk was one of mine who was still around; there weren't
many others.

The waiter glided in and out, arranging the place set-
tings, pouring the water, leaving the menus. I reached out
and flicked the rim of a goblet with a fingernail, then sat
back and grinned like a kid in the monkey house. Chet
and I go first class when we get together, and it's the only
time of year I travel that way except when the guy in the
office across the hall gives me his opera tickets.

"So what's up, Marsh?" Chet asked brightly.

"Interest rate; blood pressure; accounts payable; the
price of gold; international tensions. Everything but my
actuarial tables. How about you?"

"This and that," Chet said and frowned. "I'll tell you
later. Let's order."

I nodded and picked up a menu. Chet began with an
appetizer that went for eleven bucks, *à la carte*. I started
with the onion soup and figured I could escape for
fifty if I kept my wits about me, but Chet blew that
when he ordered wine. I decided to think about something else, so I wondered if Maximilian Kottle was
afraid to die, the camel through the eye of the needle and
all that. I decided that with the kind of money Kottle had,
you could buy an awfully big needle or an awfully small
camel or both.

After a debate with the waiter over the proper tempera-
ture for preparing beef Wellington, Chet began to bring
me up to date. His daughter was studying law in Massa-
chusetts and his son was studying fruit flies in Pago Pago
and his wife was studying Mandarin in menopause. Chet
was thrilled with each of them and, by the time he was
through telling me about them, so was I. I used to discour-
age people from talking about their domestic bliss, partly
because I saw so much of it that had gone sour but mostly
because deep down I knew my own life would be more
palatable if there were someone around to scramble my
eggs other than the fry cook at Zorba's. So it used to
depress me to hear the kind of encomiums Chet was send-
ing my way, but I've gotten over it. I still slump, though,
when I see a little kid, about nine or ten, with a Giants cap
on his head and a hole in the knee of his jeans, and I

think of all I might have learned if I'd had one of those of my own.

I tried to give Chet as much enjoyment as he was giving me, but the best I could come up with was a story about a client who wanted me to find the cat she had left back in Little Rock when she moved to San Francisco three years before, and about another who explained that his mother had died in her sleep two months earlier and wondered if he would get in any kind of trouble if he notified an undertaker at this late date to come get the body. Apparently the lemon juice he'd poured over the old girl to try to preserve her hadn't quite done the job.

The meal came and went, slowly and delectably, but by the time Chet's mouth was full of mousse and I was toying with some blackberries in cream Chet's eyebrows were still and the wrinkle on his pate had slipped to his forehead. I asked him what was wrong.

Before answering he swiped at his mouth with a swatch of gold linen, then ignited a panatela. "Are you free now, Marsh?" he asked cautiously, looking at me through smoke.

"You mean professionally?"

"Yeah."

"Not really. I'm just into something new."

"How long will it take?"

"I don't know. Maybe a week. Maybe a month. I'll know better in a couple of days."

"If I said my thing was crucial, an emergency, could you take it on?"

I thought about it and didn't like my conclusion. "I don't think so, Chet. Not right away. This other thing is kind of an emergency, too. The client's dying, and I'm into it enough to want to see it through. Sorry."

"I understand. One thing at a time. I eat my food the same way."

"What kind of trouble have you got, Chet? Hell, maybe I could fit it in."

"No. Forget it."

"Come on. What's the trouble?"

He sighed. "That's just it. I'm not sure we *have* any trouble. But if we do, it's bad."

"Who's we?"

"The paper."

"Tell me about it."

The slice of mousse vanished before Chet said anything more. He rubbed his face and then he rubbed his head and finally said, "I'd better not say anything, yet, Marsh. But listen. Will you call me when you get free of this other thing? Will you touch base before you take on something else?"

"Sure."

"Thanks. Let's leave it there for now."

"You sure?"

"Yeah. Hey. It's been nice. Let's do it again."

"Let's."

"Next time you pick."

I nodded. "Save those Ronald McDonald coupons." A half hour later I was home in bed, thrashing around on a bed full of other people's troubles, wondering when I'd last used the words "good night."

Six

The next morning I jumped in my car and followed up the second best lead I had—the address the library lady had given me.

It was raining when I started out, and raining even harder forty minutes later when I got where I was going. Along the way I slashed through puddles the way reality knifes through dreams and viewed the world through windows gray with steam. The opposing traffic spat at me, incensed at my dissenting direction. The people on the sidewalks scurried ineffectually from covering to covering or languished helplessly on the street corners under umbrellas that loomed over them like clouds of private doom.

The block of Twenty-sixth Street I was looking for ran between Guerrero and Valencia in the Inner Mission. The area is predominantly Latin, but with real estate prices in more popular areas at irrational levels, writers and artists and working people of all ethnic backgrounds are finding the Mission one of the few places left in the city where they can afford a home.

The place I was looking for was a typical San Francisco house—two levels, garage below, steps and portico on the left, bay window on the right over the garage, no yard in front. The artificial facade pasted onto this one sometime after the initial construction looked as though it was about to lose its grip. Above the broken sidewalk a telephone pole hoisted a cluster of wires high overhead, as tangled as my ambitions.

I sat in the car for a minute, checking the place out. It could have been unoccupied or there could have been twenty people living inside; in this area you couldn't tell. As I watched, the house seemed to slump even further into its own decay, confused by its past, fearful of its future, puzzled by its present. I run across a lot of *Homo sapiens* in the identical circumstance.

Just as I started to get out of the car a man rounded the corner at Valencia and came up the block toward me. He was huge, three hundred pounds at least, his face broad and overinflated, the color of a cup of cheap tea. I thought for an instant he was going into the house I was watching, but he went on to the next building instead. The sign next to the door he entered had once read "Church of Jesus Christ of Latter-Day Saints," but those letters had been pried off, leaving only a shaded outline. Over them, in black, hand-drawn letters, had been painted the words "Samoan Methodist Church."

I got out of my car and climbed to the front door of the house and pounded on it. Gunshots rang out from inside, "Gunsmoke" gunshots.

The woman who opened the door was very black and very round. Her huge flat breasts were supported only by her belt and hidden only by her apron. She took one step onto the porch, backing me up. An odor came out of the house with her, a smell I hadn't smelled since the last time I'd opened my grandmother's cookie jar three decades ago.

"You the Welfare man?" Her voice was loud, as deep as mine.

"No."

"I told them to send somebody."

"I'm not him. Sorry."

"Then you best get down off my porch." She took another step forward. My knees hit the low railing behind me and for a moment of vertigo I was sure I was going over.

"I'd like to ask you a couple of questions if I can," I said quickly, peaceably.

"Got no time for questions. I got babies in there, and bakin' too. None of 'em's gonna behave 'less I close by."

"I'm looking for the man who used to live in this house," I hurried on. "A man named Kottle. Do you know anything about him?"

"Never heard of no 'Cattle.'"

"Kottle. Karl Kottle."

"Never heard of him, neither."

I held my ground, but barely, and decided to tack. "Gingersnaps," I said.

"Say what?"

"Gingersnaps. That's what you're baking, isn't it? My grandma back in Iowa used to make them. I haven't had one in years. You couldn't spare one, could you?"

She looked at me frankly, tilting her head forward as though she were used to looking at the world over the tops of eyeglasses. Enough time went by for her to absorb me with every ounce of her flesh. "I might," she decided finally. "You wait."

She went into the house and made noises louder than Matt Dillon's perorations. When she came back there was a small plastic bag in her hand. There were three cookies in it, and she thrust them at me. I took the bag and thanked her.

"This man you want. He white or black?"

"White."

"Don't know him. Black man owns this place."

"What's his name?"

"I can't recollect."

Then, because it's so often the pragmatic thing to do, I got out my wallet. "Let me pay you for the cookies," I said slowly, slowly enough to clarify my meaning.

The fists that went to her hips loomed like gargoyles. "Now you insulting me," she said angrily. "Get off this porch. Now. 'Fore I toss you off."

I followed orders and the door slammed shut behind me, properly punctuating my stupidity.

On the way back to the car some movement caught my eye. Down at the end of the block was a grocery store, one of the Mom-and-Pop places the city is full of. A small, husky man was out front, taking some bread loaves from a delivery truck and loading them into a large wicker basket that hung from his left forearm. I went down there.

He grunted when he saw me. "You want bread?" His

accent and coloring were Middle Eastern—Lebanese, Persian, something. Inside the truck the driver was sleeping, his cap pulled over his eyes, his chin on his chest.

I shook my head. "Have you had this store long?" I asked. "I used to live here a long time ago. Just back to check out the old neighborhood. Looks pretty good."

"Fourteen years," the man said, without interest.

"Sixty-five," I calculated. "I moved out in sixty-two." I looked down the street. "A nice neighborhood. I always liked this neighborhood."

The man shrugged. "Nice. Not nice. Who knows? I been robbed three times. My friend, four blocks down, he's been robbed twelve times. Shot, even. Now they do this." He pointed. On the front door someone had scrawled the words "Down with Iran" and "Fuck the Ayatollah." "But, to do better I would have to be rich. The only rich in this neighborhood are the criminals."

I nodded wisely, as though I knew all about everything. "Say. A nephew of mine used to live around here someplace. Right up there, I think. Name was Kottle. Haven't seen him in a long time. You know him?"

"Kottle. Sure. I remember. Vienna sausages. Always eating Vienna sausages." He shook his head sadly.

"He still live there?"

"Moved. Three, four years ago, I think."

"Any idea where?"

The man shrugged and picked up the basket and carried it into the store. He jerked his head back toward the truck. "Lazy bastard. But the bread is good."

I followed him to the bread rack and helped him put the loaves on the shelves. The bread was warm and crusty, and the smell took me back to the place I grew up and the people I grew up with. I put one loaf to the side, and the little man smiled approvingly.

"Do you have any idea where Karl Kottle lives now?" I repeated. All of a sudden the question made me tired. The life led by the little grocer made me tired, too.

The man shook his head and rubbed the stubble on his chin. We finished stacking the bread in silence, and I followed him when he went over to the counter. I reached into my pocket for some money to pay for the bread. The man shook his head. "You keep. For helping."

I protested but the man's smile grew firm. I thanked him and turned to go.

"I do not know where Mr. Kottle lives," he said to my back. "But I have seen him."

"When?"

"Saturday. A week ago."

"Where?"

"Downtown. The Post Office. The Rincon Annex, I think it is called."

"Did you talk to him?"

He shook his head. "He did not see me. He was in a hurry. He seemed worried. Perhaps frightened. But then, that boy always seemed worried. He reminded me of the young men in my country."

"Did you see where he went?"

"He went into one of the buildings down there; I don't know which one. I had business. My brother was jailed by the Shah. Now the Ayatollah has released him. I send clothing, books, money. Every week."

"Does he get it?"

"I do not know."

He turned back to his shelves and began to dust them with a feather duster. I thanked him again and left, bearing gifts I felt unworthy of.

Seven

I ate lunch in my office. Bread and cookies.

After brushing the crumbs off the desk I dialed the number Shelley Withers had given me. Busy. I tried again later. Still busy.

I still hadn't gotten through to Amber when Peggy arrived for work. After straightening things that needed straightening and dusting things that needed dusting and watering the things that needed watering, she came in and placed a glass vase on my desk. In it were two rosebuds, one red, one white. Then she sat down in the client's chair to talk to the thing that needed talking to.

"So how was the feast?" Peggy didn't approve of extravagance in any form, and her grin was mocking.

"Fit for a king."

"What'd you have?"

"Pressed duck."

"How adventuresome."

"I'm a wild and crazy guy."

She laughed. "Those might be the last two words I'd pick to describe you, Marsh. The very last."

"What's the occasion?" I asked, gesturing at the flowers.

"Oh, it's raining, and Calhoun still hasn't paid his bill, and you've got a dentist appointment tomorrow. I thought your life could use a little cheer." Peggy shifted position and redraped her skirt. "What account should I charge the dinner to?" she asked briskly.

"Don't expense it."

"Come on, Marsh. Client Development. Research. Entertainment. It must fit somewhere."

"They haven't made friendship deductible yet. Forget it."

Peggy shook her head. "You must be the only man on this earth who doesn't cheat the tax man."

I looked at the roses again, then back at Peggy. The flowers were pretty and so was she. As a result I made my second mistake of the day. "You know," I said half-seriously, "sometimes I wonder why we haven't become more intimate, Mrs. Nettleton."

"You know why, Mr. Tanner," she said stiffly.

I knew, but I asked anyway. She deserved the chance to tell me.

"Because then it would stop being fun and start being love. I need fun a lot more."

I nodded and got up and poured myself a cup of coffee from the machine across the room. It took me longer than it usually did. When I went back to my desk I said, "Here," and handed her the paper Shelley Withers had given me. "Call this number every half hour until someone comes on, then give it to me."

"Yes, sir."

Peggy got up without looking at me again and marched to the outer office, leaving only the roses behind. It was the first pass I'd ever made at her, and if it wasn't the last I would lose her. Someday soon I'd have to make up for my insult, as soon as I finished recovering from hers.

It was after three when Peggy buzzed and told me someone had finally answered the phone at Amber's place. But the voice on the line wasn't Amber's, it was male and it was thick and shapeless, as though its owner had just emerged from a lengthy stupor, artificially induced. He grunted and groaned and swore and hacked, but after fill-

ing my ear with his refuse he finally muttered something I
interpreted to mean that Amber had gone to work and
that the place she worked was on Broadway and was
called "Magic" something or other.

I hung up in the middle of an effort to form a coherent
clause and looked under the listings for "Magic" in the
white pages. There were some Magic Pan restaurants and
a Magic Touch Beauty Salon and the Magic Theater, but
none of them were on Broadway. I was going to have to
go up there and look around.

A couple of decades ago I used to spend a lot of time
around Broadway. I was still in law school when I saw it
for the first time. The Famous Door and the Destination
Bagel Shop and the Coffee Gallery sheltered poets and
chess players and jazz groups and men with beards and
sandals and women with black eye makeup and straight
hair and for a boy just off the Zephyr from Iowa it was an
awesome and wondrous place. But the Beatniks foundered
on the approximation of their own ideals, and a few years
later the place went Topless.

Even that was nice, at first. The women were mostly
pretty and the breasts were mostly firm and they both
seemed to enjoy being looked at. You could alternate a
glimpse of Carol Doda's augmented aureoles at Big Al's
with a set from Thelonius Monk at the Jazz Workshop
and one from Stan Getz at Basin Street West, then catch
the Smothers Brothers at the Purple Onion or comics at
the Hungry *i*, then slip down and watch Yvonne d'Angers
roll around on a rug and wrap it all up with some late-
night pasta at Vanessi's and a later-night B&B at Enrico's.

All of it was only mildly pathetic: the customers weren't
dirty old men but only slightly soiled and the air of illicit
adventure and saucy liberation was infectious and thera-
peutic. But sex sucked up everything around it, the *i* and
the Onion included, and the jazz clubs folded and the
dancers went from Topless Schoolteachers to the Topless
Mother of Six to the Topless Grandmother to the Topless
Lady Wrestlers, and now it's the Topless Psychotic versus
the Bottomless Autistic and there's nothing fun about any
of it. No one smiles at anything, not even themselves, and
the customers are even more desperate than the club
owners. I wasn't looking forward to wandering up and
down Broadway in the rain, looking for a girl named Am-

ber who probably didn't know anything I wanted to hear voiced in the daylight.

Broadway is a night street, at its best when the neon stripes and flashing bulbs high on the marquees lift your eyes away from the trash in the gutter and the vomit on the sidewalk and the urine on the doorways and the vacant, life-numbed eyes of the people on the street. But I took a deep breath and plunged ahead, listening to the patter of raindrops on my umbrella, as irregularly insistent as the knock of salvation on the door of my soul.

I missed it the first time around. I'd stared at the Montgomery and walked west to Stockton on the north side of Broadway, looking across at the business signs on the other side, then turned around and did the opposite on the way back. There were a lot of signs to read—House of Ecstasy, Swedish Massage, Tunnel of Love—but I didn't see what I was looking for. The rain soaked me in anatomical increments: ankles, then knees; wrists, then elbows. The tires that rolled past me made sounds of mirth.

My mistake was in assuming "Magic" was the first word in the name. What I finally spotted was a sign that said "Encounter with Magic—2nd Floor." It was tacked above a dark doorway just east of Columbus, between a Bank of America branch and a place called the Garden of Eden. At street level the building was something called the Penthouse Cinema. The feature that week was *Steel Lips*.

I crossed the street and tried the door beneath the sign. It opened easily. I took the stairs two at a time, climbing over the bottle of J.W. Dant that lay on the fifth step, broken and jagged, in a pool of its own blood.

At the top of the stairs a dilapidated door repeated the information contained on the sign outside. As further enticement the management had added the word "Naked." Someone other than the management had added something, too. The word "Whores" had been painted on the sign with an aerosol can. The word reminded me of Shelly Withers' friend Randy and his rage at the bare-bottomed daughter.

A frizzy-haired girl with narrow black eyes and oily olive skin sat stiff-backed behind a tiny wooden desk. The sign outside must have referred to the décor—there was nothing on the desk and nothing on the floor and nothing on the walls. There was something on the girl, though, a purple leotard with a rip above one shoulder that created a single, pearly epaulet. Neither the leotard nor the flesh beneath it was thick enough to hide her ribs.

She looked up when I walked in, but she didn't speak. I went up to the desk and stood as close as I could, looking down into her bristly hair. That made me nervous so I looked at the desk. There was something on it after all, a worn paperback sheltered beneath her palm. Ouspensky.

"First room on the right," she said mechanically. Her eyes didn't even try to find mine.

"Amber there?" I asked.

"Who else?"

"What's Amber's last name?"

"You don't need to know her name, Charley; just her price."

"What is it?"

"Ask her. You don't have scabs, or spit on your chin. Maybe she'll give you a rate."

The first door on the right was closed. I knocked but didn't get a reponse. The wood was soft, almost mushy. Flecks of gray paint attached themselves to my knuckles. I knocked again, then turned the knob. The door swung into the room and so did I.

The place had all the cheer of the catacombs. There was only one window, and it had been painted black. Lines of light leaked through where the paint had been thinned by the brushstrokes. The effect made it seem as though someone was on the outside, scratching madly to get in.

A single bulb hung from the center of the room, forty watts at most. The rice paper globe that covered it hung too low to be an effective screen. The top of the globe was scorched the color of an overfried egg. A small table, spattered with white and blue paint, sat in the corner by the window. On it were a box of Kleenex and an alarm clock and a pile of clothes or rags. The clock ticked loudly—time marching by in hobnailed boots.

Along the left wall was a narrow cot, the kind I'd slept on during basic training at Fort Lewis, the kind that people buy for the same reason they buy used shoes. The thin mattress was covered with a white sheet that had once been whiter. On the mattress was a girl, also thin.

She was sleeping, one arm flung over her eyes, the other stretched straight out from her side and toward me, as though she beseeched my help. Her wraparound skirt was unwrapped enough to show she wasn't wearing anything beneath it. Her breaths were deep and irregular and more audible than they should have been. She was blond and had been attractive not very long ago.

I gave the room a quick once-over and didn't find anything that didn't relate to sex or squalor, so I walked over and put my hand on the girl's shoulder. She didn't move. I tried a couple of other things, but she didn't come out of it until I put my hand over her nose and mouth and held it there.

When she couldn't breathe she jerked twice, then sat up and rubbed her eyes and shook her head. The gold cross hanging from the chain around her neck swung wildly, like a crashing kite. Her yellow hair caught the yellow light and improved it. She saw me and smiled sleepily. "Whew," she sighed. "I was really out of it."

Then she remembered where she was. Her brow knit. A lip curled. "Hey. You shouldn't have come in here without knocking, you bastard." I liked her better asleep.

"I knocked," I said.

"Yeah? Well, okay. Let's get going. You want to take pictures or what?"

"No pictures."

"You can rent a camera out front. Five bucks. Two more for the film. If you want to use film."

"No, thanks."

"You bring clothes?"

"What?"

Her lips flattened in exasperation. "Did you bring some clothes? You know, something you want me to put on, dress up in. Lots of guys do that."

"I didn't bring anything."

"Well, I've got some lingerie on the table over there, stuff that other guys have left behind. You can look through it and see if anything turns you on. But no crotchless panties. Those things are sick."

I could only look as foolish as I felt. "I'll skip the clothes," I muttered. "I just . . ."

"Hold it," she demanded, and stuck out her hand. "It's ten for the encounter. That's with me naked. Ten more if you're gonna be naked, too. And I gotta notify the front."

"Why?"

"Why? Because we got some real strange guys coming up here, mister. You wouldn't believe it."

I knew that already. "I just want to talk." The cliché sounded ridiculous, like a nursery rhyme from the lips of a Roller Derby queen.

"Sure, sure. Just talk. Ten bucks, buddy, or out you go."

It seemed easier to do it that way, so I handed her the money. She got off the bed and told me she would be back in a minute and left the room. I found myself hoping that when she came back she'd say that she was surprised that someone like me would need to come to a place like this. She didn't.

When she returned her hair was combed and her lips were orange and she was fumbling with the strings that held the skirt around her. "You don't need to do that," I said quickly.

Her hands stopped moving and she eyed me carefully. "That ten doesn't get you anything but a peek, mister. No fuck, no suck. House rules. This isn't like some of the joints along here."

I motioned toward the bed. "Sit down for a second. Save the tough talk for the creeps who get off on it. I want to talk about Karl Kottle."

"Shit," she said.

The word came out easily and immediately, as though she used it often, to describe her world and to describe herself.

Eight

From the look on her face Amber had been prepared to encounter every kind of magic in that dismal room except the black magic of her past. Her features, once diffuse in the slack of apathy, now congealed into a series of emotional tableaux—surprise, embarrassment, shame, apprehension. Her hands kept pace, masking first her pubis and then her breasts, as though they were naked to my eyes and vulnerable because of it. Her own eyes swelled with an impulse that seemed less a vague disquietude than the anticipation of a specific, horrific fate.

"Are you a cop?" she asked. The question came the way it always comes, wrapped in a bag of air, to shield it from the answer.

I had answered that question a hundred times; I answered it again.

"Then who *are* you?"

Her right hand ascended from her pubis to her lips. She began to gnaw the flesh around the first knuckle of her middle finger as though it were her first food of the day.

"I'm a private detective," I said.

"What's your name?"

"Tanner."

"What are you doing here?"

"I'm trying to find Karl Kottle. I'm here because you can help me do it."

She took a moment to decide what parts of my story to believe. From the look of it she was used to making that decision, used to being lied to.

"What do you want with Karl?" she asked finally.

I shook my head. "Not yet. First you tell me why *you* want him."

She shook her head in return and dropped her eyes. In a place where so little was previously refused, it seemed ludicrous that we were now erecting standards.

I suddenly became conscious of the smells in the room, the smell of fluids gone bad, of slow and damp decomposition, of cheap thrills offered on a bed of artifice and deception. Amber retreated from me slowly, until the backs of her knees came up against the cot and she sat down on it. The bedsprings ached audibly, then were silent. I loomed over Amber like the ghost of perverts past.

"I'm looking for Karl," I repeated. "I've been hired to find him. It's nothing to do with the law. Mrs. Withers told me you were looking for Karl, too. She gave me your number. There's no reason for you not to help me. You must know things I don't; if you help me you'll be helping yourself. I'm a professional. My job is finding people. I don't need much to go on, but I need something. So far I haven't got it."

Amber sat silently during all this, a specimen afloat in a jar of indecision. I decided to treat her as someone half her age.

"You've known Karl a long time, haven't you, Amber?"

She nodded, once.

"You like him a lot, don't you?

"You want to see him again?

"Have you seen him recently?

"Have you seen him this year—this month—this week?

"Here in San Francisco?

"Did you talk to him?

"Was he all right?

"Did he tell you what he'd been doing?

"Did he tell you how to reach him?"

For the first time I got a negative response. Like the others, it was in the language of the body, not the tongue, but it was definite enough.

During my questioning Amber seemed to age, to metamorphose into the adult she was. She stood and began to pace. Her legs were thin and straight and long. With every other step her wraparound skirt surrendered a glimpse of thighs as smooth as tallow. She moved with a dancer's grace within a dancer's body. I was enjoying watching her when I had a sudden image of all the photographs of her that had been tucked into tattered wallets and then extracted by trembling fingers to perform vicarious therapies that Amber would never know of.

Although her body was lithe and free, her face was not. Her cheeks were dull and sallow, the flesh lacking the sheen of either cleanliness or hope. There were too many hollows in her face and elsewhere, voids which needed filling.

Her eyes seemed to need an extra urge to move; they lagged like a Garner melody behind the tempo of her surroundings. Only her hair had been regularly attended. It was long and straight and hung like a golden tapestry down the tapering slat of her back. It was exquisite and I told her so.

"Thanks," she mumbled absently. "I brush it four hundred strokes every morning."

"I thought you did that just before bed."

She shrugged. "I'm not in shape to brush it most nights, you know what I mean?"

"Drugs?"

"That. Other things. What difference does it make?"

"It makes the most important difference there is, Amber. There are better ways to live."

"Yeah? Name one, P.I."

Her sneer brought me up short. If I began to preach I would lose her and whatever information she might have about young Kottle. It was tempting to try my hand anyway, but my job wasn't to rescue Amber.

"Why don't we talk about Karl?" I suggested softly.

She stopped pacing and rested her hands in the curves of her hips and examined me closely. Under a load of suspicion one of her eyes canted sharply. "What's Karl to you?" she challenged.

"A job."

She snorted. "You're honest about it, at least."

"What's Karl to you?"

"Simple," she said firmly. "Karl can get me out of here. Karl and only Karl." As an afterthought her arm swept around the room in an awkward and silly gesture. "Karl can get me out," she repeated. "I know he can. Karl can do anything." There was a dream in her voice, one that had been reassembled so many times the cracks had vanished and it seemed like reality.

"Why do you think Karl will get you out?"

"Because I love him. Because I know what he needs. Because I know who he is."

"What does he need?"

"Me, mister. He needs me."

She had toughened again, and it was time to ease up. "Why don't you get out of here yourself?" I asked.

"I can't. I owe too much."

"Money?"

"That, and other things."

"Like what?"

"I don't want to talk about it. I just owe, that's all. They're good at getting people to owe them. Real good."

"What makes you think Karl can get you out even if he wants too? The people you're into sound pretty rough."

"Karl can do it. He's got money. He's got friends. His old man's a big wheel. They wouldn't mess with Karl. No one messes with Karl. Just like the old days."

"Karl can't get you out of here if you don't find him," I pointed out, not altogether accurately.

"I know, I know," Amber responded.

"So tell me about him. Tell me about the 'old days.' "

There was a pause. "Okay," Amber said after a moment. She walked back to the bed and sat down. I slid to the floor and propped my back against the wall. Amber and the sheet behind her stared at me from across the room.

"When did you first meet Karl?"

"About a century ago. He was a student at Cal and I'd

just gotten out of Lowell High. I decided I wanted to
check the action over at Berkeley, to see what all the com-
motion was about, you know? I got a job in a cafeteria,
Robbie's, right on Telegraph Avenue. Karl ate there a lot,
and we got to talking. But that's all it was, at first. Just
someone to talk to. He was a big man in Berkeley, you
know. Had his name in the *Daily Cal* every day, it seemed
like. A real hero. I was nothing. I could tell he kind of
dug me, but we didn't live together till he got back from
Canada."

"When did he go to Canada?"

"About a year after I first saw him. Seventy, seventy-
one, along in there."

"Why'd he go?"

"Well, I thought at first he went to avoid the draft, but I
guess there was more to it."

"How much more?"

"I don't know, exactly. There was some kind of trouble,
I know that. All of a sudden there were a lot of really
creepy-looking guys around asking questions about Karl.
And Karl just disappeared. I didn't see him again for over
four years."

"What was the trouble about?"

"I don't really remember. I was doing a lot of drugs in
those days, you know? Acid, mostly. Crystal, too. I don't
remember much about that time. I think someone got hurt
and they thought Karl had something to do with it. But
Karl never really talked about it, even later."

"Did you know any of Karl's friends while he was in
Berkeley?"

Amber shrugged. "He was always with a bunch of
people, but Karl was the only one who paid any attention
to me. The rest of them didn't pay attention to anything
but their own bullshit. They were real far out, that's for
sure. Sit for hours over a cup of coffee and do nothing but
talk. Wouldn't tip, either."

"What'd they talk about?"

"The war, mostly. Vietnam."

Absurdly, Amber added the last word to make it clear
to someone who had lived through more than one of them
exactly which war she was talking about. My self-image
underwent a slight adjustment.

"Can you remember any names at all?" I prodded. Amber seemed to be losing interest in me and in the conversa-

tion. She hadn't given me anything I could use yet, and if there was nothing there to get I had a feeling it was going to be a long time before I made the acquaintance of Karl Kottle.

Her brow furrowed in small, tight tucks. "I don't . . . sure. Howard was there, then. I remember Howard. No one else, though. The rest of them were just a bunch of motor mouths to me."

"Who's Howard?"

"Oh, he's Karl's best friend. They went to Canada together and everything. When I saw Karl after they got back, he and Howard were rooming together, out in the Mission."

"Twenty-sixth Street?"

Her eyes widened in surprise. "How'd you know?"

"I'm a detective; I'm supposed to know. What's Howard's last name?"

"Renn. Howard Renn."

"What's he do?"

"I don't know for sure. He used to be a poet, I think. At least that's what he said he was."

"Poets are usually something else, too, if they like to eat."

"Well, if Howard does anything else I don't know what it is. Maybe they're paying for bullshit these days."

"They pay premiums for that. Were the cops in Berkeley after Howard, too?"

"I don't think so, but I can't remember for sure."

My back started hurting so I shifted position. When I pressed my hand to the floor it felt grit and something else, something warm and sticky. I pulled it away fast. "How did you meet Karl after he came back from Canada?"

"I just ran into him by accident, out at Stern Grove, at a Ravi Shankar concert. It was weird, you know? Really blew me away."

I told her I could imagine how weird it really was. "Did you and Karl start living together then?"

"Yeah. Howard got married, so I moved in with Karl."

"How long did that last?"

"A couple of years. Till I got so strung out Karl gave up on me."

Amber's eyes glazed, taking on that distinctive aspect of someone looking inside rather than out. I kept trying to pluck memories out of her drug-fuzzed mind. "Strung out on what?" I asked.

"Speed, mostly. Karl and those people he ran with were so high-energy I just had to have something to help me keep up, you know? I guess I overdid it." She laughed helplessly. "Amber-dextrous, they used to call me. Dex-edrine, you know? Well, one day Karl just moved out. He tried real hard to get me straight, but I just wasn't together enough."

"Where did he move to?"

"I never knew. That whole bunch he hung out with were kind of underground, you know? I think a few of them were hiding from the law, and a lot more were hid-ing from drug dealers they'd ripped off at some time or another. A heavy scene, you know? Not mellow at all. They were always very secret about where they crashed and what they were into. Frankly, they were all creeps, ex-cept Karl. After he left me, whenever I'd see one of them I'd ask about Karl but they always said they didn't know where he was. They were lying, I'm sure. They didn't like me much."

"Why not?"

"Because I wasn't into saving the world. I was busy enough trying to save myself, and I was screwing that up as it was."

"So you didn't hang out with Karl again?"

"Nope."

"Then you saw Karl Kottle a week ago?"

She nodded.

"Where?"

"Right here. He came in with Howard and some other people. Just out of the blue. It was wild. I couldn't believe it."

"What happened?"

"We sat around, smoked some dope, goofed off."

She seemed about to tell me more when someone pounded loudly on the door. The voice behind it was rough and guttural. "Move your ass, baby," it said.

Amber leaned toward me and whispered. "If you want to talk some more I'll need more money."

"How much?"

"Ten, at least. It might be better if you got a camera, too. Then they won't wonder what we're doing."

I nodded and took two tens out and handed them over.

Amber bounced up and trotted out, seeming lighter and even more graceful than before. She shut the door behind her and the room started to close in on me so I shut my eyes and tried to think of other things, but all I could think of was Amber and the sheet.

When she came back Amber handed me a battered Instamatic with a flash cube on top. I looked it over. Two of the flashes had already been shot, and of the twelve pictures on the roll of film, ten had already been exposed. The last Edward Weston had apparently forgotten to take his negatives with him. I asked Amber for my change.

"Lila didn't have change. Lila never has change."

I opened my mouth to ask another question when Amber spoke again. "Maybe you better shoot a picture, so they won't come in here. They look for the flash under the door."

I put my hand on the camera and fumbled for the shutter button and pressed it, aiming at nothing in particular. Light slapped my eyes and I blinked and turned away. I'll probably do the same thing on Judgment Day. "You were telling me what happened when Karl came here to see you," I reminded her.

"Like I said, we smoked some dope Howard had with him, real heavy stuff, and everyone got silly, even Karl. Someone got a camera and one guy took off his clothes and everyone else did, too, except Karl. We started taking pictures of each other in various poses. S and M, B and D, all that. Faking it, you know? Then they just left, like they were afraid to stay in one place too long."

"Who were the people with him?"

"The girl they called Woody. I don't know what the guy's name was. He didn't say much. I turned him on, though; I could tell that."

"Hey, Amber." The door took another beating; the rough voice was back. "Luther's here. Says he doesn't have much time today."

Amber stood up and ran her hand over her hair to smooth it down. "You've got to go," she whispered. "Luther's a regular. He tips real well, twenty bucks sometimes, and I need the money." She glanced in the little round mirror that was nailed over the table beside her. "Hey," she exclaimed. "I didn't look so hot when Karl was here, but I'm lots better today. Not bad, huh?"

I agreed she wasn't bad. She preened before me like she

was on the Halston payroll and I was a big buyer in from
Des Moines. "Take my picture," she said. "Give it to Karl
when you find him. Tell him it's a present from me. Tell
him I'd sure like to see him again."

I did what she asked. The pose she struck was sophisticated and knowing, not like Amber at all. I took the film
cartridge from the camera and dropped it into my pocket
and told Amber good-bye and left. On the way out I
passed Luther. He was old and bald and fat. When I got
to the street it was still raining. I raised my face to the
clouds and let them wash me off.

Nine

It had gotten dark, which meant I should have gone home,
but for some reason I didn't want to. Maybe it was because there wasn't anything waiting there for me except
memories.

I started walking, ambling slowly, feeling stalwart and
brave to be out and about in the elements, alone and un-
afraid. The street lights turned the raindrops into molten
pods, sparks from the anvil-black sky. The puddles seemed
momentarily wounded by the drops, but they recovered
quickly.

I was supposed to have a date later that night with a
woman I'd seen frequently over the past three months, but
I was suddenly uninterested. We weren't going anywhere,
not together, and we both knew it. For various reasons
neither of us was willing to expend the energy necessary to
shove the relationship out of low gear and into something
suitable for a long-range cruise. The price of that kind of
energy has gone up lately, too.

As I sloshed along Montgomery Street I began to consider the impression of Karl Kottle that was forming
somewhere to the rear of my retinas. Smart. Idealistic. En-
ergetic. Attractive to women. Leader of men. But not perfect. A kid who took the burden of a rich and famous
father into the Berkeley of the sixties and couldn't think of
anything to do with it but toss it in the ditch.

I didn't have much trouble imagining what Karl had
been like ten years ago as a campus radical. I'd seen a lot
of them in those days, usually at the behest of the parents

of kids who had climbed on for the ride to glory and had
fallen off along the way. What I didn't know was what
Karl Kottle was like now. A lot of things can change in a
decade. He might still be an extremist like Dellinger or he
might have become a mainstreamer like Hayden or he just
might want nothing more than to sell you a little policy of
straight life so he could pocket the commission. I didn't
know, but I had a feeling I was going to find out pretty
soon. Karl Kottle was still buried, but it had begun to look
like a shallow grave.

I went in the doorway of my building and shook the
rain off my back, then walked up to the second floor.
There shouldn't have been a light on in my office, and the
door with my name on it shouldn't have been unlocked,
and there shouldn't have been a beautiful woman waiting
all alone to see me at that hour of the evening.

But there was.

I hung up my raincoat and turned up the heat and
greeted my guest. Her smile dried me off and made me
warm before the furnace had a chance.

"You look like a drowned rat," she joked. Her eyes
sparkled like the rain I had left on the streets outside. At
the end of the sentence her voice slid into the lilt of the
Deep South.

"I feel like a stewed tomato. A cold stewed tomato," I
added, "which is the most disgusting thing there is."

"I hope you don't mind me waiting like this. I convinced your secretary I was trustworthy."

"You must be a good convincer. Peggy still has doubts
about Pope John."

"We'll see," she said ambiguously.

I needed a drink and told her so and asked if she'd join
me. She shook her head. I poured three fingers of Scotch
into a glass that had originally come filled with grape jelly
and toasted her silently. Even wet and cold and tired, I
was prepared to spend the evening right where I was, as
long as she stayed there with me. From behind Peggy's
desk I looked at her over the top of a typewriter.

As the silence lengthened I saw that she wasn't as self-
assured as she'd originally seemed. As I sipped my drink I
watched the jitters break out on her, watched the onset of
that uniquely human dread of an encounter with one of its
own.

I was about to move things along when the phone rang.

It was Amber. She asked if I was alone and I told her I wasn't. She asked me to call her when I was, and left a number. I wrote it down and hung up.

"Who are you?" I asked abruptly.

The question startled her more than it should have; she must have been someone important. She pulled a Benson & Hedges package from her purse and got one out. She gave me a chance to light it for her, then lit it herself. The smoke she inhaled seemed to go directly to her breasts. "I'm Mrs. Maximilian Kottle," she said. The words followed a stream of smoke to the ceiling.

It was my turn to be startled, but I kept my mouth shut and acted like I'd known it all along. I learned how to do that in the courtroom; you never want to look surprised in the courtroom.

I looked the woman over again, from my new perspective. She was ample, tall and round, but none of her was extra. Her dress was black and wispy, with white at the neck and waist and wrists. A single diamond winked at me from the notch at the base of her throat. Brown hair brushed her shoulders in thick, silken waves. Her forehead was broad and lineless. Her eyes were big enough to hide in till it was safe to come out.

My inventory hadn't passed unnoticed. She shifted nervously and reached into her purse again and took out a pair of glasses and put them on. The lenses were rimmed with thin gold wires and gave her a scholastic, pristine air that was belied by the rest of her. She smiled hesitantly and tried to meet my eyes but didn't. "You expected someone older," she said. "Everyone does; everyone who knows my husband."

It seemed strange that a woman of her position could be shy. Her smile got all tangled up in embarrassment and her glance flitted around the room like a fly that had avoided the first swat. She must have dealt with this a hundred times, starting with the day she told her mother the age of the man she was marrying, but she still wasn't handling it well. But some issues never get easy: I still feel vaguely felonious whenever someone asks me why I've never married.

"What can I do for you, Mrs. Kottle?" I asked.

She leaned toward me, her heavy lashes shading her eyes like black awnings. "I don't ordinarily care what people think about Max and me, Mr. Tanner. I know what most of them assume, and so does Max, and we think it's funny, I guess, more than anything. Or maybe pathetic. But just so my position is clear to you, I want you to know that before I married Max I insisted that his lawyer draw up an agreement that said if Max and I ever got divorced, or if he died before me, all I would get would be two hundred thousand dollars, plus support for any children we might have."

I nodded to show I was familiar with antenuptial arrangements. They're kind of tricky to draft. Lots of times they don't hold up. Lots of times people know that before they sign them. I wasn't sure it made any difference. "Did you and Kottle have any children?"

"No. Not that we didn't try," she added firmly, a declaration of passion that she seemed compelled to make. "I signed that agreement willingly, Mr. Tanner; I have a copy of it right here, if you want to see it."

I shook my head. "That won't be necessary, Mrs. Kottle. I believe you. I always believe women at this time of night. It's later on when I start to have problems."

I smiled to show it was a joke, but you've got to be careful these days, some women have given up humor till the ERA goes through.

"I'm glad you know where I stand," she said. "And you may call me Belinda."

"Why are you here, Belinda?"

"I'm here about my husband, of course."

"I guessed as much. What about him?"

"He told me he'd seen you."

"Did he?"

"He also told me what he'd asked you to do."

"Did he?"

"Yes," she said primly. "He did, Mr. Tanner."

"So why are you here?"

"I'm not sure how to put it. I'm here because I want you to be careful."

"Of what? Of whom?"

She paused a moment. "Of Karl, I guess."

"Do you know Karl?"

"No. I've never seen him."

"Then I don't understand. Why are you so afraid of him?"

"I'm not afraid of him. I'm just afraid for Max. For what might happen to him if you find Karl."

I let those words tour the room on their own for a while. Belinda Kottle seemed afraid, but then most of the people I see are afraid of something or other. Sometimes they're afraid of me. "Maybe you'd better tell me exactly what's bothering you," I said softly.

She sighed and leaned against the couch. "I'll try. Oh, I shouldn't even be here. Max will be furious. You won't tell him, will you?"

"I don't think so."

"Promise?"

"No promises. Come on, Mrs. Kottle. What's the problem?"

She moved her large body this way and that, straining the threads of her dress, causing a hip to be crushed by the arm of her chair. One thigh appeared, round and white and firm, beneath a lacy black tent. I asked if she wanted a drink now. She shook her head. The telephone rang while I was pouring another for myself.

This time it was Hedgestone, Max Kottle's executive assistant. He asked if I was free to see him that evening. I said I wasn't. He asked if he could come by in the morning. I told him not before ten. He said he'd look forward to seeing me then. When Mrs. Kottle asked me who it was I lied.

I'm a believer in a zero sum world. When the status quo changes then someone gets more and someone else gets less. It's true for nations and it's true for families. All of a sudden lots of people in Max Kottle's entourage were interested in knowing whether the status of Max's long-lost son was about to change. I thought I knew why.

"Talk to me, Mrs. Kottle," I said brusquely.

"I think maybe I should talk about money," she said slowly.

"So do I."

"Max is a rich man, Mr. Tanner."

"I know."

"No, you don't. Not precisely. I don't even think Max knows how rich he is."

"I've seen the annual report for Collected Industries. I know what you're talking about, Mrs. Kottle."

"But that's not the half of it. That's just his public money. In private he has much more. Today he spent the morning talking with some Arab. Yesterday it was the Chinese. Last night a Greek wanted to fly over and have breakfast with him. For Max the world is no larger than Union Square."

"So Max is up there with the Sheik and the Shah and the Pope. So what?"

"So I want to make sure you realize that if you find someone who calls himself Karl Kottle, and if you introduce that someone to Max, that someone may soon end up with a great deal of money and all that goes with it. I've never met Karl but I'm not entirely ignorant about him. Just after Max and I married, the first Mrs. Kottle dropped in on me one day. We talked about a lot of things; she was very nice, actually, in a sarcastic sort of way. She told me a lot about Max and a lot about Karl. A lot about herself, too, by accident. Someone like Karl could do a lot of damage with several million dollars to play with, Mr. Tanner. I don't think that ought to happen if it can be avoided. I want my husband remembered as the great man he is, not as a sentimental fool."

No one could accuse Belinda Kottle of that trait, but I didn't point it out. "Are you suggesting it might be better if I didn't find Karl?"

"Not at all. I'm only asking you to consult me after you do find him, so that we can be sure we know who and what he is before we unite him with his father. Until all the facts are known, Mr. Tanner, it would be well for Max and Karl to remain as they are."

"Strangers."

"Exactly."

I shrugged. "I'll keep the thought in mind. I'll also keep in mind that if Karl doesn't show up at all, then *you* may end up with millions to play with."

I'd insulted her and she knew it. She stood up, angry, then hurt, then confused. "The agreement, Mr. Tanner. I wasn't lying. I did sign that agreement."

"Read the sports page, Mrs. Kottle. Contracts aren't worth the price of the staples these days. There are a hundred lawyers in this town alone who would contest Max Kottle's will for a twenty-percent contingency without even reading it first. Hell, I'd do it myself if I was still practicing law."

"Are you a lawyer?"

"I'm a member of the bar, but I don't work at it."

"Why not?"

"I forget. Something about hypocrisy, I think, but I'm

not sure whether it was mine or theirs. It's not important. I just can't see that your husband needs all the help you're trying to give him, Mrs. Kottle. The man's built an empire. Now you say he can't be trusted to decide how to treat his son."

"But things have changed. He's dying."

"Maybe his perspective is better for it, has that ever occurred to you?"

She stood up. "We're getting nowhere." She walked to the door and stopped and looked back. "I don't think I like you very much, Mr. Tanner."

"I don't earn my living being liked, Mrs. Kottle."

She flipped her wrist to show me what she thought of that statement. "I haven't mentioned the fee I'm prepared to pay for the consultation I suggested. Should I go into it?"

"I don't think so."

She nodded briskly. "I'll wait to hear from you."

I could still hear her footsteps when I called my dentist and told his answering machine to cancel my appointment. The machine seemed to be expecting my call.

When I dialed the number Amber had left me, the voice that answered wasn't Amber's. Rightfully or not I matched it with Lila, the frizzy-haired girl who had been sitting at the front desk when I first encountered the Encounter with Magic. The voice was flat and nasal, a bleat of boredom. I asked if I could speak with Amber.

"She's busy."

"It's most important that I speak with her," I said unctuously.

"It may be important to you, Jack. To me it's important that Amber give her john all the jollies he paid for."

I sighed. "When will she be finished?"

"Who knows? He brought a movie camera and some Girl Scout uniforms. He could be in there for hours. Hey. Your name Tanner?"

"Yes."

"Amber gave me a message. She says the guy you want used to hang around some joint called Cicero's down by the Embarcadero."

"Anything else?"

"That's it. You're pretty hot for Amber, huh?"

"Sizzling."

"Well, Amber's all right, if all you want to do is leer,

but she's a vegetarian, Jack. I got other girls who'll do anything your heart desires. Tea Party. Circus. You name it."

"I'll keep it in mind."

"Do. I guarantee, after an hour with Laurel your mind won't be the same. Gives you a whole new perspective, you know, when a chick sticks her tongue up your ass. Think about it, Hot Rocks, and come see me."

The phone clicked. Miss Frizzy was right about the new perspective, but I already had mine. I got it several years ago when I was helping a man from Seattle locate the twin daughters his wife had skipped town with. It took a lot of time and a lot of money but I finally got a lead. LaVerne Blanc suggested I check out a magazine called *Kiddie Kapers*. I found it in a Tenderloin smut shop. Beginning on page sixteen was a three-page spread featuring a pair of girls, identical and naked and puzzled, and an equally puzzled and naked boy, doing what you'd expect to find them doing in a magazine like that. The twins were eight years old at the time. It cost the guy from Seattle two years and twenty thousand bucks to convince a judge to take custody away from the mother. The mother published the magazine.

Perspective. There's a lot of it out there. Once you get it, it stays with you forever, like malaria.

The last call I made was to my date. I told her I was too tired.

Ten

On the way to the office the next morning I stopped at a camera shop on Columbus and dropped off the film I had taken from the Encounter with Magic. The owner of the shop was a kid named Jerry who did nice work at reasonable prices and would do it in a hurry if you were willing to pay extra. I tossed Jerry the cartridge and he laughed. "You hock the Nikon, Marsh? Business must be pretty bad. I got a Yashica I'll loan you next time you go out."

I explained enough of the situation so Jerry wouldn't worry about getting paid and told him to get the prints back as soon as he could. He told me to check with him the next afternoon.

As I was about to leave, Jerry asked me to wait. "Check this out," he said, and handed me a print enlarged to eight by ten.

It was a portrait, face only, black and white, high-contrast glossy, shot through a long lens of at least two hundred millimeters. The subject was a girl, with one of those faces that gets pasted onto billboards and stapled into magazines and tacked onto closet walls by kids who have reached puberty a year before their parents suspect it. I whistled. "Who is she?"

"That's just it. I don't know."

"Who dropped off the film?"

"I don't know that, either. Some guy. Carrie waited on him, but she doesn't remember much. I tried to run him down, but the address and phone number he left don't exist. And his name's not in the book."

"You want me to find her, is that it?"

"Hell no, Marsh. I'm going to find her myself."

I chuckled. "Let me know if you need any tips out of the John Marshal Tanner *Crimebusters Manual*. For you they come free of charge."

"No tips. The fun's all in the search. Hell, when I find her it'll turn out she's married to some Standard Oil Vice President. You know how it goes. You're okay as long as you're still looking; it's when you find it that the trouble starts."

I knew. I told him so. I went out the door and took Jackson Street to my office.

I had an hour to kill before Hedgestone was due so I squandered it the best way there is next to watching the tube: I talked on the phone.

First, I called a woman I knew at PG&E and had her run Karl Kottle and Howard Renn through the billing tapes. The computer didn't kick out anything on Karl, but there were two Howard Renns and I wrote down the addresses of both and promised the woman her usual fee—a stinger at Perry's and an ounce of Bellodgia.

Then I called the Alumni Affairs Office at the university in Berkeley and put on my important executive voice and spewed out some jargon about a major new fund-raising effort that focused on the graduates of the sixties and the concerns that were so dramatically expressed in those difficult years, and so on and so on. Then I asked for the last known address they had for Karl Kottle, who was an heir

to an important fortune, as we all knew, and a potentially
key contributor to the drive, as I'm sure she could understand.

The girl on the other end of the line made a pro forma
defense of the confidentiality of the alumni records but she
wasn't being paid enough to risk her job in defense of an
abstraction and she wilted when I cast her as the only ob-
stacle between the university that employed her and a mil-
lion-dollar gift. But the address she gave me was a decade
old. I thanked her anyway and told her I'd tell her boss
how helpful she'd been. That didn't mean anything to her,
either. First to last, her voice was as flat as Kansas.

One of the Howard Renns was in the phone book, at an
address up on Edgewood Avenue. It smelled right. The poetry business must have been picking up—it was one of
the nicest nooks in the city, a bit of Berkeley and a dash
of New England thrown together in a blender and airlifted
to the side of Mt. Sutro, discoverable by invitation only. I
added Renn to my list. Since I couldn't get a lead on Karl,
I was going to have to start picking on his friends.

I grabbed the telephone again and called the only cop in
the city I was sure I could trust. His name was Charley
Sleet. He was a good cop and we both knew it. Charley
was a witness for the prosecution in one of the first criminal cases I ever defended. The charge was armed rob-
bery—a liquor store in the Tenderloin. My client was
young and black and as tough as teeth. He told me he was
minding his own business, strolling along Mason, when the
cops swooped down and tossed him into a patrol car and
hauled him to the precinct house and kept him awake for
the next forty-eight hours with questions and more physical forms of inquiry involving their toothpicks and his nostrils.

This was before the days of *Miranda* and *Escobedo*; police methods had to shock the conscience of the judge in
order to void a confession. Most judges were pretty un-
shockable by the time they'd been on the bench a few
years and I didn't think we had a prayer, mainly because
in those days the story the cops told on the stand had
about the same relation to truth as *Star Wars* has to
Dispatches.

But Charley Sleet had surprised me. He told it exactly
the way it went down, with my client nodding his head
beside me all the time, and the confession was tossed out

and I'd won my first case. Since then I'd always started with Charley when I needed a favor from the cops. Charley would help me out when my request was legitimate and tell me to fuck myself when it wasn't, and that's as good as it gets between private and public police.

When Charley came on the line I told him I'd buy him lunch anywhere north of Market. He suggested Hoffman's. I said it didn't qualify. Charley said I was picking nits just like a lawyer. I said I'd see him there in two hours. When he asked me what I wanted, I told him I wanted to know what the cops had on a guy named Karl Kottle. He said he'd check. I said no one should know he was checking. He swore and said it was my turn to buy.

By then it was time for Hedgestone to show and, on the dot, he did. When I told him he was punctual, he told me he was proud of it. From the tone of his voice it wasn't the only thing he was proud of. Then he told me who it was he'd brought with him.

"This is Professor Monroe Hartwig, Mr. Tanner," Hedgestone proclaimed. "He holds the William Willis Chair in International Economics at Stanford. I'd like him to speak to you a bit later."

"I look forward to it. Have a seat, Professor. Just throw that junk on the floor."

The professor's consultant's fee overcame his repugnance at the litter on the couch. While he arranged himself I looked Hedgestone over. He was tall, as thin and straight as a chopstick. His suit—gray, herringbone, priceless—fit him as well as disgrace fit Nixon. The only white in his hair lingered over his temples the way smog lingers over L.A. Whenever he wasn't talking his chin began to levitate. As he eased himself into the client's chair he wore the expression of a man about to sit on a frog.

I walked over and closed the door. When I got back behind my desk Hedgestone was looking up at the Klee and deciding not to comment for fear of complimenting its owner. Then he gave me his best smile, his very best. I put it in my hope chest to save till I was in a better mood.

"Thank you for seeing us, Mr. Tanner," Hedgestone began warmly. "I know someone of your reputation must be very busy."

His blue eyes changed shades perpetually, in textured waves, like bird feathers ruffling in the breeze. I guessed he was fifty because he looked ten years younger; a liberal application of money camouflages at least a decade. I asked Hedgestone how I could help him.

"May I be blunt?"

"Please do."

"As I told you when I arranged for you to see him, I am Mr. Kottle's Executive Assistant."

I did something to show he hadn't lost me yet.

"That title, of course, can mean many things. What it means in Mr. Kottle's case is that he has the world's foremost authority on the Eurodollar market, and the only economist in the Western Hemisphere who speaks both Arabic and Portuguese, at his beck and call twenty-four hours a day."

"Namely, you."

He smiled immodestly.

"Okay. You're the greatest thing since Bernard Baruch. So what?"

Hedgestone made a pup tent with his fingers, then began tapping the tips of them together. "You're looking for Mr. Kottle's son," he stated smugly.

I let the smugness float past. It stuck somewhere on the wall behind me. I hoped I could get it off. "What if I am?"

"I'm here to make a suggestion."

"Good. Outside assistance is always welcome, even from amateurs."

Hedgestone tolerated it, but just barely. "My suggestion, Mr. Tanner, is that you fail."

"Why?"

"It's very simple. You know Mr. Kottle's condition. What you may not know is that his personality is undergoing dramatic change. The pattern is known. The psychology of the terminally ill is coming under increased study."

"I've read Kübler-Ross," I said. "Some of it makes sense; some of it doesn't. Like most things."

"Then you know the stages. Mr. Kottle has moved through the denial, the anger and the fear, Mr. Tanner. They were bad enough. But now he is in a state of passive euphoria. He romanticizes everything. He seems eager to die, once he has been united with Karl, if you can believe it. He is no longer competent to manage his affairs. Unfortunately, the courts as usual are lagging behind the developments of abnormal psychology."

"I don't know. If you have to be anywhere near psychology at all it's probably better to be behind it, don't you think?"

"No, I don't think. But that's not important. I'm not asking you to accept a theory of the mind, Tanner. I'm simply asking you to take steps to prevent a potentially disastrous development. Do you know what the worldwide consequences would be if Max Kottle left his empire to a . . . a revolutionary?"

"Let me guess. Cataclysmic."

"Exactly."

"Let me guess again. That's what the professor is here to talk to me about."

"Correct."

"Two for two. How do I do it?" I looked at the professor. "Where did you go to school?"

"B.A. at Wisconsin. Ph.D. at Harvard. Postgraduate work at the London School of Economics."

"Any government experience?"

"A year with OMB."

"How about on the international front?"

"Two years at the World Bank. Three years at the Brookings Institute, specializing in international credit transactions."

"Very nice. Gentlemen, this is one day I'll for sure record in my diary."

"Why?" Hedgestone asked suspiciously.

"Well, I've been leaned on by hoods and by space cadet junkies and by hotheaded husbands, but I've never been leaned on by an economics teacher from Stanford."

I think it was the "teacher" that got him. I barely got it out before the professor was up off the couch and over to the door, telling Walter it was a mistake to have come. But Hedgestone wasn't so easily offended.

"I'm willing to pay you fifty thousand dollars to make sure young Karl stays in whatever obscure little niche he's chosen for himself until his father dies and his will is accepted for probate."

I smiled.

"A hundred thousand."

I chuckled.

"Two hundred."

I shook my head. "There's only two things in this world a man should never do, Hedgestone. He shouldn't pay money to fuck and he shouldn't take money to fail."

"Nonsense. Every rule has its exceptions. This one could be most profitable."

Sometime in there I got mad. I think it was the way he kept wrinkling his nose, as though he was smelling the trappings of my nest and finding them cheap and offensive, both morally and chemically. "I don't know about the Arabic and the Portuguese, Hedgestone," I said, "but I do know you're the only man in this hemisphere with an asshole as big as the bay. It's not so bad that you're trying to buy me off, but it's tacky as hell that you're using my own client's money to do it. Now you and your professor get out of here before I wrinkle your suits. And take that phony accent with you."

Hedgestone smiled mildly. "The accent is quite genuine, I assure you."

"How the hell would you know?"

Hedgestone considered the situation but failed to come up with a counter. He stood up. "Good day, Mr. Tanner. If you change your mind I can be reached at this number. It's a private line."

He flipped a white card on the desk and followed the professor out the door. I hoped he heard me tear it in half.

Eleven

Since I was walking down Montgomery Street, the heart of the city's financial district, I naturally started thinking about greed. Not about greed for money or power, the common forms, the greed we expect to encounter the way we expect to encounter the light bill, but a third variety, one not always appreciated either by the one who wields it or by the target of the exercise. This is the greed for moral suasion, the often unconscious impulse to dictate the habits, the desires, the behavior of others. It inflicts more psychological damage than either of the other forms because it is the variety most capable of evading our defenses. Perversely, we more willingly allow someone to dictate how we live than we allow that same someone to make a few bucks at our expense. Moral charlatans are welcomed with hosannas; welfare cheats are jailed with dispatch.

In Walter Hedgestone and Belinda Kottle I had seen two capable practitioners of ethical evangelism. Their importunities were to have persuaded me that the ailing Max Kottle was both unwise and addled, that by assisting him in locating his son I was compounding the tragedy of his decline, and that the greatest good for the greatest number would be accomplished by a slight but significant alteration in my pursuits.

But Walter and Belinda had made two mistakes. When the greatest good for the greatest number coincides with the greatest good for the person telling me about it, I never go along. Also, I'm not in business to achieve the Humanistic Calculus; I'm in business to serve my client. Lots of times the interests of the client and the masses don't coincide. Once in a while they're completely at odds. So be it. Max Kottle's spouse and Max Kottle's factotum had succeeded only in making me determined to do what the dying old man wanted me to do: find his son.

Charley Sleet was waiting for me at the bar. The customers were three deep, as usual, and they were mostly men, also as usual. The food at Hoffman's comes hot and heavy and Germanic and the atmosphere keeps pace. So did Charley Sleet. He was as thick as the goulash and just as reliable. His jaw was square and his head came close. His stomach rested above his belt like a medicine ball on a golf tee. The cops use Charley the way the Steelers use Lambert—he goes where he's needed. Over the years Charly's done enough favors for the movers and shakers around town—favors that often involved calming the victims of various sexual peccadillos—that he's become immune to department politics. They don't mess with Charley and he returns the favor.

Charley already had a beer and after I got a Bloody Mary I asked him how life was among the forces of law and order. "We're gaining on the bastards, Marsh," he said loudly. "We're gaining on them."

"How can you tell?"

"The smell, Marsh. The city doesn't smell quite as bad as it used to. Haven't you noticed?"

"I thought it was the rain."

Charley shook his head. "Hit the streets, Tanner. Quit lying around moaning over why you're a cheap-suit shamus instead of the Clarence Darrow you always wanted to be and hit the streets. Breathe the air. Feel the soil. Talk to the folk. Live, Tanner. Live."

"Christ, Charley. You must be the only cop in the world who still venerates the *folk* after thirty years on the force."

"You got to distinguish the bastards from the folk, Marsh. That's all there is to it. Some people are bastards and some people are folk. As long as there's more of the latter than the former, things are all right. When it gets the other way around I'm moving to Australia."

"They won't let you in."

"Hah. One good thing about being a cop for thirty years. You learn enough about enough people so that you can get in any damn place you want."

"You ought to write a book."

"Hah. They'd never believe it. Never, ever."

"Who?"

"The folk, of course. What's the point of writing a book if the folk aren't going to read it?"

I made a bad joke about Charley and the pulpit and ordered another Bloody Mary and asked Charley if he'd come up with anything on Karl Kottle.

"Why else would I be here?"

I laughed. "Because you're a lonely old man."

"Hah. We rousted the hookers from in front of the St. Francis again last night. When I left they were all over the station house, cackling like a pen of turkey chicks. A cop is never lonely, Marsh."

Charley was protesting too much and we both knew it. His wife died five years ago and since then he's been a cop twenty-four hours a day, roaming the streets of the city like a foster parent to us all, a nomadic life more akin to the derelicts and pushers he sometimes has to run in than to the citizens he was hired to protect. I think Charley Sleet is a saint, but it's not the kind of thing you mention to anyone.

I was about to ask Charley what he had on Kottle when they showed us a table. Charley ordered franks and beans and I ordered sauerbraten and we both ordered sourdough. When the time was right I asked Charley if he'd ever heard of a man named Howard Renn. Because his memory was as substantial as the rest of him, Charley answered in about five seconds.

"A poet, right?"

I nodded.

"Hangs out around North Beach. I see him around. We haven't got anything on him as far as I know. Although just maybe . . . hell. Half the time I can't remember how to unzip my fly anymore, Marsh. Too many gray cells pickled over the years." Charley laughed grimly. "You know how relevant poetry is to what I do for a living, Marsh? As relevant as spats."

I shook my head, then asked Charley if he knew anything about a girl named Amber who worked at the Encounter with Magic on Broadway.

"Broadway. I don't do vice anymore, Marsh. Haven't got the stomach for it. Too many girls dancing in those clubs I saw last at eight o'clock Mass. Last time I made a bust up there three white girls with razor blades and butter sticks were doing things to two Jap guys you wouldn't believe if I showed you a movie of it. Bastards. All of them." He shook his head. "I know about four girls named Amber. They're all junkies."

"This one might be, too."

"What's she look like."

"Blond. Thin. Pretty about five years ago."

"That describes every one of them. They only eat when someone feeds them, which is never. You know what I found yesterday, Marsh?"

"What?"

"Girl OD'd on smack."

"What's new?"

"She was pregnant. Just before she croaked she apparently decided to give the fetus a hit too. The syringe was sticking out of her belly like a dart. How about that?"

"How about that."

"Her boyfriend watched her take the hit, then watched her die, then called the police."

The image bounced around the room for a while, tarring everything it touched, then I asked Charley what he found on Karl Kottle.

Charley pushed himself away from the table and looked at me like I was one of the bastards and not one of the folk. "You looking for this Kottle guy, Marsh?"

"I might be. Why?"

"You're not the only one. He's wanted."

"Who by?"

"Alameda County."

"What charge?"

"Murder one."

Charley folded his arms across his chest and studied my reaction. I hoped I wasn't giving one, but Charley looks like that when we play poker and he always beats my ass. I asked for the details.

"It's an old one, Marsh. I didn't get a chance to talk to the guy who has the case, but here's the gist. Kottle was real political back in the sixties. Got hauled in during some of the antiwar marches at the Induction Center and the Army Terminal, but no time served. Charges all dismissed, apparently. They usually were, in those days. That's the only record on him except this other thing."

"Tell me about the other thing."

"Well, at some point in there, May of 1970 as I recall, the ROTC building at Berkeley was torched by person or persons unknown. Pretty clearly a political act. Late at night. Slogans painted on the building. Lots of protests beforehand, demanding ROTC to shut down. Fairly typical stuff for those days. There was just one problem."

"Someone was inside."

"You hit it, Sherlock. A girl. Not political, not even employed at the ROTC joint. Just a student who snuck in there at night to study, is the way it looks. Overcome by smoke and died. No one even knew she was there till the firemen found her two days later."

"What's the connection to Kottle?"

"His group struck the match, is what it comes down to. He was the head of something called the Student Antiwar Brigade. They were the main ones taking on the ROTC."

"Doesn't sound like much of a case."

"Then how's this sound? Kottle wasn't seen in Berkeley again after the fire. In any case, Kottle's the only one charged with first degree. A couple of other guys were charged with second and one of them went to trial but he was acquitted. Kottle's the man they want, according to the guy I talked to."

"Who's in charge of the case?"

"Cop named Lanahan, in Berkeley."

"Do they have any information on Kottle's present whereabouts?"

"Nope. It's not on the front burner any more, of course, although there's apparently lots of pressure from the father of the dead girl to keep the case active. If something comes in the computer will spit it out, that's for sure."

"You tell anyone I was interested, Charley?"

"You know better than that, Marsh. Who's your client?"

"You know better than that, Charley. Anything else on Kottle?"

"Nope. That help you any?"

"Not a damn bit."

"I'd like to know it if you find the guy."

"I know you would, Charley, I know you would."

I lit a cigarette and thought briefly about what Charley had told me. It probably meant that whatever Max Kottle's dreams were, they weren't going to come true. If I found Karl chances are the cops would find him too. In fact, I had an obligation to tell them where he was. And if I couldn't find Karl, chances are he was hidden away so deeply no one could find him, not before Max died. The underground in San Francisco was still pretty effective. It hid the Weathermen and it hid the SLA and it was still viable enough to hide a single man who was smart enough and desperate enough to want to stay hidden.

Charley glanced around the room at the thinning crowd and leaned forward toward me, propping his elbows on the table. When he spoke it was as close to a whisper as Charley can get. "You got a lot of sources around town, Marsh. You hear about anything big going down?"

"Big how?"

"Big this. Cops worry about a lot of things, you know, and one of the things we've been worried about most over the past couple of years is terrorism. The Red Brigades, Black September, that kind of chickenshit operation. Kneecapping. Bombings. All that stuff. Well, we may be about to get a taste of it right here in sweet San Francisco."

"What makes you think so? I haven't read anything about it."

Charley nodded in agreement. "The reason is, the papers and the TV haven't gotten wind of it yet. I can trust you on this, can't I, Marsh?"

I nodded. Charley was as serious as I had ever seen him.

"Over the past few years," he went on, "the police commission has met in secret with the various people and organizations who are the most likely targets of terrorist activity. Wealthy individuals, politically sensitive businesses, politicians, people like that. A code has been worked out so we can respond to a suspected terrorist attack without alerting the media as to what has really happened. That Aldo Moro thing in Italy really got to people. All of the ones we approached have gone along. We've convinced them that if we can keep the stuff out of the papers we can put a stop to it pretty fast, even if some group does get started. Hell, those punks don't go to the crapper unless someone agrees to put it on the tube."

"So what happened, Charley? Who got hit?"

"Last week someone put a bomb in a restroom at Laguna Oil, down on Sansome. There was the usual note beforehand, full of threats and boasts and demands and like that."

"Anyone hurt?"

"Hell of a blast, but no injuries and not much fire. They gave ten minutes's warning."

"Wait a minute. I read something about that. The *Chronicle* said it was a short in the electrical system."

Charley smiled. "That's what we wanted them to say. Laguna Oil wanted them to say that, too."

"What makes you think they're going to strike again?"

"Because we got word that some new group is in the market for weapons. We think it's the same outfit. They want military stuff, grenades and launchers and M60s and M16s. The word is out, and you know as well as I do there's been enough of that kind of ordnance stolen from armories in this state to supply them with everything they want. All they need is bread."

"Do they have a name? Generally they pick a name."

"They call themselves the Sons and Daughters of Isaiah. The SDI."

"Son of SDS, out of SLA."

"That's about it."

I thought a moment. " 'I have nourished and brought up children, and they have rebelled against me.' "

"What the hell's that?" Charley asked.

"The Lord according to the prophet Isaiah. Chapter one. My mother was a Baptist.

"Mine wasn't."

"What do they want, Charley? What's their particular blueprint for universal salvation?"

Charley shook his head. "That's not clear. They want Laguna to stop importing oil from overseas, and to divest its retail operations, and to roll back prices on domestic

crude. And employ more black youth. And on and on.
Lots of ranting and raving about inflation, the poor, the
environment, Israel. Hell, to listen to them you'd think
Laguna Oil was the only one shitting on the earth."

"How many Sons and Daughters are there?"

"Who knows? But if this thing gets some publicity
there'll be more than enough to do some damage. There's
a lot of chiefs and a lot of Indians in this town, Marsh.
Enough to make a hell of a tribe."

"What's that mean, Charley?"

"I mean there's all those people who a decade ago were
spending every minute debating peace and war and sexual
freedom and civil rights and all that, shutting down
schools and confronting the cops. Now all they confront is
the next mortgage payment and all they debate is which
flick to see on Friday night. They're the chiefs. Then
there's the younger ones, the Indians, the new kids in town
with big holes in their middles that they can't fill themselves. We've been lucky for a long time. The people filling those holes have been basically nonviolent, the
Erhards, the Krishnas, like that. But for a lot of those kids
that hole can be filled just as well by tossing a firebomb as
by wearing saffron bedsheets and playing finger chimes. If
the Chiefs and the Indians ever get together we're in for
some long nights."

"What do you want me to do?"

"Just keep your ears open. If you pick up anything we
can use, let me know. You remember Zebra. I'd just as
soon that didn't happen again."

Zebra. The name still chilled. The Death Angels, blacks
killing whites, at random. Twenty-three victims over a six-
month period in this city alone—hacked, stabbed, shot,
butchered, raped, maimed, kidnapped. The city had almost
closed down, the nighttime streets filled only with the fear
that leaked out from behind locked doors and shaded windows. The cops had tossed the Fourth Amendment out the
window and searched almost at will. Most of the city fa-
thers had gone along. When a half dozen businessmen
have their legs shotgunned out from under them, and the
rest spend half their time imagining the sex life of a para-
plegic and double-checking the due date on the disability
premium, a lot more than the Fourth Amendment will be
in jeopardy.

I told Charley I'd do what I could and we stood up and

shouldered our way out the door. We promised each other we'd get together soon and then Charley took off, ambling down Market Street toward his car, a hulking bear of a man who, like every cop in the world, eyed the people in his path with eyes as hard as fists.

Looking for the bastards.

Twelve

Montgomery Street had lengthened considerably over the lunch hour—it seemed to take forever to get back to the office. Along the way the Kottle case sloshed around in my mind, its elements dispersed, a floating slick of puzzles and questions that were badly in need of a catalyst. The puzzle that was Karl Kottle had taken on a new dimension, a new and grotesque thickness that I didn't like. Instead of the rebellious youth I thought I was seeking, Karl was instead a fugitive, quite possibly a murderer, a man on the run from his past, a man with nothing to lose. It would make him harder to find, and when I did find him it would make him harder to handle.

As I climbed the stairs to my office it occurred to me that the case was probably over. As much as he wanted to see his son, I doubted that Max Kottle would want to jeopardize the boy's freedom by taking the chance that the cops would follow my path to Karl and take him away from both me and his father.

I said hello to Peggy and sat down at the desk. As though I had depressed a joy buzzer, the telephone rang. It was Chet Herk. After a preliminary skirmish or two he got to what was on his mind. "You remember the other night at dinner, when I asked if you could take on something new?" he asked.

"Sure."

"Your situation changed any?"

I thought about it. "Not yet. Why?"

"Because my problem hasn't gone away. I've got to do something, Marsh. If you can't help me, give me the name of someone who can."

I sighed. "I might be able to help you in a few days, Chet. The thing I'm on is going nowhere. Either I'm going to get taken off it or I'm going to have to hit the pavement twenty-four hours a day till I dig something up. I was just about to call the client and see what he wants me to do. If you can wait awhile I might be free."

"I better not wait. If you get loose give me a call. I have a feeling it's going to take more than one set of eyes to find this needle. San Francisco's a hell of a haystack."

"Who's missing?"

"Who said anyone was missing?"

"You did."

"The hell I did. Give me some names."

"Well, when I need someone I usually try to get Jessie Tadlock, if he's free."

"Tadlock. Yeah. He's the one found the kid a few years ago, right?"

"Right. Also, you remember Harry Spring?"

"Harry. Yeah. Good cop. Hell of a way to die."

"He was a good investigator, too. His widow, Ruthie, took over his license. She's good, too."

"I don't think this is anything for a woman."

"Chauvinist."

"That's what one of my girl reporters tells me every day. But what the hell. Everybody's got to be something, right? I'll call Tadlock."

"Tell him I sent you."

"Why? You get a percentage?"

I laughed and we made small talk for a while. After we agreed to meet for a drink in a couple of days Chet hung up. I reached into the file drawer of my desk and hauled out the folder with the receivables in it and spread the various statements over the desk top. Someday I'll paper the bathroom with uncollectable accounts.

As I was arranging the statements in descending order of collectability Peggy buzzed me. "A Mr. Kottle is on the line," she said.

My nerve endings sparked briefly across the gap of my afternoon lassitude. "Which Mr. Kottle?"

"Maximilian. Your client, remember?"

I told her to put him on. I should have known I couldn't be that lucky.

An electronic second passed; switches clicked, wires linked, then Max Kottle spoke to me, his voice arid, without ornament. "Sorry to bother you, Tanner, but I've had a hell of a day. Spent the morning with my lawyers, haggling over the precise language with which to inform the world, and more precisely Wall Street, that I am not long for this earth. Apparently they don't want to make me appear too dead, since there's a statistical chance I'll remit, but then they don't want to mislead people by declaring me fully alive. A troubling problem in semantics, but everyone but me seemed to be enjoying themselves. This came after the night I spent in the hospital being bombarded with cobalt rays. Right now I'm nauseous as hell. You know what I take for it?"

"What?"

"Marijuana."

"No kidding?"

"Works, too. My nurse told me about it. But don't tell my doctor. It's not officially prescribed."

"Mum's the word."

"So. On that cheery note I'm calling to see if you have any news for me. A man who is himself regressing inevitably seeks out signs of progress in others."

If I could have made him better by telling a lie I would have, but he would want the gaps filled, the connections made, and I wouldn't be able to do it. "I haven't found him," I said simply. "I'm sorry."

"Don't be," Kottle rasped. "I should have started this process a long time ago. It would have been much easier then, wouldn't it?"

"Who knows? If we always did what we should, think of the people who would be out of work."

"Do you have anything at all to go on?" he asked.

"A couple of things. In a few minutes I'm going to see a man who knew Karl in Berkeley and who's been seen with him fairly recently here in the city. Also I've been told Karl used to hang out in a bar down by the Embarcadero. I'm going to check that out, too. Nothing hot, but warm enough."

"Is that all?"

"Yes, but it's something. Karl's been seen here in San Francisco within the past month. I'll find him, Mr. Kottle. Sooner or later."

"Who saw him?"

"I don't think I'll disclose that. It wouldn't help; it could hurt."

"Who could it hurt?" Kottle scoffed.

"Does it matter?"

Kottle didn't respond so I pushed on. "Your son is

wanted by the police," I said. "You should have told me about it."

"How did you find out?" Kottle said hotly. "I told you not to consult the police. Apparently you disobeyed my instructions."

Kottle's tone was raw and peremptory, despite his ailment. All of a sudden I got mad again. Men like Max Kottle amass a myriad of things over their lives—money, power, influence, beauty, you name it. The only thing I've managed to accumulate is a small pile of dignity, carefully scooped and scraped together over the years. It's nicked and scarred in places, eroded in others, incomplete, but a pile nonetheless, small and sturdy and mine. Walter Hedgestone had stomped right on it by offering a bribe, and Belinda Kottle had taken a piece off it too, and now Max was implying I was less than competent and less than free to do things as I saw fit.

"Your check bought some hours of my time, Mr. Kottle, it didn't buy you the right to tell me how to do my job. I got the information I needed from the people I needed to get it from. The police don't know any more about Karl today than they did a week ago. But an investigator always needs to know whether the person he's looking for is wanted by the cops. It makes a difference where and how he looks. You didn't bother to tell me, presumably because you thought I'd turn bounty hunter and give Karl up for the reward, am I right?"

"Something like that."

"Either you trust me completely or not at all. Which is it? I've got other things I could be doing."

Kottle's voice was heavy, suddenly lifeless. "I trust you. You have my apologies."

"Great. With them and a dollar I can buy a gallon of gas. Are there any more tidbits you thought it prudent to keep from me?"

"No. Nothing."

"Okay. I'm going to send you a bill. On it will be the words 'For legal services and consultation.' Pay it right away."

"I have more lawyers than I can count already, Tanner. What's the point?"

"The point is that as your lawyer I can keep what you've told me confidential. I always do this in a police case. Makes the game a little clearer. When you play with the cops it's nice to know the rules."

Kottle was silent for another moment. I watched a spider climb the wall across from me, a spiny nugget of terror. "I'm afraid I made a mistake in not trusting you," Kottle said finally. "As a matter of policy I trust no one but Walter and Belinda. When Lathrop mentioned your name to me he said you were discreet and loyal. I should have believed him."

"Lathrop Lewis?"

"Yes. You know him?"

"I know of him. I didn't know I was on his recommended list."

"I was stupid to doubt his word. After all, the worst thing that can happen already has."

There was nothing I could say to that, except to tell him he was wrong. In the silence I began to wonder when they would get me, those little Storm Troopers, to wonder when the carcinoma would begin to scurry through the shadows of my lungs and the folds of my kidneys and the creases of my brain, to wonder when I was going to die. I looked for the spider. He had disappeared.

"I'll leave you to your business, Mr. Tanner," Kottle said. "Pursue it in your own way. I won't interfere. Just keep me informed."

I told him I would and I told him I was sorry I'd gotten mad and he hung up. I looked down at the past-due accounts and decided I didn't want to deal with them, so I called Peggy in and asked her to put them back in the file. I also asked if there was anything I needed to know before I left for the day. She told me there were just nine shopping days left till Christmas. The telephone rang again. It was Mrs. Kottle. Belinda.

"You talked to him, didn't you?" she asked breathily. Her eagerness tickled.

"Who?"

"My husband."

"I can't seem to remember. What if I did?"

"Please, Mr. Tanner. I have only his best interests at heart. You have to believe me."

"The only thing I have to do just now is assuage some of my creditors. I'm working for your husband, Mrs. Kottle. If he wants you to know what I tell him he'll inform you himself. The last I heard there was nothing wrong with his vocal chords."

"That's tasteless."

"You're right."

"This is ridiculous. I didn't explain it right the other afternoon. We're off on the wrong foot. May I see you again, and make a second effort?"

"I'd be happy to see you again, Mrs. Kottle. You can come by my apartment tonight. I'll fix you a drink and put on some music and we can talk about anything you want except one. You're a beautiful woman. It'll be the best evening I've spent in a long time. But if you think I'll tell you anything about your husband you're wrong."

She paused. "Yes," she said at last. "I probably am. But if you think I care for anything or anyone except my husband, you're wrong, too."

The phone went dead in my ear, leaving an echo of frustrated purpose. I hoped I had underestimated Mrs. Kottle, but I couldn't afford to wonder about it.

I glanced at my watch, then made a call. With surprising rapidity Sergeant Lanahan of the Berkeley police was on the line. I told him I was a graduate student in sociology at Cal and that I was doing my thesis on the war protests of the late sixties. I told him I was interested in Karl Kottle especially, and wondered if the police had any information on where he might be now.

Lanahan sounded young and happy about it. "Kottle, huh? If I knew where he was I'd get a cell ready."

"Is he still wanted for the death of that girl?"

"How'd you know about that?"

"I've been researching some old newspaper articles," I explained. "The *Gazette* and the *Tribune*, mostly."

"Well, Kottle's still wanted, all right. My guess is he's in Canada, but he could be about anywhere, I suppose. He's smart as hell. A silver-tongued devil on top of it. We won't find him unless he wants to be found or he trusts the wrong person."

"You sound like you kind of admire the guy, Sergeant."

"I won't say I admire him, but he's capable as hell, I'll admit that. I used to monitor all those rallies and marches back then. I was a rookie. Got all the shit details. Looking for incitement evidence, was what it amounted to. Anyway, Kottle was the best of all those guys, maybe next to Savio. He didn't insult your intelligence, you know? And he didn't go for the trashing, either. His crowds never went off wild."

"Then maybe he didn't start that fire after all."

"That's not my job, to say whether he did or didn't."

"But what do you think?"

"What I think is he *could* have started it, since it was the ROTC. He'd go that far. But he wouldn't have done it if he'd known that girl was inside. No way. Some of the other ones, hell, that wouldn't have even slowed them down. But Kottle, he was a better type of individual."

"Do you still have any pictures of him?"

"Somewhere. Hey. I've talked too damn much already. Do your research someplace else. And spell my name right. Lanahan. All *a*'s."

He hung up and I got my car and headed for the nearest freeway.

Thirteen

I skirted downtown and headed into the heart of the city, then abandoned the freeway at Fell and whizzed west along the Panhandle of Golden Gate Park to Stanyan and then turned left. At the Haight Street intersection some old memories bestirred themselves and I slid back to another time. I pulled into the parking lot at the Cala Food Market and stopped the car, in the grip of senses seldom used.

Back in '67 I lived in this part of the city. It was the summer of the Flower Children and the Grateful Dead and the Hog Farm Collective and Captain America, and by day Haight Street was a festival of drug-eased love and joy. Young boys with hair like Hayworth and young girls with no hips roamed the sidewalks, exchanging peace signs and daisies and soulful stares and illegal substances, all offered and received with unquestioning acceptance, without doubt or fear. During the day, when the sun was shining, it looked harmless and peaceful and somehow better than what any of the rest of us had going.

But even at the beginning there was a dark side to all of it, there always is, and as usual the dark side came out at night. I'd see one aspect of it whenever I'd come home late. Everytime I drove along Stanyan, around midnight or after, I would see them right across the street from the market where I was parked. Swaddled in the fog, huddled together against the cold and wet, a score of little rag bundles lay like dead dogs on the concrete sidewalk that led down into the park. They were the kids from Toledo and Little Rock and Duluth, the kids who'd run off to San Francisco to find on the streets of that mostly mythic city whatever it was they weren't finding at home. The runaways.

Some of the kids, a few, actually found it for a while—the self-respect all of us crave and most of us used to develop at an early age back before the Beverly Hillbillies and the Rotary Club became more interesting to parents than their children were. But a lot of kids never hooked onto the good side of Flower Power and instead got progressively sicker and more exhausted until they were burned out and left for dead by the ones who had got there early and were so far into themselves they couldn't see anything but their own desires. Some young lives were lost and some old hearts were broken before it ended, but still and all we, all of us, are a little better off for what those kids planted inside us a decade ago, that paramecium-sized idea that it didn't always have to be the way it always had been.

I stayed where I was a few minutes more, remembering a past that seemed a better time for both the city and for me. Twelve years had elapsed since then, twenty percent of my life, probably, in theory my most productive period. But in practice, well, in practice there were no prizes, no awards, no books written, no paintings painted, no buildings built, no machines designed, no cures discovered. No tax shelters, no Keogh Plans, no Krugerrands. Just a five-thousand-dollar CD earning half the inflation rate and a six-year-old Buick chugging gas the way winos chug Thunderbird and a Paul Klee original that hung in my office inside a walnut frame because once, a long time ago, I'd managed a miracle for someone with imagination and good taste.

Twelve years.

At one time that seemed an expanse of time beyond the powers of contemplation. Now it seemed like a belch.

I started my engine and went on about my business, which was to talk to Karl Kottle's old friend Howard Renn. The poet.

Edgewood Avenue runs along the base of Mt. Sutro, on its northeast edge, just below the University of California Medical Center and just above Kezar Stadium, where the Forty-Niners used to play before some visionary gave us Candlestick Park. I'd lived about a hundred yards from Renn's house back in '67, down on Parnassus Street in a duplex over a girl who'd owned the skinniest, ugliest dog I ever saw: an Italian greyhound. I still have nightmares about the dog and I still have dreams about the girl.

Howard Renn lived in a large, Maybeckish brown-shingle house that perched like a grackle above the small green lawn that sloped up to meet it. A narrow flight of steps split the lawn and hooked the house to the walk. I squeezed the Buick between a Mercedes and a Volvo, after begging their pardon, and walked up the steps through a gauntlet of pink petunias. If there was another poet living on this block his name was Rod McKuen.

It was a storybook place: windows trimmed in yellow, chimney splashed with red, porch steps streaked in white. The grass was clipped shorter than my hair and the flower-beds were weedless and geometric. The air around me smelled of rare essence—money well spent. The man who opened the door, however, looked more like a serf than a lord.

He was short and fat and bald. A ring of black and gray hair circled his head like surrey fringe. His thick beard was bristly and salted, his nose red and bulbous, his hands round and meaty, with stubby fingers the shape of kosher wieners. His eyes were black and vibrant, out of the same box as Rasputin's. He just stood there, blocking my view of anything but avoirdupois.

"Mr. Renn?" I stuck out my hand. "My name's Tanner," I said cheerily. "I'd like to talk to you a minute."

"Read the sign." The words were brusque, like the gesture that went with them.

"What?"

"The sign."

He gestured to his left again and I looked. A small, sparkling, black-and-white, glow-in-the-dark plate was tacked to the house just above the mailbox, at eye level. "No Solicitors."

"I'm not a solicitor," I said quickly. "In the profession I used to pursue, solicitation was unethical."

"Well, now, what have we?" Renn bubbled. "A legal

eagle? A master of the healing arts? Or perhaps merely a strolling minstrel, a roving ambassador, a vaudevillian manqué. Surely not the Avon Lady?"

"I'm an investigator," I said with irritation. "I'd like to get some information from you."

Renn inhaled, swelling his belly. "I am a veritable mountain of information," he announced grandly. "My corpuscles are inflamed with knowledge. I have information about Emily Dickinson's peculiar punctuation and information about the inherent fallacy in the Warren Commission's 'single bullet theory' and information about the American complicity in the slaughter of the Tupemaros. Which will it be? Come now. Don't be shy."

Renn wasn't trying to be funny, he was trying to be Brecht. I put a stop to it. "Turn it off, Renn. Save it for your next quatrain. I want to know about Karl Kottle. If you don't talk to me now, the next guy that rings your bell will be a cop. And he may just solicit you and your tummy right down to the Hall of Justice."

I wasn't about to call a cop, of course, not at this stage of the game, but Renn didn't know that. The satiric glint in his eye flew away soundlessly and his eyes narrowed. One hand rose to his chest, balled into a fist, then opened again, a pink and mutant morning glory. His mouth opened and closed as well, fishlike.

I waited. "You *are* Howard Renn, aren't you?" I asked finally. "I'd hate to think I put up with all this for nothing."

Renn hesitated, then nodded.

"You were in school at Berkeley ten years ago?"

"Yes. No. For a while, I mean. Nothing relevant was occurring in the classroom in those days. The only true knowledge was in the streets." Renn paused, shaking his head. His eyes looked past me. "Have you been there lately?"

"Berkeley?"

"Yes. The streets are empty. Did you notice? People selling belts and tie-dyed underwear. Sproul Plaza groans with the verbs of commerce. I never thought it could happen. I never thought that what we did would disappear so quickly." Renn laughed hollowly. "I had a girl here the other night. She thought Mario Savio was a varietal wine. I could have strangled her. My God. Karl shed blood on

University Avenue. There should be a monument on the spot. Instead they sell strawberry smoothies."

Renn's eyes moved away from mine, became glazed exemplars of his dismay at the nation's terminal inadequacy. When they found me again they were softer, less wary.

"Tell me about Karl," I said easily.

I had tried to slip in under his defenses but I hadn't quite made it. He began to pant. His brows jumped simultaneously, again and again, like window wipers. White bubbles gathered at the corners of his mouth. He swiped at them twice with the back of his hand. "Who are you?" he asked.

"My name's Tanner. I'm a private investigator. I'm looking for Karl Kottle. You know where he is." I made it a statement, a charge.

"No, I don't."

"Yes, you do."

Renn shook his head in a second denial. Suddenly a voice came from somewhere inside the house, somewhere deep and below ground, from the sound of it. "Is that Woody? If not, get rid of her." Renn turned toward the sound, then back to me. He seemed fearful.

"Leave. Go. I know nothing of Karl Kottle. I write poetry. Sonnets. Laments. Epics. Haiku. I know nothing that would interest a man like you. Please leave."

"You're lying. You mentioned Karl just a minute ago, when you were talking about the old days in Berkeley. When did you see him last?"

"I told you. I've never seen him. I don't know who you mean." His eyes went back to the interior behind him.

"Come on, Renn," I urged. "You and Kottle are in the history books. You ate at Robbie's, you orated on the steps at Sproul Hall, you stomped down Telegraph Avenue like moral conquistadors. Kottle was Quixote and you were Sancho Panza. Don't play games with me."

In the silence I altered my tone. "There's nothing to worry about, Renn. I simply want to give Kottle a message. We don't even have to meet. Just have him call me. Tanner. I'm in the book under 'Investigators.' Here's my card."

"No," he said. "No."

With the flush of panic on his face he knocked the card from my hand and slammed the door. The white card fluttered off the porch and drifted toward the lawn, lurching

spastically, a wounded gull over a small green sea. I
watched it come to rest on the grass; it landed upside
down. I walked back to my car.

Howard Renn was lying. I was so certain of it that I
drove down to where Edgewood dead-ended into a eucalyptus grove and turned around and parked again,
hoping Renn would rush out and drive off and I could tail
him to Karl Kottle, just like in the movies.

It didn't happen. The eucalyptus choir sang an *a cap-
pella* canticle as I waited beneath it. Time drifted by, tugging behind it a sky that was a blackboard in need of
erasure. The sidewalks and the street were as barren as
bread.

I squirmed around, trying to keep warm, then squirmed
again. As I did so I looked out the window to my left,
directly across the street. A woman was looking at me, a
young woman in an old Mustang. A seaman's watch cap
hid her hair and gave her a masculine, Dickensian aspect.
With wide blue eyes she examined me frankly, filing my
face away in an already bulging file of faces.

I raised my eyebrows in a question. She looked away
for a moment, then opened her car door and came over to
my own. I rolled down the window.

"She was there, wasn't she?" the woman asked. The
voice was nasal, ill.

"She's everywhere," I cracked. "Who are you talking
about?"

"I *know* she's there. I was late today, but I know she's
in there. She probably spent the night."

"Lady, who are you?"

She put her hands on her hips, stretching her sweater
tautly along her slim body, and thrust her chest forward,
challenging me. "You were in Howard's place. I saw you.
You must have seen her. Why won't you help me?"

Incipient hysteria upped the last question an octave
above her normal range. I raised a hand to back her up,
then got out of the car. She was shivering, from equal
parts cold and anger. Abruptly, she broke into tears. I put
a hand on her shoulder. She pulled back for an instant,
then sobbed and pressed against me. I put my arms
around her and tried to make my chest a comfortable
place to be.

When the convulsions stopped I asked her who she was.
"I'm Judy Renn," she stuttered. "Howard's wife. He's di-

vorcing me. He has our child. He took her from me. I
want her back."

"He kidnapped her?"

"No, not exactly. He got his lawyer to get some preliminary something-or-other. My lawyer says if I take her
they'll put me in jail."

"He's probably right."

"He says the only thing I can do is prove I'm a fit
parent and he isn't. He says women's lib has made it
harder for women to keep their babies."

"He's probably right about that, too."

"I can't let Howard win. He's such a slob. So totally ir-
responsible. I can't let him do this to me, not on top of all
the rest of it."

"What's the rest of it?"

"The years, all the years. We lived on nothing for ages.
Howard wrote those stupid poems and spent his nights
hanging around bars and coffeehouses, while I worked my
tail off. Three different jobs at once, sometimes. Howard
never lifted a finger. His art was all. Art. Garbage, is more
like it. How could I have been such a fool?"

"Love."

"I know, I know." She shook her head miserably.

"But what happened?" I asked. "The place he's in now
isn't exactly a hovel."

"His father died. A dentist. Howard inherited everything, including that house." She laughed quickly at herself. "I was still stupid even then. I planted every one of
those damned petunias. Can you believe it?"

"Are you okay now?"

She nodded. "Thanks for the squeeze."

"Do you come here every day?" I asked, suddenly
aware that this woman could help me a little, too.

"When I can."

"You're collecting evidence of his unfitness, is that it?"

"Now that he's got money the fat slob has those Union
Street women crawling all over him. I'm making a list and
taking pictures. I've got to beat him."

"A detective would do it better."

"I can't afford a detective."

"You're probably better off, at that." I took out the picture of Karl Kottle that Max had given me and showed it
to her. "You ever see this guy in your husband's place?"

She took the picture from me and turned it to the

streetlight and studied it for a minute. She frowned, then handed it back. "That's Karl, isn't it? He's changed quite a bit, but that's Karl. Karl Kottle. Isn't it?"

I nodded. "When did you see him last?"

"I've seen him lots. He used to come over for dinner, when I was with Howard. He was so sick, I always liked giving him a good meal."

"How was he sick?"

"I'm not sure. He just looked real weak and all. I tried to fatten him up, but it didn't work. I haven't seen him since I left Howard, though."

"You know where Karl lives now?"

A siren suddenly squealed into life up at the medical center and Judy Renn started and stepped away from me. "I think I'm getting into something here," she said suspiciously. "Who the hell are you, anyway?"

"Nobody."

"Welcome to the club. I don't think I'd better talk to you anymore, Mister Nobody."

She turned and walked rapidly toward her car. I yelled for her to wait but she just increased her speed. As she opened the door she thanked me for the shoulder to cry on. The door of the Mustang slammed, squashing my source. She slumped down in the seat, her eyes on the side mirror, spying on her future.

I got back in my car and started the engine. Just then Howard Renn and another man came out and got in a blue Volvo and drove off. I tagged along, just like in the movies.

Fourteen

I skulked along behind Renn and his friend as they lurched through the city, trailing taillights through rainy streets the way I used to trail rabbits through snowy fields when I was a kid and my grandfather had a farm and a shotgun and taught me to use them both. Like everything else, it seemed more fun when I was young.

As it turned out, Renn was going my way. After driving to the foot of Mission Street he pulled into a parking lot between Steuart and the Embarcadero and got out. As I watched, the two of them went halfway down Steuart and turned into the back door of a building and disappeared.

I still hadn't gotten a good look at the guy with Renn. He was big and curly-haired and wore a red lumber jacket and jeans. As far as I could tell he was no one I knew.

I found a place to park and went around to the front and counted off the buildings. The one they'd gone into was Cicero's, the bar where Karl Kottle used to hang out, according to Amber. Things were heating up.

There were several reasons why I shouldn't have gone inside, most of them having to do with secrecy and surprise, but there was one good reason why I should: I still didn't have any idea where Karl Kottle was, and someone in there very likely did. I pushed open the door.

It was dark inside, bar-dark. A line of men sat side by side, each separated from the other by a barstool's worth of space and time, which in places like Cicero's is all the space and time there is.

At the far end two women, one young and one old, held hands and whispered over two glasses of headless beer. The bartender stood beneath a Hamm's sign, polishing a stem glass with a limp cloth. He probably hadn't poured anything into a stem glass in a decade. High in the back of the room a black-and-white television set showed some people dressed like vegetables jumping up and down and hugging a man wearing a suit that was shiny and a condescending grin that wasn't. If the sound was on I couldn't hear it.

There were some booths along the wall opposite the bar, and a row of tables in between. Two heads were visible above the backs of the far booth. The one facing me belonged to Howard Renn.

I walked over to the bar. The floor made crackling noises beneath my feet, the cry of shrinking souls. I edged onto a stool. For the next five minutes the only sound I heard was the white noise of despair, made up of a lot of other people's tones and a few of my own.

Finally the bartender walked down toward where I was sitting. He was tall and slim and his skin was as white as a cueball just out of the box. He had the air of haughty aloofness bartenders learn about the same time they learn how to mix a Tequila Sunrise without looking it up. "What'll it be?" he asked casually.

"Beer. In the bottle."

"We wash our glasses."

"I'll still take the bottle."

"Bud?"

"Fine."

He went back to the Hamm's sign and bent down and came back up with a tall brown bottle and flipped off the cap and set it on the bar. I pretended not to get the hint that he wanted me to come and get it. He swore under his breath and grabbed the bottle and came back to my end and banged it down in front of me. I handed him a ten and told him he could keep it all if he'd give me a couple of minutes of his time.

He glanced quickly down the bar. When he didn't see anything that hadn't been there for at least an hour he folded his arms and leaned against the counter across from me. The bottle of Galliano behind him made him seem pinheaded.

"My name's Tanner," I began quietly.

"Phil."

"Nice place, Phil."

"It's okay."

"You own it?"

"Nope."

"Been working here long?"

"Nine years next month."

"Who's the owner?"

"You a cop?"

"No."

"Health Department?"

"No."

"Beverage Control?"

"Private investigator."

"No kidding."

"No kidding."

He unfolded his arms. "Who you after?"

"Guy named Kottle. Know him?"

His eyes boiled hard, then rolled toward the back of the room and then rolled back to me. "Kottle. Never heard of him. Any reason I should?"

I shrugged. "I heard he used to hang out here."

"Why you want him?"

"If he's the Kottle I think he is, he's going to come into some money. Rich aunt died up in Red Bluff. Executor hired me to find her heirs."

The barman laughed, loudly and without humor. "How many times a month you figure I hear that line? Huh? Christ, you collection guys are all alike."

I smiled. "Okay. No rich aunt. I'm not a collection agent, though. I think Kottle would want to talk to me. Where can I find him?"

"Beats me, buddy. Thanks for the ten."

The bill slipped out of sight beneath his palm and he walked back down the bar, chuckling to himself. The line of men didn't move, didn't speak, didn't breathe, didn't exist. The barman poured some cheap bar whisky into a cheap shot glass and set it in front of the third man from the end. The man stared at it the way people stare at their own blood.

I stayed where I was and drank my beer. The two women slid off their stools and moved to the door, still whispering and still holding hands. By the time they got outside the older woman was crying. A while later a kid in a gray sweat shirt and jeans came in, looked around, and took the stool the old woman had vacated. A while later another man came in and sat in a booth facing me. He stared my way for a minute, his gaze parting the gloom like a comb. He was young, thirties, with blond hair and bright blue eyes, the left seeming larger than the right. His face was thin, his neck long, his shoulders narrow and sloped. He could have been Karl Kottle in disguise and he could have been someone I would never see again or want to.

I drained the bottle. An old woman shuffled in, a different one, scraping her soles in the grit, muttering to herself every step of the way. She didn't sit anywhere, but stood in the middle of the room, staring at the floor, her hair matted and caked, her chin wet with spittle. No one paid any attention to her and no one paid any attention to me. When she left she took my interest with her.

"Think it over," I called down to the bartender, loud enough to be heard by everyone in the place. "I know Kottle comes in here. It's worth money for a lead to him. Good money. Pass the word. The name's Tanner."

If anyone heard what I said they didn't show it. I looked in the mirror behind the bar, at the reflection of Renn and his friend, but didn't get either the reaction or the glimpse of the friend I was hoping for. I was about to go over and sit down with them, to pour a little salt on whatever open wound I could find, when suddenly Renn stood up and waved his arms back and forth. "Split!" he yelled. "Take off!"

I spun around on my stool and almost fell off it. Over in the doorway a short blond girl and a taller black-haired man were running outside, their backs to me, the man tugging the girl along behind him like a kite he was trying to get airborne.

I took off after them, stumbling a bit as my foot caught in the stool next to me. "How about the beer?" the bartender yelled after me. I told him to take it out of the ten. He told me what to do to myself.

By the time I got to the street the man wasn't in sight. I could have gone looking for him, and I probably would have, if I hadn't spotted the girl climbing into a little white Triumph that was parked next to a freeway piling. I waited until I saw her pull out into the Embarcadero heading north, then ran to my car. I drove after her, hoping the traffic would hold her up enough so that I could catch her. By the time she turned west on Bay Street I had.

The rush-hour traffic stuttered along beside me like a flock of palsied sheep, bleating regularly but hopelessly, oblivious of their fate. The air inside my car grew noxious, making my nose itch. The people in the cars around me did this every day. If you asked them why, they'd have a reason.

All of a sudden I felt lonely. My home was just above me, on Telegraph Hill. I wanted to go up there and slip into something warm and comfortable, like a Marquand novel or a rerun of "The Rockford Files." I blinked and kept on driving.

It was slow going. When she turned onto Marina Boulevard I figured we were heading over the Golden Gate, and I was right. Twenty minutes later, when she took the Sausalito exit, I figured she was going somewhere I had been before. I was right about that, too.

The Triumph climbed toward Edwards Avenue and by the time I caught up to it, it was parked across from the home of the first Mrs. Maximilian Kottle, Shelly Withers, authoress. The blonde must have been the one whose naked derrière I'd seen three days before, the one Randy had called a whore.

I pulled over and cut my engine and my lights and tried

to decide what it all meant. Fifteen minutes later I decided
it didn't mean anything, yet. I hadn't been running on
anything but bluff when I'd told the bartender I thought
someone at Cicero's knew Karl Kottle, and for all I knew
Howard Renn had warned the girl and her friend off because they were about to deal some cocaine or perform
some other deed equally inconsequential as far as I was
concerned.

Still, the link was there, and links often—though not always—make a chain. The trouble with chains is, if you
follow some of them you find something nice hooked onto
the other end, but if you follow others you just go round
and round, finding nothing but your own frustration.

I got out of the car and walked up the steps and
through the hedge to a point where I could see the house.
No one went in or out. From time to time some shadows
moved behind the linen curtains, a faint and lissome
shadow play, and then were gone.

The bay lapped like a wolfhound at the shore below, the
sound dissonant with the mindless roar of the commuters
on the freeway above. Then all of a sudden the thing I
heard best was the sound of a woman singing about love
and sadness. It sounded like Carole King. The sound was
on a record and the record was scratched, like the singer's
heart. The sound came from deep inside the house. I figured the girl with the formerly bare behind was in for the
night, so I went home.

Fifteen

The apartment was cold and empty so I decided to build a
fire, the first one of the winter. I had enough old *Chronicles* to paper train the zoo and enough hickory and plum
logs to build an ark: I tend to overanticipate my enthusi-
asms. It took some time for the chimney to begin to draw
properly, but within the hour I was as toasty as a flea on a
sheepdog.

I poured a drink and put on Mozart's D Minor Concerto
—Köchel 466, Rubenstein, with the Beethoven cadenzas.
The logs in the fireplace hissed at me like cats on the
veldt. The music and I were slightly sour, slightly melan-
choly, and just ever so slightly glad to be that way.

Across the street an engine roared, the signal for the neighbor girl to run out and hop into a customized Camaro and slide over till she was indistinguishable from the slick-haired driver so they could roar off for an evening of disco delight. The girl's name was Debbie. I'd only spoken to her once, on a Sunday when I was out washing my car and she came over to ask if I wanted to buy some hash.

My jacket and tie and shoes were on something other than my body and I was on my third helping of Scotch and my second helping of Oreos when the doorbell rang. I opened up and looked into the cavernous eyes of Belinda Kottle.

"Hello," she said.

"Hello. Slumming?"

"Not at all. I just had dinner with some friends down on Green Street and I wanted to see you. Am I disturbing anything?"

"Only solitude."

"Solitude can be very precious."

"Not to me. I could hold a fire sale. Come on in."

She gave me a smile I'd remember for a while and swept into my living room.

She was dressed for the evening—long gold gown, emeralds at throat and lobes, hair swept up onto her head and swirled into some kind of knot that was held in place by a gold pin the size of a Ticonderoga Number 2. I helped her off with her little jacket and pushed some papers off a chair and asked her to sit down. Then I asked if she would like a drink.

She shook her head. "I've had my limit already this evening."

"No limits allowed here. How about a B&B? Just to ward off the chill."

She tried to be mischievous. "The chill outside or the chill inside?"

"This is the warmest place in town," I said.

"Well, I'll have a little taste, just to be sociable."

I went to the kitchen and washed the dust off a liqueur glass and filled it with thickness, feeling more than a little guilty because, like a kid at his first fraternity party, I felt suddenly eager for Belinda Kottle to become intoxicated in my living room.

I went back and handed her the glass. "Here's to crime," I said.

"Here's to punishment."

We both laughed; then we both didn't. "How's your husband?" I asked in the uncomfortable silence.

"The same. Worse. Who can tell? I feel so guilty when I leave him, but sometimes I just have to get out of there. Do you know what I mean?"

"Sure. Your husband does, too."

"I know. It's just that it seems so wrong to have a good time with Max so ill."

"You're not doing Max any good by becoming miserable yourself."

"I keep telling myself that."

"Good. But just so you don't feel too bad I won't bring out the hats and horns."

"You're kind."

"Not really. If I was kind I wouldn't be sitting here wondering if there was any chance of getting you into the bedroom."

I wouldn't have said it if I'd been sober, and I probably wouldn't have said it even then if I hadn't been anticipating another attempt by Mrs. Kottle to prevent me from doing the job I'd been hired for. But it was still lousy.

Her eyes were closed. "I suppose I deserved that, for the way I acted before."

"No you didn't."

"Well, there isn't any chance, you know. Of that."

"I know."

"Can we leave it there? Can we forget it?"

"Let's. I'm sorry."

"Don't be. I came to show you something."

She fished around in a sequined clutch bag, then pulled out some papers and handed them to me. There were eight of them, and they all said the same thing, in block printing, done in crayon by someone who didn't want the handwriting traced: "You will die for what you have done."

"Hallmark's got something for everyone, don't they?"

"I don't think these are funny at all, Mr. Tanner."

"Where'd they come from?"

"My husband. That is, they were sent to him, once a year for the past five years, postmarked January second."

"Does he know you have them?"

"No."

"Why *do* you have them?"

"The other day I tried to persuade you to be cautious

about uniting Max and Karl. I didn't do a very good job of it and I thought these might help."

"How?"

"Max is convinced Karl sent them. He's also convinced they're nothing to be concerned about. I think he's being foolish. Karl is not a child. If he really did make these threats he's fully capable of carrying them out."

I nodded. "But given the circumstances it doesn't make much difference, does it?"

"If what you're saying is that Max will be dead soon, perhaps you're right. But surely you can see that if Karl did send these it could be very painful for Max to be confronted by all that hate. I only want to spare him. Do you understand me now?"

I understood her. In my stocking feet, in the firelight, in the warm apartment, I could understand anything she cared to say.

She rearranged the lamé that spilled over her thigh like well-pulled taffy. I watched her do it. Right in the middle the telephone rang. I crossed the room and answered it.

"Mr. Tanner?"

"Yes, sir."

"This is Max Kottle."

"Yes. How are you?" It took some effort, but I managed to keep my eyes off his wife.

"Fine. I've heard from Karl."

"Really?"

"Yes. I'm overjoyed."

"That's great. I'm happy for you."

"Thank you."

"Where is he?"

For the first time there was something other than ecstasy in his voice. "I'm not sure. He said he would call again tomorrow. I think he wants to see me. At least I hope he does."

"I'm sure he does. Well, I don't think I've earned all that retainer you gave me. I'll check the books and remit the excess in a few days."

"No. Keep it all. I insist. For all I know he could have called because of something you did."

"I doubt it."

"In any event, I wanted results and I got them. Keep the fee."

"If you insist."

"I do. Well, I won't take any more of your time, Mr. Tanner. Thank you for all your efforts."

"Sure. And good luck to you. I hope it works out all right."

He laughed crisply. "Thank you. I'm sure it will, one way or another. Now that I've heard from Karl, nothing else matters, if you know what I mean."

"I guess not," I said.

"You should be encouraged, you know. Apparently no man is so abandoned that his last wish cannot be gratified."

"That's nice to know."

"Isn't it? Well, good-bye, Mr. Tanner."

"Good-bye."

The dying man hung up. I went back and sat down across from his wife. "Business at this hour?" she asked.

"Another satisfied client."

"Service with a smile, is that it?"

"Sometimes, when I'm on retainer. I think you'd better go, Mrs. Kottle. I'll keep your concerns in mind. Somehow I don't think there's going to be a problem."

"How can you be sure?"

"I can't be sure, but I can be lucky."

"What's that mean?"

"Hell, I don't know. You'd better go. I'm not as certain of my ability to keep my hands off you as I was a few minutes ago."

She looked at me with some puzzlement and then stood up and gave me her hand while she looked around the room with full confidence she would never see it again. "Nice place," she said.

"No it's not."

"Well, it could be."

"Not as long as I'm the only tenant."

She looked me over. "I'm starting to like you better," she said. She gave me a smile to take to bed with me, and was gone.

I stoked the fire and thought about love and death and their accoutrements and then went over to the phone and called Chet Herk and asked him if the thing he was worried about would keep till Monday. He thought it would. Since he was spending Monday with some Bank of America bankers, we arranged to meet in the Carnelian Room at five thirty that evening.

I hung up the telephone and went to the bedroom and threw a change of clothes into my AWOL bag and got in the Buick and drove down to Carmel. I spent the entire weekend in a cabin that had once been owned by a woman named Sara, a woman I'd liked and maybe loved, a woman who'd killed someone else and then herself and had left the cabin to me in her will. Over a year later I was still uneasy about having accepted the bequest, but more and more the place is good for what ails me as long as I don't think too much about her.

By the time the sunrise brought Monday morning with it I felt refurbished. The drive home was slow and halting, but I was enjoying it anyway when I turned on the radio while waiting for a light to change in Morgan Hill. The news rolled around five minutes later, and there it came, flat and emotionless, sandwiched between a story about a flash flood on the Russian River and a story about a show-business wedding.

Maximilian Kottle was dead.

Of a lingering illness.

Services pending.

I pulled into a vacant parking lot and shut off the engine and brought Max Kottle to mind. I didn't know him, not really. And he was of a class I despised, or at least mistrusted, but there was something he had wanted to do before he died and I hoped he had been able to do it. And more than that, I hoped it had happened the way he had imagined it would, that he and Karl each had found part of what they sought, maybe the most important part, maybe the only part there is. I hoped it had happened just that way.

By the time I started the engine again I had almost convinced myself that Max Kottle had been ready to die.

Sixteen

If you can't see it from the top of the Bank of America headquarters you can't see it from anywhere in the city, or so they like you to believe, but on Monday evening the clouds were thick, swirling gobs of gray and the most visible thing in the windows was your self, the precise thing a lot of the people around me had come up there to escape.

There were other people in the place, too, of course: the tourists down from Redding to do their Christmas shopping in stores that ridiculed everything about them except their money, the hardware salesmen in town for the Snap-On-Tool convention getting juiced enough to open up the possibility that something would happen to them that evening that was different from anything that had ever happened to them before, the secretaries sitting across from their bosses listening to the rushed endearments they had heard a hundred times before because it was the last time they would have a chance to until after the holidays. All of these and more. Me, I was just waiting for Chet Herk.

My highball was oversized and overpriced. I sipped it slowly, thinking of nothing but the visible, watching the maneuvers to see or to be seen. In the fifty-one stories beneath me were some of the most powerful people in the city—financiers, advertisers, lawyers, developers, consultants, brokers—promoters of everything from themselves to nirvana. I didn't know a soul in the place.

Chet came in some ten minutes after I'd ordered my second drink. He was red-faced and round, rolling his way past the hostess and the other imbibers the way a bowling ball rolls past the six-seven-ten. A few faces turned to him in wonderment, white moons briefly shining in the bargloom, but Chet didn't notice. When he reached his objective, me, he muttered a greeting and sat down.

"What a day," he began. "Christ. Talking about money is my second favorite thing. My first favorite thing is poking myself in the eye with a fork. What a crock. 'Financing statements, subordination clauses, sale and lease-back agreements, chattel mortgages.' Thank God it wasn't *my* money they were talking about."

"Whose money was it?" I asked.

"Greer's."

"Who's Greer?"

"The publisher. It's his paper and the bank's money at this stage of the game I guess, and if the paper starts making a profit again they'll both be happy. But if it doesn't, the bank will own the paper and a yacht and a house at Sea Ranch and a condominium at Tahoe and Greer will get to sell pencils for the rest of his days. At least that's the way it sounded to me. Those bankers have hearts like Sno Cones."

"You sound like you could use a drink or ten," I said as Chet puffed and wheezed to catch his breath.

He nodded. "What I need most they don't sell up here."

"What's that?"

"Peace of mind."

"I don't think you can buy that. It's kind of like free samples. It comes in the mail, addressed to occupant, free of charge, but you never know when."

"I guess. Hell, I wouldn't know peace of mind if it stuck its hand in my shorts and jerked me off. I'm probably allergic to it anyway. That and every piece of flora between here and Truckee."

I smiled and Chet relaxed a bit, too, his body settling further into the Naugahyde, the planes of his face moving like drops of oil on water, rearranging themselves in more familiar patterns. A waitress glided over to our table and Chet told her to bring him a fifth of Beefeaters with an olive in it and she smiled tolerantly and faded away without a sound.

Chet and I chatted for a while about sports and the weather and the Ayatollah and even more important things, and then he coughed and looked at his watch and said, "Okay, Marsh. Let me spill it, huh? I've got to get this off my mind or I'm going to explode. Plus, I have to be in Hillsborough by seven to tell some guy who made a fortune in electronic Ping-Pong games why he should put fifty grand into the *Investigator*, so I don't have much time."

"Fire away."

Chet cleared his throat, making noise enough to pave the way for *Caesar's Gallic Wars*. "You know who Mark Covington is?"

"Sure. He's that hotshot reporter on your rag, isn't he?"

"That's the guy. You ever meet him?"

"No."

"I figured not. Mark's a loner. I mean a *real* loner. Kind of a prick, too, to be honest. But he's the best investigative reporter on the West Coast right now, maybe the best anywhere, next to Sy Hersh."

"So what about him?"

"He's disappeared."

"How long ago?"

"Almost a month."

"Any ideas?"

"None."

Chet looked at me earnestly, as though I just might tell him he was mistaken, that it was all a misunderstanding, that it wasn't real. Unfortunately, by the time people get around to me reality is usually graven in stone, immutably and forever.

Chet wiped his pate and rubbed his nose and downed half the martini the waitress had placed in front of him and looked around to make sure no one could overhear what he was saying. What he saw were a lot of people listening only to themselves.

I looked around, too, and what I saw was a black face I thought I recognized. She was sitting at the other end of the room all by herself at a table by a window, attracting stares the way fire engines attract kids. Her lowered eyes looked into her drink or into something even more murky, and when she didn't look up when the next group of customers arrived I decided she wasn't waiting for anyone. But I still hadn't quite figured out where I'd seen her before when Chet started talking again.

"I'm sure you guessed from what I said about the bankers that the paper's in trouble, Marsh. Costs are out of sight, plus people aren't reading the kind of thing we do anymore; the inner workings of government bore them and the scandals just confirm their suspicions. Our circulation is way down. Covington's the only thing that keeps us going, really. He's probably going to get a Pulitzer this year and that plus the other stories he's bound to dig up are the only things that keep us from folding the tent."

"Are you absolutely sure he's missing?"

"I wasn't until ten days ago. Mark drops out of sight fairly often, for obvious reasons. But there was an editorial board meeting last week, and a staff meeting afterward, and he wouldn't have missed them for anything. Budget problems. Greer wanted to cut way back on the slush money, you know, the dough we use to follow up leads, pay informers, that kind of thing, and Mark was going to fight the cutback all the way. Also, Arnold's been flirting with the so-called neoconservative line on various issues and Mark couldn't stand that, either. But he didn't show."

"And no one else has seen him?"

"No one I can find."

"How hard have you looked?"

"Well, not too hard, I guess, mainly because I'm not sure where *to* look. Covington leads a pretty low-profile existence. He didn't want to be known, felt it would hamper his undercover work. Other than his wife and the people at the paper, I'm not sure who to ask."

"So you want me to check it out?"

"Can you?"

"I guess so. Like I said on the phone, I'm as free as an osprey these days. But why not the cops?"

"Fuck the cops. I won't let them in the door, not since those Supreme Court bums gave them license to snoop around in our files. The only way a cop's going to get inside the *Investigator* is over my dead body."

"Overreacting, aren't you, Chet?"

"The hell I am. Wake up, Marsh. Look at what's going on. Reporters go to jail for not revealing their sources. Cops are given the right to paw through newspaper files anytime some half-wit Muni Court judge says there's probable cause. Any nut who files a libel suit can depose a reporter for days on end about why he wrote what he wrote. They're even talking about *licensing* newsmen. The free press is dying in this country, Marsh. The Bill of Rights is about as respected as a role of Charmin."

"Come on, Chet."

"No. You've got me going now, Marsh. I know you're probably not up on what those guys have been doing since you're not practicing law anymore, but read up on it. The Fifth Amendment's shot to hell—anything you put on paper can be used against you. The Fourth Amendment—shit, the cops can search anywhere. And the First—reporters in jail, Marsh. In *jail*. I tell you, Nixon's going to have the last laugh after all. Those justices are *fascists*. All of them."

Chet's face was as red as a radish. "Look on the bright side," I told him. "You're going to have a lot of help pretty soon."

"From whom?"

"The lawyers. I see where the Attorney General has started asking for warrants to search lawyers' offices for evidence against their clients. When the cops start rummaging around in the lawyers' files the feces will hit the propeller real fast. Besides, Burger can't live forever."

"The hell he can't. Guys that nasty *never* die. They pickle in their own bile."

I laughed. "I feel for you, Chet, but you news guys made the same mistake the lawyers made."

"What's that?"

"You strutted around for too damn long acting like privileged characters. You told everyone you were exempt from the rules. Well, folks are getting tired of being told how special you are. This is the Age of Narcissism. Everyone's as good as everyone else. Better start disguising your pedestal a little instead of trying to jam it down everyone's throats. But what's all this got to do with Mark Covington?"

Chet clenched his fist and starting pounding on the table. "Just this. There's three members of the South Bay Planning Commission and two real-estate developers and a psychiatrist and a couple of door-to-door outfits that have criminal convictions on their records because of Mark Covington, and the people they were bilking or seducing aren't being bilked or seduced anymore, and unless guys like Covington can keep on doing their jobs without the cops sitting on their shoulders like goddamn vultures, that kind of curruption is going to be more pervasive than the happy face."

"You sound like the cops sounded the day after *Miranda* came down, Chet. If you listened to them you'd believe there'd never be another arrest in the history of the world."

"And you're starting to sound like Agnew, Tanner."

"Touché, Chet. Touché."

The splash of my little joke finally washed Chet's face out from red to pink and he gulped the rest of his martini in one swallow. "I've got to go," he said quickly. "Can you come down to the paper tomorrow morning? Greer will be there, and I want him to know I'm bringing you in on this. He'll have to pay your fee. I've been on half salary for six months."

"That's rough," I said, suddenly sad that Chet had felt he had to go through with our fifty-buck dinner the week before, that he hadn't felt he could level with me. "In the meantime," I went on, "get up a list of Covington's enemies. If all those people you mentioned have bit the dust because of his snooping, there must be enough motive floating around to choke a hippo."

"You're right about that. Hell, there are a few people in

our own office who wouldn't shed a tear if Mark never
drew another breath."

"Sounds interesting. Tell Greer my rate is fifty an
hour."

"Jesus. He might not go that much, Marsh."

"I have to put a quarter in the machine to get his paper,
Chet. He'll have to feed my meter, too."

"I'll see what I can do. See you, Marsh. And thanks for
listening to me. Maybe I'll get some sleep tonight."

We shook hands and Chet moved off toward the eleva-
tors at half the speed of his arrival.

I finished off my drink and was about to leave, too,
when I remembered the black woman down by the window. She was still there, and when she cocked her head to
look at her watch the position of her head and the scowl
on her face reminded me of where I'd seen her. I got to
her table before she saw me coming. "You know Doctor
Hazen," I announced to the top of her head.

When she looked up she was already frowning, already
annoyed, already closing down anything that might have
been open. She didn't say anything with her lips but her
eyes said, "Get lost."

"May I join you? Just for a moment?"

She looked me over carefully, her features unyielding as
teak. If she was trying to decide whether I was, after all,
the reason she'd come up to that sky-high bar, I don't
think she'd reached a decision by the time I seized the ini-
tiative that was dangling somewhere between us and pulled
out a chair and sat across from her.

Her eyes stared at me coolly, communicating more bale
than interest. One hand cupped her chin. The fingers were
long and tapered, black on top and buttery on the bottom,
the nails long and yellow-white, like old paper. Her wrist
still wore the three thin bracelets I remembered from before, flimsy rings of allure. But her face still wore a visible
mask of antipathy.

"My name's Tanner," I said calmly. "You were on duty
at Max Kottle's place a week or so ago."

"I remember," she said. "He's a memorable patient."

"Miss Durkin, isn't it?"

She nodded.

"It's kind of dreary out tonight, isn't it, Miss Durkin?"

"In *and* out."

I put on my disarming smile, such as it was. "May I buy you a drink?"

"No, but thank you."

I glanced at the table. A single glass, a single napkin, a single swizzle stick. Miss Durkin had a low limit. She didn't trust herself; she didn't trust me. I started to wonder what I was doing there, why I seemed bent on making a fool of myself. While I did that Miss Durkin's head lowered, but not before I saw a tear flip over the edge of an eyelid.

"What's wrong?" I asked quietly.

"Nothing at all."

"Tell me about it."

"No. Don't be ridiculous. I don't even know you."

"That's the point, isn't it?"

She smiled, but it was a wan, lifeless exercise.

"Then I'll take a guess," I said. "You came here to take a look at other people and then at yourself, to help you decide whether you liked who you were and what you had become. About five minutes ago you reached a decision. What you decided was that you were off the track, out of control, heading right for the concrete abutment. Am I close?"

She chuckled humorlessly. "Close enough. What I decided was that my life makes me sick. Sitting in this place makes me sick. Men like you on the make for black women make me sick. Everything makes me sick."

I leaned toward her. "Let me tell you something. I don't know whether you're a good nurse or not, but I know enough to tell you that nothing anyone in this room is doing or ever has done is more important than what you do. And besides," I added, "anything will make you sick if you look at it too closely. Even aspidistra."

"Aspidistra? What the hell does that have to do with anything?"

I laughed. "I don't know. The word just popped out. That happens to me a lot—words pop out. I'm not sure I even know what aspidistra is."

"Really?"

"Really."

"A house plant."

"Oh. Well, if one walks in and sits down at the bar in the next few minutes, point it out to me. I like to improve my mind."

Miss Durkin laughed this time, which I guess is what I wanted her to do. At that instant she seemed—brown, ivory, bristly, regal—a species I had never encountered before.

"What is it really?" I asked. "A man?"

She shook her head. "I kind of set men aside when I went to nursing school and I'm certainly not in the habit of worrying about them. Not that I enjoy sitting here being hit on by a different guy every five minutes." The contempt on her face was broad enough to encompass me.

"Problems with the job?" I asked.

She paused. "I suppose that's it, more than anything. I came out of the Fillmore District and worked my little black ass off to get that RN's cap, and now instead of being back helping the people I grew up with I work for a doctor with an office on Sutter Street who has only one patient and who wishes he were a sculptor instead of a radiologist. Not exactly the direction I planned to take, way back when."

"Seems to me you shouldn't have to justify the color of the patients you see."

"Hah. You should talk to some of the cats in the bars I used to hang out in. I'm not real popular with some of my racial brothers and sisters."

"You can always go back to the Fillmore, can't you? Or work at San Francisco General? You'll be hip-deep in black suffering the minute you set foot in *that* place."

"I tell myself that, but I don't really know anymore. I may have gotten too used to the way I live these days. I hope not, but it could be true. This suit I'm wearing cost three hundred dollars. I don't have anything else that nice but I have this. In the old days I went to school barefoot."

"Maybe you ought to run a little test on yourself. Work part-time at a neighborhood clinic or something. Check out the sensibilities."

For the first time some warmth broke through, melting the chocolate, making it irresistibly delectable, better than anything Blum's ever made.

"You white boys are smarter than you look," she said smiling. "That's just what I had decided to do when you so rudely intruded upon my private little drama."

That ended it for a time. I sipped my drink and she toyed with her swizzle stick. I think we were both measuring the new environment, checking for weak spots, alert for traps for the unwary. I didn't find any myself; I couldn't tell about her.

"Tell me more about your boss," I said, just to move things along. "He sounds a bit strange."

She shrugged. "He is, I guess. I feel sorry for him, actually. Clifford's a disappointed man. He really and truly set out to win the Nobel prize. God's truth. And he says he might have gotten it, or come close—his theory had something to do with manganese and superoxide levels in cells—but then something happened and his research got fouled up and he couldn't get funding. When he knew he'd never get the prize he kind of lost interest in medicine. Not completely, of course. He's Chief of Radiology at Bay Area University, and he's a Fellow in the College of Radiology, but most of what he does is administrative. The passion for medicine just isn't there anymore, not even at the tertiary level. So, he's decided to become a sculptor. You should see his studios. There's one at the office and one in his home. A foundry, a kiln, some kind of generator. Hunks of metal all over. What a place."

"How's his art work?"

"Terrible. I hate to say it, but it's true. No one will show it. Poor Clifford takes his little slides around to all the galleries, here and in New York and L.A. too, and no one's interested. It drives him crazy, and keeps him bankrupt, but he plunges on. Someone always says something that's just encouraging enough to make him keep going. Unfortunately, the poor man's taste is all in his mouth." She shook her head in sympathy. "I posed for him once," she went on. "Something called the lost wax process, I think. I came out looking like a cross between a pine cone and a Brillo pad."

I laughed with her and told her Clifford must be totally devoid of talent if he couldn't make anything out of such a lovely source of inspiration and she thanked me for the compliment and I told her there were several more from where that came from if she played her cards right. She told me she'd never been lucky at cards. I told her I had a system that I'd be happy to teach her. She said that might be fun. Then I backed away. We seemed to be going somewhere but we didn't know the road. We wouldn't get there if we took it too fast.

I made conversation. "You said Doctor Hazen had only one patient. Max Kottle, I suppose?"

"Oh, I was exaggerating a little, of course, but since Clifford became Chief of Radiology he's had to do more administrating than treating patients. He keeps old friends on, but not many others."

"Old friends and rich friends."

"I suppose that's part of it. Clifford always seems short of money, even with patients like the Kottles."

"The Kottles? You mean he treats Mrs. Kottle too?"

"Not her. Karl."

"Karl? How long's he been treating Karl?"

"For years. Every three months."

"When's the last time he saw Karl, do you know?"

The swizzle stick stopped spinning between her fingers. "I don't think I'd better say anything more about that," she said, suddenly wary. "Clifford's a bear about confidentiality. You're working for Mr. Kottle, and I was especially instructed not to say anything to Max about Karl."

"I'm not working for Max anymore."

"Why not?"

"The problem he wanted me to solve suddenly solved itself."

"Really? How?"

"I thought you'd be one of the first to know."

"Why?"

"He died. Max died."

She hadn't known. I hoped her sorrow was a bit more than professional. "I was off this weekend and Doctor Hazen didn't come in today. The great Max Kottle dead. It's too bad, actually. For a rich guy he was all right."

"Let's get back to Karl," I said. "What's wrong with him? Why does he see Hazen so often?"

Her lips froze in two red stripes. "No. If you ask any more questions about Doctor Hazen or his patients I'll leave. I mean it."

I held up my hands in surrender. The Kottle case was closed, Max and Karl had been united to some degree or another before Max died, and whatever might have happened in the past was as cold as day-old soup. I had to work at it, but I left it that way.

I asked Miss Durkin her first name and she told me it was Gwen. I asked if she wanted to go to North Beach for dinner and she said, "Why not?" Later, when I asked if she wanted to see my beer can collection, she said, "I suppose I should, shouldn't I?" I didn't have any beer cans, but it didn't seem to bother her, at least not at first.

Then, right in the middle of what I thought was a perfectly adequate kiss, she leaned back and looked at me and said, in words brought with her from the Fillmore, that she didn't want to ball me that night, she just wanted to sleep on my couch. Because I was mad at her I let her. From the creaks and groans of the couch I knew she had a hard time getting to sleep. I had a hard time, too, until I went in and picked up her three hundred dollar suit off the chair where she had draped it and hung it on a wooden hanger in the closet, right next to my bathrobe.

Seventeen

We must have readjusted our expectations sometime during the night because we were both pretty perky the next morning, laughing and joking over the flapjacks like a couple of "Laugh-In" rejects. Somewhere along the line we decided to walk to work, since the sun was out and all, and we skipped down the Filbert Steps like the ingenue and the swain out of something by Busby Berkeley.

The bay that spread out before us was a blue-green mat with "Welcome" printed on it. The world seemed bathed, rendered, cleansed. I felt the same way. At the corner of Battery and Union Gwen continued toward town and I trotted up the steps toward the entrance to the Bay Area *Investigator.*

Chet Herk's paper was published out of a squat, square brick building on Battery Street a few blocks north of Broadway. Its neighbors were the Ice House, Barsocchini's and Soraya's Oriental Rugs. Once upon a time the building had been a cheese factory, and if you inhaled too exuberantly you could still smell something that had curdled long, long ago.

There was a sign over the door, black on white, hand-lettered to look as though it had been set in giant type:

> When there is much desire to learn,
> there of necessity will be much arguing,
> much writing, many opinions; for opinion

in good men is but knowledge in the making.
                    Milton, *Areopagitica*

I pulled open the door and went inside. An entryway of sorts had been established just inside the door. A couple of folding chairs and a card table were scattered around in clubhouse modern. The rock poster on the wall was supposed to create a with-it atmosphere, but the effect was institutional, penal more than anything. Across the room was a brick wall, and on the wall were two words, each with an arrow beside it. The "Production" arrow pointed down, the "Editorial" arrow pointed up. I went up.

The stairway was steep and narrow, the walls covered with names and slogans and epigrams that had seemingly been scrawled while the draftsmen were on the move, following one or the other arrow. One slogan read "Truth is a complete defense." Below that someone had added, "The Forty-Niners have no defense at all. If they stop telling lies they'll lead the league."

I was trying to decipher some more of the writing when I was interrupted by a tall, urgent-faced boy who was galloping down the stairs as fast as he could go. I pressed against the wall to let him by, but I don't think he even noticed me. He was holding some sheets of copy in his hands, but I couldn't read what they said. From the look on his face they announced the imminent disintegration of the planet.

The second floor was an open loft that had been subdivided into a maze of cubicles, each cell walled off from the other by half-plywood, half-Plexiglas partitions that rose six feet off the floor. The Plexiglas was frosted, making the figures behind the panes ghostly blurs of light and dark. Overhead, bands of fluorescent lights irradiated everything. I felt as though I had stumbled into a place under investigation by the antivivisectionists.

I poked my head inside the first cubicle I came to. The woman inside was short-haired and negligently attractive, with eyes that immediately seemed to challenge me to keep a secret, any secret, from her for over five minutes. She raised her brows in a question but before I could say anything she began thumbing madly through the telephone book, slapping pages aside as though she were brushing dust off the family album before showing her baby pictures to the new boyfriend.

When she paused a moment I asked where I could find Chet Herk. She raised her hand to make a gesture, then stopped in mid-motion. Her head cocked and her eyes narrowed and her lips puckered. "I'll take you there," she said, slowly and speculatively. She slid off her chair and smoothed down her jeans and struck out her hand. "I'm Pamela Brown."

"Pamela," I repeated, bowing.

"Miss Brown to you," she replied, grinning.

"Billie Holiday. *Circa* 1935."

"Hey. Not many people know that."

"Not many people listen to good music. I'm Marsh Tanner."

"Charmed, I'm sure. It's down this way."

She led me out of the office and down the corridor, loping along in strides I had to work to keep pace with even though her legs were half as long as mine. From the rear her body was round and firm, packed tightly in a denim wrapper, good for a long shelf-life. Her waist was half the circumference of her hips.

Halfway down the hall she allowed me to catch her. "Have you come up with anything on Mark yet?" she asked casually. Too casually.

"Mark who?"

"Come on, pal. Mark and I were real close. We worked side by side in this madhouse for three years. I'm as worried about him as anyone around here, Chet included."

"Lucky for Mark. Whoever that is."

"Well, if you're not here about Mark you must be here about whatever it is that has Chet so uptight this morning."

"Is Chet uptight?"

"Very. The question is, why?"

"I don't know."

"I don't believe you."

"I don't care."

"Well, fuck you and the horse you rode in on, buddy."

"Likewise, I'm sure."

We considered each other for a moment, dogs eyeing the same bone, then we both started to laugh. "One of those days," Pamela Brown said. "I'm sorry."

"Come on."

"Me, too."

She turned and hurried on down the hall and I fell in at

the rear and rode in her wake, listening to her sandal's slap her heels.

At the end of the corridor we turned right and then left and stopped beside a wooden door with the word "Herk" printed on it in red helvetica letters. "Here we are," she said. She knocked three times, sharply, then turned the knob. A voice inside said "Come" and we did.

Pamela Brown blocked most of my view, but over the top of her head I could see Chet half-buried behind the pile of papers on his desk. "Some guy named Tanner here, Chet," Miss Brown declared. "You want me to sit in?"

Chet smiled benignly and told Pamela that no, she didn't need to stick around. She frowned and started to say something but changed her mind and shrugged and stepped back. "There you go, Tanner. But if you *are* here about Mark Covington, stop and see me on the way out."

I nodded politely and thanked her politely and went past her into the office and shut the door behind me. Miss Brown's sandals began slapping her heels again, but not right away.

Chet nodded grimly and gestured to a chair in front of his desk and asked me to sit down. "Greer should be here any minute," he said wearily. "I haven't been able to talk to him since Friday, but I think he'll want you to go ahead on the Covington thing. He won't have long to think it over, though. Someone dropped a bombshell here this morning."

"What kind of bombshell?"

Chet was about to answer me when his telephone rang and he slid into a discussion with someone on the other end about the size of that week's press run. I let my eyes wander and my attention wander along with them.

Chet's office was a monument to the newspaper business and, although he didn't intend it that way, a monument to Chet Herk as well. The walls were streaked with front-page headlines clipped from the original papers in which they'd appeared: Dewey Wins/MacArthur Fired/Kennedy Dead/Man on Moon/Nixon Resigns/Mayor Killed. Beneath the headlines were stacks of newspapers, side by side, ringing the room like a limestone fence. The papers on the bottom of the piles were curling and yellowing with age. On the opposite wall books occupied their shelves haphazardly, as though thrown into them from across the room. Here and there were bronze medallions and brass plaques and shiny white certificates that testified to Chet Herk's place in the journalistic pantheon. None of them were prominently displayed. Chet was immodest about every history but his own.

He hung up the phone and looked at me. "We got this letter," he said gravely. "From something called the Sons and Daughters of Isaiah."

I perked up at the name, but as I was about to ask a question the door opened and a man came in. He was small, tiny in fact, with white wispy hair and a thin face with a chin that pointed down and a nose that pointed up. His left eye had a black patch over it.

"I hear something's up," the man said as he marched to the center of the room. His voice rattled the panes. His walk came close to a goose step.

Chet nodded. "This is Marsh Tanner," he said to the man. "Marsh, this is Arnold Greer. Our publisher."

I stayed where I was and so did Greer. He made no move to sit in the chair beside me and no move to change his expression, which was haughty and watchful. "Marsh is a detective," Chet continued. "Used to be a lawyer. We met years ago, when I was with the *Trib*. He's the best in town."

"Are you?" Greer asked bluntly. I checked, but he didn't seem to be joking.

"It all depends on what you want done," I said. "For some things Jessie Tadlock's the best and for other things Ruthie Spring is."

Greer was tactless and proud of it. "Our thing is trying to get a reporter back from wherever he's gone without letting our competitors know he's been missing. Who's best at that?"

I decided to be macho, too. "Me," I said.

"What's your fee?"

"Fifty an hour."

"That's too much."

"No it isn't."

There was some silence then, and I just let it build. I didn't like Arnold Greer much, and if it weren't for Chet I would have walked.

"Okay, Tanner," Greer said heavily. "I'm good for a week. No more. If you haven't found him then, forget it. Okay by you?"

I shrugged. "Normally it wouldn't be. I don't like taking

on jobs in increments. It's like the Late Show. I don't start watching unless I'm sure I'm going to be around for the finish." I looked at Chet. He looked at me. "In this case I'll make an exception."

Greer nodded. Chet looked relieved. "Welcome aboard," Chet said. "I know you can wrap this up in a hurry. Like I said, Mark's been gone for almost a month. I've written out his wife's name and address for you, since she was probably the last person to see him. She's the only one outside the paper I can direct you to. In the office Mark's only real friend was Hal Arndt, our sports man, and his only real enemy was Pammy Brown. Her you've met."

I nodded. "What was that about, anyway?"

"Oh, Pam's Mark's heir apparent. She thinks she should get the stories Mark gets, that her byline should get equal space with his, that kind of thing. Her problem is, she's not that good. Not yet. His problem is, he's told her so. More than once."

"You're not saying she'd do away with Covington just to take over his space in the paper, are you?"

I expected Chet to laugh but he didn't. "I'm not saying that," he muttered grimly. "But Pam's damned determined. Sometimes I think she'd do anything to get ahead, starting with a slash at my balls."

Chet seemed a little more involved in that subject than was healthy so I switched streams. "What was Covington working on recently? The last thing I remember was the piece on that charity, what was it?"

"The Order of Nineveh."

"Right. Five million collected and only two hundred thousand made it down to the poor, wasn't that about it?"

"Exactly. But hell, every story Mark wrote flushed out a new covey of enemies. It'll take you years if that's all you have to go on."

"What was he working on when he disappeared?"

"I don't know," Chet said. "As far as I know, no one does. Mark had lots of leeway. Unless he needed money he'd only show up when he had a story. We'd print it and people would scream and shout and Mark would disappear until the next time. Do you know anything, Arnold?"

Greer shook his head, silently, his eyes on mine.

"Did he have an office here?" I asked.

"He had one but he never used it. I checked it out last week, Marsh. Empty."

"Where does he work?"

"Beats me."

"So what you're saying is there's not much to go on."

"That's what I'm saying."

Greer turned toward me, smiling tightly. "Since you're the best in town I'm sure we'll hear from you soon."

"You will if you're listening."

Greer started to respond, but turned back to Chet instead. "Now what's all the uproar?"

"We got this letter," Chet began. I should have left but I didn't. I was interested, for no particular reason except that I began to hope the letter meant trouble for Arnold Greer.

"Who wrote it?" Greer asked.

"Some group that calls itself the Sons and Daughters of Isaiah."

"Who are they?"

"Never heard of them."

"What do they want?"

"They want us to publish their manifesto. They say if we don't they'll blow up the building."

Greer scoffed dryly. "Talk's cheap. Always has been."

"In this case it may be more than talk," Chet said soberly. "They claim that ten days ago they planted a bomb at the headquarters of Laguna Oil, over on Market. They say it went off, but that the company and the cops got together and covered it up, made it seem like an accident. They say this time they won't worry about killing people, that if a bunch of us die the cops won't be able to stonewall it."

Greer began to pace. "This manifesto," he said. "What does it say?"

"Well, they use a lot of rhetoric—call themselves the heirs of Bakunin and the Naradnaya Volya and all that—but at bottom what they seem to want is for the oil companies, all of them, to stop importing foreign oil. Totally. They say their cadres in L.A. and Houston and New York are prepared to strike immediately if their demands aren't met."

I looked at Greer. A line of shiny sweat had begun to form along his forehead. He swiped at it with his palm and in the process brushed the patch away from his eye. There was no eye, though, only a hole, black and fathomless. The flesh around it was white and lined with red scars, a piece of horrific scrimshaw.

Greer adjusted the patch and the hole disappeared, though not from my mind. "We get these things all the time, Chet," he said nonchalantly. "Why do you think this one's legit?"

"Because they gave us something we can check. One way or another we ought to be able to get the straight dope about Laguna Oil."

"That's true," Greer said, "and I know just how to do it."

"How?"

"Call Max Kottle."

I blurted a question. "Why him?"

"He owns Laguna Oil. Every last barrel of it."

"But Max is dead."

Greer looked at me oddly. "Oh. Yeah. The Big C. Too bad." He looked at Chet. "Try Walter Hedgestone."

Eighteen

Chet and Greer launched a discussion of journalistic integrity and the news worth of extortionate demands and honor and truth and like that, and like most debates over principle it was predictable and self-serving. I excused myself and went out into the hall, wading through the weeds of the Kottle case that had sprung up around me like thistle. I thought about those weeds for a while, thought about whether I should do something about them, and finally decided not. They didn't amount to much—a few questions, mostly—and I never did like to pull weeds, even as a kid, especially if no one was paying me to pull them.

I went back to the place where I'd first met Pamela Brown and tapped on the side of the cubicle and waited for her to look up. She did. Her eyes began to gleam, polished with a buffer of triumph. "I thought I'd be seeing you again, Mr. Tanner. Come in and have a seat."

Pamela Brown leaned back and put her feet on the corner of her desk and clasped her hands behind her head. Her breasts flattened beneath her T-shirt, which rose above her navel. The word on the T-shirt was "BITCH." I'd never seen anyone take so much pleasure in being right. "The Covington thing, correct?"

I nodded. "What do you know about it?"

"What I know for sure is that I couldn't care less if the guy never comes back. Now tell me how shocked you are."

"Not much. He's in your way, isn't he?"

"That he is."

"Anything else going on there, besides professional jealousy?"

Her eyebrows lifted. "Like what?"

"Oh, like sex, for example."

Her eyes widened. "You do come out with it, don't you?"

"Don't you?"

She laughed and nodded, then picked up a pencil and began to gnaw on the eraser end. Her eyes closed. Wisps of hair danced down the slopes of her face. Somewhere down below us, way down below, something began to rumble. Walls and things began to rattle and creak. I thought it was an earthquake, maybe even the big one all of us are waiting for, but then I figured it out: the press had begun its run.

"I'm probably a fool to talk about it," Miss Brown said slowly, "but what the hell. Sex. Mark did take me under his wing, so to speak, when I first started here. And like an idiot I snuggled right in there, all warm and cozy and dry, or so I thought, even though after a few bouts with professors in college I swore sex wasn't going to have any role whatsoever in my career. It can help for a while, but in the long run all you get is fucked. Well, I should have stuck to my guns. I found out that every girl in the office had been under Mark's wing at one time or another over the years, so I backed out."

"Any withdrawal pains?"

"Sure. There always are, at least for me. But it had to be done. Mark, of course, hardly noticed I was gone."

"And since?"

"Since then it's been like Frazier and Ali between us. Tooth and nail, all the way. If I thought it would help me beat him to a story I'd scratch his eyes out."

"Who's under his wing now?"

"Who knows? I stopped keeping track a long time ago, when I started having to take off my shoes to count them up. My guess is Mark's libido has dropped below the boiling point at long last, but maybe he's just dipping his wick somewhere else. He's not around much, I know that. But I don't worry about it."

"Anymore."

"Right. Anymore."

"Any chance an irate husband could be responsible for whatever happened to him?" I asked. "Assuming something has?"

She shook her head. "It's possible, but I doubt it. Mark wasn't a home wrecker, particularly. God knows there are enough single girls around this town, a pirate like him wouldn't have any trouble keeping the steerage full."

"You don't happen to have a picture of the pirate, do you?"

She grinned. "No, but it's funny you should ask. He was buggy on that, you know? Refused to have his picture taken. Ever. I saw him give fifty bucks to one of those street photographers on Union Square one day, just to get the negative back. Mark took his work seriously. Too seriously, probably."

"More seriously than you take yours?" I asked.

She frowned, a mixture of two parts anger and three parts sadness, from the way it looked. "They don't like me, Tanner. The men. They think I'm some kind of freak, but I'm not. I'm just someone trying to make something of myself the best way I can. I'm just like them—in ability, ambition, arrogance, greed, all of it—but because I'm a woman they can't accept it. You can't either, can you?"

"I don't know. I'm not in a position to be threatened by anyone, male or female, so I don't worry much about it. But I'm no better than the next guy. When I act like a prick it's usually because I'm afraid."

"Yeah, well, fuck 'em. Fuck 'em all."

She pulled a phone book across the desk and began to flip through it angrily, ripping one of the pages, crumpling another. "Just one more question," I said. "What do *you* think happened to Covington?"

She looked up. "You really want to know?"

"Yes."

"He's under cover. It's just a guess, but that's what I think. Deep cover."

"You sound like a spy."

"This business is a lot like the spy business, don't think it isn't."

"What do you mean, exactly?"

"I mean I think Mark's assumed a new identity, maybe even a new face. There's a plastic surgeon on every corner these days. After a half-day session with one of those boys I could sit right here and you'd swear you'd never met me before."

"Why would he do that?"

"The Big One, of course. The game breaker. The Big P."

"What's that?"

"Pulitzer. Posterity. Call it what you want. Mark's done it all on the local scene. I mean, I hate the bastard, and I think I'm better than he is, but still, he *has* done some fantastic pieces. The series on the Water Project should have gotten him the Pulitzer last year. It would have, if it wasn't for those kids up in Point Reyes who took on Synanon."

"Any idea what the Big One is?"

Her eyes slipped shut again, the eraser went to the mouth, seconds ticked by, metronomic, loud. "Are you any good?" she asked finally.

"Yes," I said.

"Are you trying to do anything other than find Mark Covington?"

"No."

"Will you keep it a secret if I give you a lead? I'm supposed to hate Mark's guts, you know," she added sarcastically. "I'd hate for anyone around here to learn I'd helped find him."

"I'll keep the secret."

"So you say. So you say."

She got up and went to the entry to her cubicle and looked up and down the corridor, then went back and sat down, pulling her legs under her and crossing them into a lotus position. "Okay," she said. "Here's the deal. I'd go after this myself, you understand, but I've got something hot that's about to break, and I've been working on it for six weeks and I hate to let it go. So I'll give you a tip, if you promise that when you get something firm, anything, you'll tell me so I can be the first to write it. Deal?"

I didn't even think about it. "Deal," I said. I wasn't sure I meant it, but I said it.

"Okay. Check out the Biloxi Corporation."

"Biloxi? What's that?"

"I don't know. But the last time I saw Mark was here in his office. I heard him say that name on the phone. When he saw I was standing where I could hear him he hung up."

"Biloxi," I repeated. "Anything else?"

She shook her head. "Anything else I might say about Mark would tell you more about me than about him."

"That's usually the way it works."

The telephone rang and I got hurried directions to Hal Arndt's office before Miss Brown picked it up and started taking notes in a rapid scribble. As I left her office she was telling the person on the other end that she would go to jail before revealing his name to anyone.

As I turned down the hall Miss Brown called out for me. "Hey, Tanner. You know, you're the only one around here who ever asked me what I thought about Mark's disappearance. Thanks for that, okay?"

Hal Arndt was in. He was a thin, haggard man with the drooping air of a frustrated jock. His face was lined, his fingers stained with nicotine, his hair trimmed to within a centimeter of his scalp. I stood in the doorway and watched as he thumbed his way through *The Sporting News.* His desk was in the exact center of an office that contained at least twenty souvenir balls of various shapes and sizes and textures, arrayed like planets in a modest solar system.

I knocked on the wall and Arndt peered around the edge of his tabloid, sloe-eyed and weary. "Have a seat," he offered. "You the guy from Stanford?"

I shook my head. "I'm the guy who wants to know about Mark Covington."

Arndt swore and lowered the paper to his desk and sighed. "I was hoping to spend the afternoon talking about football."

I apologized. "I'm told you and Covington were friends."

"So?"

"So I've been hired to try to find him. I'm sure you know he hasn't been seen for a while."

Arndt frowned, then shrugged. "I considered Mark a friend. I'm not sure what he considered me. He never said."

"When did you see him last?"

"A few weeks ago. Five, maybe."

"Where?"

"Here."

"Anything unusual?"

"Just being around Mark was unusual. He was an unusual man. But there wasn't anything you would find useful."

"What's he look like?"

"Tall. Dark hair. Thin. Like Dolph Schayes. Remember him?"

"Sure. How come you got along with Covington when no one else could seem to manage it?"

Arndt smiled. "One, he liked sports. Two, he didn't have anything I wanted, and vice versa. Three, I never called him, he always called me."

"Where do you think he is?"

Arndt shook his head slowly. "Nope," he said. "It's too soon. When someone shows me evidence that Mark's in trouble, then I'll talk. Till then I'm going to do what I always do when someone asks about Mark."

"What's that?"

"Keep my mouth shut."

"Chet Herk thinks Covington's in trouble."

"Chet Herk thought the Cubs would win the pennant."

Arndt was one of those men who knows his life will never see a big battle but only lots of little ones and so has resolved to fight those to the death. I started to leave but then changed my mind. "I just spent some time with Arnold Greer," I said. "What's the story on him? The eye, for instance."

Arndt took a minute to decide whether there was any reason not to talk to me, then decided there wasn't. "The eye," he began. "Well, Arnold lost the eye in Africa a few years back. He went to Biafra while the war was on over there, real Ernie Pyle stuff, you know? Took along his own little band of mercenaries, out to save the Ibos. But Arnold went a little too far into the bush and got himself captured by one tribe or another, I forget which. The old chief thought Arnold was a spy for the bad guys and tried to get him to talk. The way Arnold tells it, they poked his eye out with a red-hot bayonet. The way Arnold tells it also, he never made a sound the whole time."

"You believe the story?"

Arndt shrugged again. "Why not? Arnold's a tough little bastard, I know that. He'd be real pissed off at getting captured, as much as he hates to lose. I could see it happening like that."

"What's Green doing running a newspaper? Seems a little tame."

"It is, but then everything's tame these days except rugby and hang gliding. Arnold's perfectly willing to devote his time and money to achieving social change as long as it has his name on it when it happens."

"I get the feeling the paper's in trouble financially."

"Could be. They don't talk to me about anything but the point spread around here. Chet's pretty worried these days, I can tell that."

"Why?"

"It's obvious. He's fifty years old. If the paper folds he's out of a job. There's not much market for fifty-year-old editors these days. The newspaper business is a young man's game."

"Name one that isn't," I said.

"Quoits."

Nineteen

The Covington house was a small, white-stucco, tile-roofed place on Quintara Street in the Sunset District, just off Thirty-third Avenue. Like the other houses in that area it was surgically sterile and eclectically ornate and enough like its neighbors to be indistinguishable to anyone except its owner. If you wanted to live incognito, as Mark Covington apparently did, there was no better place in the city to do it.

I trotted up the stone steps and rang the bell. The wind whistled overhead—cold, wet, salty, aromatic—hinting of romance and danger and decay. I put my hands in my pockets and waited.

After a minute I rang again. Some sense told me an eye had just nestled next to the peephole and that I was under inspection by someone who inspected everything. I straightened up and tried to look like something more intriguing than a vacuum salesman.

The door opened, but not far. The chain was still

latched, drawn taut across the six-inch opening like a rein on the occupant's curiosity. I tried not to look dangerous. I've been told I don't do it well.

A face appeared, or rather a part of a face, hidden partially on each side by the door and the jamb, the center panel of a neogothic triptych. It was a woman's face, and the most obvious thing about its puffy features was that it had been sleeping, sleeping soundly, drug-soundly. I told the face I was sorry to bother it. Then I told it I had come to talk to it about its husband.

That bit of information seemed to exhaust the face even further. It nodded resignedly. The door closed, the chain rattled and the door opened again, freely this time. I went inside, bidden only by implication.

The face looked at me from atop a slim, unobtrusive body that was wrapped in a silken pink robe that was Macy's idea of what they wore in Japan. The face and the body both seemed on the rim of collapse. "I've come to ask you some things about your husband," I repeated earnestly.

"Mark," the face said, and the face finally became a person. If her husband was as dead as the tone she used to name him I was wasting my time and hers.

"Do you have a few minutes, Mrs. Covington?" I asked.

"I don't . . . there isn't . . . Oh, well. I guess you might as well sit down."

She inclined her chin toward a chair that was camouflaged by a blue damask spread that lay over it like a shroud. I sat on it anyway and watched Mrs. Covington. Her skin was dappled from circulatory sloth. Bands of black cupped her eyes like nests. Her lips were dry and cracked. Lines of gray stretched through her hair like vapor trails. She was unlovely and knew it.

She went to a horsehair couch across from me and sat down. The furry bristles on the cushions had been trimmed and dyed in places to make *fleurs-de-lis*. One of the arms was worn to the nap, which was dark and grimy. The reading lamp on the table beside the couch had a ceramic base and a silken shade. A string had been tied to the lamp chain and the end of the string pinned to the arm of the couch with a golden safety pin. When Mrs. Covington reached up to pull the string her hand shook. In the fresh penumbra of light beneath the lamp were a pair of wire eyeglasses, a dish of mints and three bottles of pills. Both the bottles and the pills looked plastic.

I tried to get comfortable but couldn't. "I've been asked by Chet Herk at the paper to try to locate your husband," I began. "I believe he talked to you about it, is that right?"

"I believe so."

"I thought you might have some information I could use."

"I doubt it," she said wearily, stupidly. Her tone implied she hadn't been useful in a decade.

I spoke quickly, before her infectious helplessness spread, rendering her mute. "First of all, no one at the paper had a picture of your husband. I wonder if you would mind lending me one. You'll get it back in a couple of days, after I have it copied."

She smiled at me cheerlessly. "I'm not sure, actually, that I have one. I certainly don't have anything recent. Mark was adamant about that."

"So I've been told."

She drifted into memory. "I bought a camera once. One of those little ones you can put in your pocket. But it disappeared the next week. Mark said he didn't know anything about it. He was lying."

She looked at me directly then, for the first time, as if to tell me she knew how absurd it was for her to be telling me that her husband lied to her, that she knew such a confidence was not appropriate in our circumstances, but that she was beyond caring what I or anyone like me might think of her or of anything else.

"How about some wedding pictures?" I asked. "Anything at all would be helpful."

"Wedding pictures," she said listlessly. "Of course. In my circumstances one tends to forget about weddings and things of that sort. It might be fun to see them again."

She retreated toward the rear of the house, shuffling along in fluffy white slippers, leaving me in the mausoleum that was her living room. Nothing in view indicated who the occupants were or ever had been. The white leatherette Bible on the coffee table was perhaps a clue to what one of them wanted to be, but it seemed too pristine to have ever been anything but a formless hope.

I picked up the pill bottles. Darvon. Percodan. Valium. Nerves and pain. No sleep, no energy, no strength. A prescription personality, identical to those foisted on mil-

lions by doctors seeking only to subdue symptoms and
drug companies seeking only to broaden dependence on
their wares. In any place but their own minds they are indistinguishable from the dope pusher on the corner across
from the high school.

My legs felt stiff and atrophied so I got up and walked
around the room. Pictures of birds and flowers on the
walls. A collection of tea cups. A crocheted sampler that
read "God is Love," suggesting that homilies are more
likely to be true if they are written down. No books, no
photographs, no souvenirs, no mementos. Time had passed
unremarked by anything except the tick of a clock.

Mrs. Covington came back as I completed the circuit.
She was clutching a large black book to her chest. The
word "Photos" was stamped on the cover in gold. She
handed the book to me, insistently. "Look inside," she demanded. "Look." Her voice was harsh and urgent.

I opened the cover and turned some pages. Here and
there a few snapshots clung to the stiff black pages, one of
a church, another of some flowers on an altar, but for the
most part the pages were blank except for the little gold
triangles that had once anchored the missing pictures to
the album. "He took them," Mrs. Covington said fiercely.
"Even the wedding pictures. He took them and didn't even
tell me. My God. Can you imagine?"

I could imagine it as easily as I could breathe; the
woman was a magnet for cruelty. I shook my head sympa-
thetically, and it wasn't entirely an artifice. Mark Covington was becoming less appetizing as the day wore on.

"That's pretty nasty," I said. "Could there be any photographs somewhere else?"

She stiffened visibly. "Even if there are I refuse to look
for them. If you want to know what my husband looks
like just watch for a man that acts as though he hasn't
made a mistake in his entire life except in choosing the
woman he married. When you find him, you've found
Mark."

"I know a lot of people who'd fit that description."

"Pity you. I only knew one. One is enough."

I stood up and Mrs. Covington did the same. Her eyes
flicked back toward the bedrooms, then returned to my
face. I didn't think it meant anything except that she
wanted me to leave. "By the way," I said, "does your husband have an office here at home?"

"No. He works at the paper. He never brings work home. He rarely brings himself."

Mrs. Covington obviously didn't know that her husband rarely appeared at the office. A mystery. *E pluribus unum.* "Are there any friends of his I should talk to?"

"Friends? Mark didn't have friends. They were a luxury he could no longer afford, as he put it. His own brother and sister-in-law live half a mile away. We haven't seen them in two years. Not that I minded," she added bluntly.

I tried to show some sympathy for her but it was difficult, like trying to show sympathy for a slug. "It can't be easy, being married to a crusader," I said.

"Fanatic would be a better word. Mark fancies himself a cowboy, I think. Riding into town all by himself, cleaning up the corruption, then riding off into the sunset without even waiting for the thanks of the poor townspeople. Of course he does have his name painted on his saddle."

"Your husband sounds a bit romantic."

"He's a child, is what he is. If you knew his mother you'd understand how he got that way."

I didn't want to get into that at all. "What do you think happened to him?"

"Nothing. I think he just left."

"Left what?"

"Everything. Me, for starters. His job. His mistress. His car payments."

The litany of her husband's abandonments seemed enervating. For a moment I thought she was going to fall. I put a hand out to steady her. Through the thin, cool robe her arm felt like a stick of bamboo. "I think you better leave now," she said wearily. "I need a nap."

"You've already had a nap."

"So? I'll have another. I like naps. Is that a crime? Is it a crime that a woman's husband leaves her? Is it? Why don't you investigate that crime, huh? There's a crime for you."

I moved toward the door, aware of the hysteria behind me, left like an excess pickle on the Blue Plate Special. I pushed open the screen, then turned back to her. "Just a couple of things. You said 'mistress.' Does your husband have a mistress?"

"Of course he does."

"Who is she?"

She shrugged. "Any name I'd give you would be at least

a year out of date. I stopped keeping track some time ago. There seemed little point in being Mark's scorekeeper."

"What about his car? Is it here?"

"Out in the drive. The beige one."

"May I look in it?"

"Why? Are you a used car dealer? You don't look much like a used car dealer, Mr. Tanner."

It was a joke, a small one, but it was the only likeable thing I'd seen her do. "I don't deal in used cars, Mrs. Covington," I said. "I deal in used lives."

"Well, you've come to the right place," she said, then laughed roughly at the jape. "The car's unlocked. Have a ball. Don't wake me when it's over."

She swept the pill bottles off the table and jammed them into her pocket and slithered out of sight toward the bedroom. I let myself out of the house, hoping I was leaving more than that behind me.

Twenty

The Saab was several years old, the color of sand on a dusky day, dented and scratched and corroded from more than a half-decade of jousting in the city's lists. I walked around it once. The rear bumper hung loose and a taillight was cracked and a windshield wiper was missing. When I opened the door it groaned the way a girl I once knew groaned just before she fell asleep.

A layer of dust had settled over everything inside. I set to work among the treasures in the tomb, fumbling first with the litter on top of the dashboard. I disturbed some sunglasses, some bank deposit receipts, a pen, a book of matches and a stick of gum. Chewed. In the glove compartment several maps, more matches, a first aid kit, a tire gauge, a briar pipe and a partially consumed roll of Life Savers coexisted peaceably if not neatly.

Elsewhere was only trash: empty hamburger bags and pop cans and candy wrappers, artifacts of the twentieth century. When I found a baseball glove tucked under the front seat I began to like Covington a little better.

What I was looking for was something that would lead me to the piece that was missing from the puzzle of Mark Covington, the piece that showed where he worked, where

he thought, where he dreamed. I took a deep breath and
tried again, opening the door and checking the service
sticker on the end plate. It had been stuck there by the
Saab dealer on Van Ness. Predictable, thus not helpful. I
got back in the car and pulled up the floor mats and
peered in the ash trays and folded the seat backs forward.
Only dross.

I thought about asking Mrs. Covington for the keys to
the trunk. I thought about it twice. But I didn't want to
see her again, to get into the trunk or to get anything else.
Then I remembered you could fold down the rear seat of
a Saab and create a flatbed that extends directly into the
trunk, so I crawled in the back seat and fumbled with
some levers and knobs and finally figured it out in four
times the time it would have taken anyone under the age
of twenty.

The seat pulled down like the lid of a coffin. Just before
I struck a match to see what was back there I had a vision
of a body, a dead body, folded neatly and packed tightly
in a mobile crypt. I found a body in a trunk once, but not
this time. There was nothing there but a half-inch of dirt
and a case of empty wine bottles and a dirty feather pillow.

I shook out the match and pulled my head out of the
trunk and got out of the car. It had started to rain again,
the weather turning as inclement as my case. I leaned on
the car door and let the rain besmirch my sport coat and
my professional reputation.

I was about to close the door and go on to the next order of business, which was lunch, when I noticed something white sticking out from beneath the armrest on the
opposite door. I leaned over and looked.

The Saab people had put a little pocket under there, a
six-inch deep pouch that ran the length of the door just
under the arm rest. At some time or other Covington had
stuffed an oily rag inside it, which was what I'd seen.
There were also some tools—pliers, Crescent wrench, Phil-
lips screwdriver.

I looked in the other pocket. It was stuffed full of cus-
tomer copies of credit-card receipts, all crumpled and
rolled and wrinkled and soft from the moisture in the air,
the consistency of crepes. I pulled them out by the hand-
ful.

They made a large pile on the passenger's seat. It took
me awhile to straighten them out, one by one. Most were

oil company receipts for gasoline credit-card purchases, several more than two years old. Almost the whole batch was from the same place—a Texaco station at Thirty-third and Noriega, four blocks away. But five of them were different, from another place, a place that didn't seem to relate to either Covington's house or to the newspaper, a place on Pierce just below Union, a place in an area of the city where many a cocksman before Covington had established his digs. Absent another alternative I hopped in my Buick and headed that way, stopping only for lunch at Zim's.

This one was an Arco station, owned by a guy named Bud, or so the sign said. I didn't see anyone who looked like a Bud, but the bay doors were open and there was a kid in the back doing something to the universal joint on a two-year-old Ford. A radio was blasting away. Disco. I went back anyway.

The kid's name was Larry. He'd been working for Bud for about a year, ever since he'd dropped out of Balboa High after being suspended for taking a swing at the assistant basketball coach. No, he couldn't ever remember it raining this much before Christmas, yes, the gas situation was still a bummer what with Iran and all, and yes, he sure liked cars, worked on them all his life.

Under the pretext of waiting for Bud to come back I moved him from Indy cars to Formula One to NASCAR stocks to the super modifieds they ran down at Watsonville. As soon as I could I worked in foreign cars—German, Japanese, then Swedish. Volvo, then Saab. They were pretty good cars, in fact I had a friend who owned one, a beige one. All kinds of things wrong with it—bumper, taillights, wipers. As a matter of fact, my friend lived right around here. Tall, thin, dark hair, good-looking. A newsman. Maybe Larry knew him.

And Larry did. Larry filled his tank every other week or so. Larry also knew exactly where my friend lived, because he'd seen him go in there one day last summer with a foxy-looking chick on his arm who had a set of bazooms that wouldn't quit. Two blocks up, then left toward Steiner. The apartment building with the little tree out front. That was it, wasn't it?

I hoped so.

I thanked Larry and told him I couldn't wait for Bud any longer. On impulse I pulled out a five and gave it to

the kid. Ever since they took the cop off the beat the gas
station attendants are the only people in town who know
what's going on.

I was out of the service bay and halfway to my car
when something coming over the radio yanked my attention to it. I don't know how the news report began, but the
way it ended was that the body of a man named Howard
Renn had been found early that morning by some joggers
in the Portals of the Past area of Golden Gate Park, dead
of a gunshot wound to the head. He'd been dead at least
forty-eight hours. Investigation was continuing.

And so the city had one less poet and one more mystery. For the second time in as many days the radio had
told me about death, had told me that people I had seen
and talked to no longer existed. Max Kottle and Howard
Renn. Father and friend to a boy named Karl. Father and
friend: what a man needs most till he gets past puberty.
And maybe even then.

As I walked along the sidewalk the weeds of the Kottle
case grew higher and thicker around me, threatening to
block my view of anything else. I pushed them back,
though, out of my way and out of my mind.

For the time being.

Twenty-One

The apartment house with the little tree out front was
called the Parkway Arms. The name was written in
golden cursive on the glass panels in the double-door, one
word per side. An iron grate protected the glass, but not
enough to keep some local wags from reaching through
and adding a yellow "F" as a prefix to the second word.

The tree out front was a bottlebrush and the building
was one of those financed with a lot of leverage, which is
to say with a lot of other people's money. The walls would
be as thin as eardrums and beneath the veneers on the
cabinets and tabletops would be planks of pressed sawdust.
Over the years I'd lived in a lot of places just like it.

After making sure no one was interested in what I was
doing I crossed the street and walked up to the entrance.
To the right of the door was a bank of tin mailboxes, each
with a white name-tag on the top and a tiny round button

on the bottom. Above them all was the wire mesh of the speaker that hooked into the buzzers and the lock system. I read the names quickly. There were twelve of them, but none was Covington or anything like it.

So I went over the names again, more slowly. Four were single women, or at least were surnames preceded by a single initial. Five were couples, and three of the five were unmarried. Which left three single men: Winkles, Briley and Zenger. Apartments 2, 7 and 10, respectively.

I pushed the button under number 2. The speaker hissed and crackled and almost immediately a man's voice asked me who I was. I told him I was from the Census Bureau, making a preliminary survey to determine whether we needed to revise any of our canvassing procedures before beginning the 1980 census.

The voice was doubtful. I added that, because this preliminary canvass was so vital, and because participation was voluntary, we were empowered by an Act of Congress to pay twenty-five dollars to those people who agreed to talk with us. The voice told me to come on up, and the buzzer squawked.

Apartment 2 was halfway to the back of the building. The hallway was dark and smelled of cheap paint and burned food and medicines applied externally. I knocked once and the door opened immediately behind my fist.

The man who looked up at me might have been five feet tall if he'd stood on a brick. He was sandy-haired and stooped but his flesh was as smooth as an eggshell and his eyes were bright. He might have been fifty and he might have been seventy. I stuck out my hand and he took it in a surprisingly strong grip.

"Smarts a little, huh?" the man said happily as he studied my reaction.

I admitted it.

"Used to be a jock," he said. "Thirty years. Santa Anita. Hollywood. Bay Meadows. You name it. Got to have good finger strength to rate a horse, you know. Haven't been up since sixty-two, but I've still got the grip. Rubber balls, that's the secret."

"Feels like you could handle Shoemaker or Cauthen any day of the week."

He shook his head. "I wasn't that good. Never even made the Derby. The Flamingo, once. Clam Digger, the horse was. Sixth. Second at the clubhouse turn, but died in the stretch." He paused, clearly reliving the run for the wire. I didn't disturb him. "But what the hell," he continued finally. "I'm still walking. A lot of the boys aren't. People don't realize how dangerous the sport is."

I tried to show I understood, and tried to figure how I was going to get out of there in a hurry.

"Come on in," he urged. "What do you want to know?"

"Now let me see." I pulled out my notebook, careful not to show the little man that the pages were blank. "You're Jacob Nestor, is that right?"

He smiled. "No, that's *not* right."

"It's not?"

The smile stretched into a grin. "Not by ten lengths. I'm Eddie Winkles."

"Winkles. Are you sure? Just let me check." I flipped some pages. "No, you're Jacob Nestor. It says so right here."

Eddie Winkles giggled and put a hand on my wrist and tugged me further inside the apartment. "Come over here," he said. "Now look." He pointed to the wall to my left.

I looked. On the wall was a giant photograph, life-sized or better, of a young jockey dressed in blue-and-white silks, gripping a crop with his left hand, a black number 3 pinned to his chest. He stood in the sun, his face round with a half-grin that said he had had a lot of luck a lot of times and was planning on having a lot more. The name Eddie Winkles was printed below the picture in white block letters.

I shook my head helplessly. "There's evidently been a terrible mistake at the Computer Center. No use asking you anything more, I guess. I'd better check with the office." I put my notebook away. "Wow. I'll probably have to check the whole block this afternoon." I shook my head with the oppression of a bureaucrat faced with extra work. "Well, I guess that's why we make these preliminary checks. Someone's head will roll for this one."

"If they're smart," Winkles said, "they'll let the heads stay on and chop the cord to the computer instead. Those damned things are going to kill us all."

"Computers? How?" I thought I knew, but Eddie clearly wanted to tell me.

"Nuclear war." Eddie's gaiety had vanished like sheets

at a white sale. "Two of those babies are going to get mad at each other one of these days, one of ours and one of theirs, and before they're through we'll all be dead."

"I never thought of it that way before."

"Well, you better start. I didn't bring two hundred nags to the winner's circle by being dumb. We'll be living on borrowed time till they invent a computer that says ouch when you kick it. I've got some pamphlets on it right here. Put out by a guy in El Paso. You ought to read one."

I told Eddie I had to get back to the office and bid a hasty good-bye, then took the stairs to Apartment 10, the apartment whose occupant had the same name as John Peter Zenger, the first man in America to go to jail in defense of the freedom of the press.

This time my knock went unanswered. I waited three minutes, checked to see that no doors had cracked open in front of eyes that had nothing better to do than see what I was up to, then knocked again. In the resultant silence I pulled out a credit card and ran it up the crease. No dice. I pulled out my picks. The second one got me in.

One room and a bath. Hot plate and ice chest. Typewriter and desk. Bed and chair. Lamp and rug. Phone and radio. And enough file cabinets to have stored every piece of mail I've ever received. It wasn't the Ritz, but it wasn't the Motel Marvelous, either.

I took a quick survey. The closet contained a few colorless clothes that had been bought off a pile instead of a rack and something repulsive that turned out to be a fake beard and hairpiece. The bed was small and soft, the sheets rumpled and discolored by dirt and semen and whatever it is women secrete during sex besides tears. Various items were tacked to the walls with straightened paper clips—articles about a tire company that sold tires that disintegrated and a car company that sold cars that blew up and others of that thrust, some of Covington's own pieces clipped from the *Investigator*, posters of television women in bikinis, the famous Wirephoto of Vice President Rockefeller flipping the bird to a heckler, an aerial view of the city, a green-and-black National Geographic Photomosaic of the contiguous states and a technically precise but emotionally sterile nude drawing of a woman who was definitely not Mrs. Covington.

The desk was just as useless. On its top were the standard references—Bartlett's, Brewer's, Fowler's, Webster's—and its single drawer contained only writing materials and a roll of stamps. I began pawing through the file cabinets.

It would have taken me a week to inspect every paper in the files so I began by checking the folders themselves. The file labels were a bibliography of Covington's career, a list of the exposés that had made him the most respected and most feared reporter in town. El Gordo Fire Department. Stanlock Development Corporation. South Bay Transport. Carl Putney. On and on, names that had been obscure until Covington exposed their corruption the way dentists expose nerves. And there were other names, names that had been famous in San Francisco for a century, names whose files bulged with indecipherable commercial data or pitifully pornographic photos, names that brought to mind news headlines and society page layouts and television closeups of wide-eyed, sweating faces and promises of reform and denials of responsibility and affirmations of change. Names and more names, and beneath them, in manilla wrappers, the flotsam and jetsam of psychological truth.

I kept rummaging, learning a lot of things I didn't know and a few I didn't want to. But after a half hour I hadn't found anything more pertinent than a reminder of how many people there were who would enjoy seeing Mark Covington assume another form of existence. Then I moved to the fourth cabinet. There, in between the folders for the January Club and the Lake Tahoe Gamesmanship Preservation Society, was a folder bearing a single name— Kottle.

I took out the file and opened it up. There were a lot of things about Max in it, mostly old news clippings, and I didn't learn anything from reading them. But there was also one other thing, a volume of poems, slim and thick-paged, with uneven edges and a stiff blue cover. The title of the volume was *War Baby*. It was published by the Sunflower Press. The author was Howard Renn. The dedication page read simply, "to Karl."

I thumbed through the volume. The poems were short, not the Ginsbergian soliloquies I'd expected but terse, bitter epithets of formal rigidity. One poem in particular caught my eye. *Zarathustra*:

Corsair
Condor
You who soared
Above us all
On wings of words
And led a thousand
Breathing dreams
Through streets
Of blood and bondage,
Is there now
A nest for you,
Or must you fly
Again aloft
To meet a fate
So certain, so elite?

I tucked the file back in the cabinet and turned out the lights and left. On the way out I remembered I'd forgotten to give Eddie Winkles the money I'd promised, so I slipped three bills into his mailbox, feeling more a felon than a samaritan.

Twenty-Two

I settled into my apartment the way aspic settles into a mold and called my answering service for the first time that week. All the messages were irrelevant annoyances except one. Two days ago, while I was still in Carmel, Howard Renn had called and left a message that he wanted to see me. Now he was dead. If I hadn't gone out of town he might be alive. It could be that simple, if I let it be, or it could be more complicated, the way it really was.

The spaghetti in my stomach began to burn, a cinder of displaced remorse. After two more drinks I let myself think again. After one more I called LaVerne Blanc.

LaVerne used to be a reporter, then a columnist, but he got next to the bourbon a little too frequently and now he publishes a gossip sheet that prints more fiction than fact and makes the *National Enquirer* look like the *National Geographic*. Oddly enough, despite its intellectually bereft contents and its déclassé layout, LaVerne's paper still manages to find its way into most of the Pacific Heights mansions and Marin County split-levels through one door or another. I almost always make a pass at LaVerne in a missing persons case. He doesn't always come up with something helpful, but he always comes up with something.

When you call LaVerne you're not taken seriously until the phone has rung ten times, so it was almost a minute after I dialed his number before LaVerne picked up the receiver. "Speak," he demanded.

"Marsh Tanner, LaVerne. How's it going?"

"I feel like I've been shot at and missed and shit at and hit, Tanner, which is an improvement from yesterday. Not that anyone this side of my sainted mother-really gives a damn. Who's on your mind?"

"Mark Covington."

"Blades."

"What?"

"Blades. That's what we used to call him."

"Why?"

" 'Cause of the way he chopped up anything and everything between him and a story."

"When was this?"

"Mid-fifties. Covington wasn't born with a byline up his ass, you know. He scratched for crumbs at City Hall and the Hall of Justice like the rest of us chickens before he made it big."

"Friends?"

"Me and Mark? Never were and never will be."

"Why not?"

"Try to imagine how you'd feel going out for a few beers with God Almighty after work every night, Tanner. Well, that's the way I felt around Blades—kind of on edge, you know? Why the interest?"

"Can you keep a secret, LaVerne?"

"Come on. I kept my daughter's first Wasserman a secret through two husbands. What's up besides my pecker?"

"Covington's missing."

"Presumed dead, I hope."

"No presumptions, just questions."

"Well, I ain't heard nothing, but then I tune out when that guy's name comes up. I'll pay attention for a few days. That it?"

I'm not sure what made me go on, except that when I'm talking to LaVerne I develop an urge to run every name I know through his data bank, just to see what pops out. Other people have a similar urge when they find themselves alone with their friends' medicine cabinets. "How about Karl Kottle?" I asked.

He thought it over. "Nothing. Any relation to Max?"

"Why?"

"Max I knew, rest his soul. Used to go through the girlies like Sherman through Georgia. Insatiable. Nothing in the past few years, though. He must have been sleeping with his money. Which probably gave him a better screw than the bitch I got in the next room. Too bad Max kicked off, though. All the personality in this town's dropping dead."

I didn't bother pointing out to LaVerne that Max Kottle had been happily married during his last years; LaVerne had no interest at all in the norm. "How about Howard Renn?" I went on.

"The poet?"

"Yeah."

"He's dead, too. What'd you do, Tanner? Open a mortuary?"

I laughed in spite of myself. "Come on, LaVerne. You hear anything about Renn or what he was into when he died?"

"I know his wife was all over him like a bad smell because he threw her out when he came into some bread. I also know in the old days you couldn't take a shit in a public john without Renn popping out of the next stall and reading you a poem about cosmic screams or some such crap. But Renn was a sixties man. Haven't heard of him in years, other than his obituary."

"Pete Zenger."

"Who?"

"Zenger."

"Wait a sec. There's something on that one. I think . . . no. Nothing. I don't know nothing about no Zenger."

"Hey. LaVerne. You sounded scared there for a minute."

"I ain't been scared since fifty-two."

"What happen then?"

"I had my first DT."

"What about Zenger, LaVerne?"

"What about Zenger is that you'd best keep your nose out of that business. It's big and it's as nasty as an elephant with adenoids and it's no place for people who get off on breathing. Now that's it. No more. I got to go feed the fish."

I gave up. "Keep smiling, LaVerne."

"At my age, the only thing worth smiling about is an effective laxative."

After LaVerne hung up I puttered around for a while—filling the sugar bowl, taking the stains out of my coffee cup, throwing out the stale bread, sewing a button on my topcoat—keeping ahead of whatever it is that doing those things keeps you ahead of. I had hoped that my unconscious mind would utilize the fallow period to sort and resort the impressions it had collected over the past twenty-four hours and come up with a brilliant place for me to start the next morning, a shortcut to Mark Covington, a way to bring an early end to a job I was tired of, an end to trying to find people who didn't want to be found.

But my unconscious was uncooperative. All it did was present me with images of kids, kids with weapons—automatic rifles, white phosphorous grenades, electro-explosive devices—kids massing on the Marina Green, clutching the tools of modern terrorism, shouting, chanting, eyes ablaze with thoughtless fervor, preparing to bring a city to its knees in a pool of the blood and guts of random victims.

When I had finished with both my daydreams and my domesticity I put on a robe and slippers and poured another drink and sat down in the only comfortable chair in the place and looked out the window at the nothing that was there. Sometime later I fixed another drink. Automatically. It bothers me when I do things automatically, but I suppose it doesn't bother me enough. When you get past forty nothing bothers you enough.

Time settled over me like a shawl. Elsewhere in the city people were dining and dancing, drinking and laughing, touching and talking, exchanging the bits of themselves that is the currency of love and friendship. I wasn't doing any of those things; I was all by myself. If a bomb dropped in the neighborhood it wouldn't kill anyone I'd ever spoken to more than twice. I tried to tell myself it wasn't important. That was too hard, so I did something easier. I told myself I didn't care.

On the way back from the liquor cabinet I made another effort to focus my thoughts on Mark Covington and what I knew about him and what I needed to know, but it was still no dice. Within seconds I was sharing the room with a phantom, a woman who had been in my apartment and had left enough of herself behind to build an image out of, a woman recently widowed, a woman named Belinda.

My thoughts were en route to a place I shouldn't have been going, so I resorted to the best thought-killer of them all—the television set. Ten minutes later there was a fresh drink in my hand and Lou Grant was screaming at Rossi and *vice* was screaming so loud at *versa* I barely heard my door bell ring over the pointless din.

I marched to the door and opened it recklessly. That's because I was tough. I had nothing to fear because I could not be harmed. Or maybe I had nothing to fear because I could not be harmed enough. In any case I opened the door and looked into the face of my most recent dream.

I invited her in and apologized for my informal attire and my informal habitat and anything else she found offensive. She looked at me funny. "Are you drunk, Mr. Tanner?" she asked archly. She looked drunk herself, or at least jostled by something extraordinary. "You can't help me if you're drunk."

"Oh, yes I can," I said. Drunkenly.

Her eyes rolled and she searched for things, first in me and then in the room, that could help her. When she didn't find any she turned to go. "I've made a mistake," she said. "I'm sorry. I shouldn't have bothered you."

She had the door open before I could get to her, but she was still in the apartment when I put a hand on her arm. "Don't go," I said. "I'm all right. I've been having a mixed drink and it didn't agree with me. White Label and self-pity. The combination's toxic, but not irreversibly. I'll make some coffee. Sit down. I'll put on some clothes. Please."

Given her stage of agitation I thought she'd leave anyway, but I was wrong. She marched to the couch and sat down without a word, stiff and wary, and waited for me to do as I'd promised. I put on some water and ground some beans and went to the bedroom and got dressed. I was ready before the coffee was.

Five minutes later I handed her a mug. The contents were too hot to drink so she put it on the table beside her, moving mechanically, heedlessly, her mind on something neither of us could see.

I told her I was sorry to hear about her husband, that I'd tried to reach her when I heard he was dead but couldn't get through, that I hoped his last hours with Karl had gone well. She didn't seem to hear a word of it. The steam rose off her coffee like the veil off a reluctant bride. I wanted to hold her hand. I looked at her carefully, trying to anticipate her needs, trying to remember that she was Mrs. Maximilian Kottle. But the thing I remembered best was my own desire.

She wore a tan skirt and nut-brown top, boots, belt. No jewelry, no makeup. Her hair wasn't a slum, but it hadn't been tended since daylight. I guessed her visit was a whim. What I couldn't guess was what had prompted it. I was certain it had more to do with her than with me.

When she finally spoke it was with a voice that had gained strength since her arrival. "You seemed to be a man I can trust. I hope it's still true. I'm counting on that, Mr. Tanner. Just so you know. I'm counting on that very heavily. More than anything, I don't want to cause further grief."

Tears welled up and she groped in her purse for something to dab them with. When she didn't find anything she loosened her grip on the purse and it fell to the floor. A lipstick cylinder spilled out and rolled across the room. "Damn. Oh, dammit all." The words were overloaded.

My handkerchief was clean if not white and I reached out and handed it to her. She reached for it, but when she felt my hand she took it instead. She held it for a long time, tightly, relentlessly, until the tears dried. "I'm here about Karl," she said thickly, giving me my hand back even though I didn't want it.

"How is he?" I asked.

"He isn't. That's the whole trouble."

"You mean he took off again?"

"I mean he was never here. Max lied to you. He didn't hear from Karl. He hasn't even spoken to him. He just wanted you to stop looking."

"Why didn't he just take me off the case?"

"He was afraid you might suspect something, that you might keep looking in spite of being fired. He didn't want that, at any cost."

"Why not?"

She clenched her fists in her lap and leaned toward me. "Karl's been kidnapped," she said. "They're holding him for ransom. They want two million dollars. And Max is going to pay it."

"Max is dead."

"No he's not. That whole story was a lie, too. He's alive and he's got a suitcase full of money and he's waiting for a call from the kidnappers and he needs help and I don't know who else to turn to. Will you help? Please?"

Twenty-Three

The ravage of disease may appear more tellingly on the face of its witness than its victim. From the look of her, Belinda Kottle had endured every pang and wrench of her husband's affliction until it had become virtually indistinguishable from her own. Her eyes burned, their rims seared red, their sockets scorched black by the heat of her grief. She had lost weight and, more pitifully, her will seemed to have vanished with the flesh. She was a blank page, awaiting script.

Whatever my inclinations, I couldn't waste time charting the wounds on my guest. There were a thousand questions to be asked and I wasn't at all certain I was in shape to ask them or that Belinda Kottle was in shape to answer. "Let's go back to the beginning. What was the first thing your husband heard about Karl?"

"He got a telephone call. Friday. At the apartment."

"How did they get through? It can't be that easy to reach your husband on the telephone."

She clenched her fist, as though to squeeze out memories. "It came over Max's personal line. I answered it. The voice said it had word about Karl. I told Max. He thought it was someone you had talked to. He took the call immediately. Eagerly. You should have seen his face when they told him they were holding Karl for ransom. It was horrible. Horrible."

The gods restaged the horror on Belinda's face, fashioning a mask, forcing it upon her, warping her features. I inched forward to the edge of my chair and reached out and touched her knee. She took my hand and raised it to her face. My fingers grew damp with the second wave of her tears. "What was said on the telephone?" I asked softly. "Exactly."

Her words were halting, without inflection. "Very little was said," she said. " 'We have your son. We are not afraid to kill if it becomes necessary. We will do so if we do not receive two million dollars within the next five days. We are giving you time to get the money together without arousing suspicion. You will not hear from us again until you are instructed where to deliver the money.' That's all I can remember. Max didn't get a chance to say a word."

"Male voice?"

"Yes. Deep. Educated. Confident."

"Did you hear the conversation?"

She nodded. "Max put it on his speaker phone. It was like a séance. None of us moved. None of us breathed."

I hoped that was as close to a séance as it would ever become.

"Was there any background noise?"

"Not that I could hear."

"I don't suppose the call was recorded by any chance."

She shook her head. "Max does record some calls on his business line, but he can't do it on his personal one. There wouldn't have been time, anyway. It was a very brief conversation."

"Who else was there when the call came through?"

"Walter Hedgestone and me. That's all."

"Did they put Karl on the phone?"

"No."

She looked at me. I didn't look back. "Did they offer any proof he's alive?"

Her eyes widened at what had passed unstated. "Alive? Why wouldn't he be alive?"

There were a lot of reasons not to tell her, and maybe I should have yielded to one of them, but she had made the decision to come to me and she was going to have to make another decision before the evening was out and I wanted her to know it all. "Sometimes the victim is dead before the ransom demand is even made," I stated evenly. "Leopold and Loeb did it that way, to name one case."

A little sound came from within her, a little sound of anguish. "Then how can I possibly know what to do? How can Max be sure he's doing the right thing, the thing that will get Karl back?"

"He can't be sure," I answered. "No one can. That's the beauty of it. There are at least three ways to proceed, and if it goes bad you will wonder for the rest of your life what would have happened if you'd done something different."

"My God," she said, so softly I barely heard her. Her eyes were closed and she was breathing heavily through her nostrils, making sounds as forlorn as a departed train. "What would you do?" she asked finally.

I shook my head. "I don't know. Since I don't have money or family I'll never have to find out." There was silence then, space enough for each of us to contemplate our histories and our fate if we wished to. "Was there anything else about the call?" I asked. "Anything at all?"

Her brow furrowed prettily, in spite of it all. "Oh, yes. They had a name, a silly little name, as if that would make it all right to do what they were doing. Max thinks it's a political thing. Extremists, or something."

The tumblers were falling into place despite my inebriation. "Let me guess," I said. "The Sons and Daughters of Isaiah."

Her surprise turned quickly to suspicion. "How did you know? How *could* you know?" She was almost screaming.

"It's nothing sinister," I said quickly. "It's just that I've stumbled over that group several times lately. If the stakes weren't so high I'd think it was a Parker Brothers game."

"Well, who *are* these, these Sons and Daughters?"

I shrugged. "I don't know. Max is right as far as I can tell. I think they are some kind of terrorist group, but their ideology's a little vague. They bombed Laguna Oil and got mad when the press didn't report it. Then today they presented some manifesto to the *Investigator* and demanded it be published or they'd blow up the building or some such rot. That's all I know. Maybe if the paper prints what they want we'll learn more."

"Max owns Laguna Oil," Belinda said quietly.

"I know he does. Interesting, isn't it?"

"But what does it mean?"

I didn't know and I told her so. Then I asked if her husband knew she was here.

She shook her head. "He won't have to know, will he?"

I considered it. "Probably not. He's not a client anymore. But if this gets nasty, nastier than it already is, there are legal and ethical requirements that could pop up. I never like to predict who will have to say what to whom."

Belinda nodded and fell silent. I sipped my coffee, making a noise in the process. It was the only sound in the room.

As I watched her, Belinda looked out the window, as though an answer to it all floated out there, suspended somewhere above the street and below the stars. I looked out there, too, but I didn't see anything but air. Black air.

"Max is going to pay," Belinda said dreamily.

"Does he have the money?"

"Yes."

"Has he told the cops?"

"No."

"Why not?"

"The man who called told him not to. He said he would know immediately if Max contacted the police or the FBI, and would slit Karl's throat if he did. You should have heard his voice. Max believes him. So does Walter. So do I."

"Two million," I said.

"Two million," she repeated.

I didn't say anything for a while. There wasn't much I *could* say that would comfort Belinda or her husband. The odds of coming up winners in a kidnapping are never good, and they're getting worse. I thought of some of the recent ones—Exxon paying fourteen million for one of their executives, Firestone paying three million for one of theirs, a German company sixty million for three of theirs—on and on, with the cards entirely in the hands of the terrorists who could decide to take the money or, like the Aldo Moro case, to prove a deadly point.

Suddenly I thought of Charlie Sleet and the group he had told me about, the group on the make for guns and explosives, the group that was going to pay cash, big cash, for that kind of ordnance. It seemed possible that the Kottle kidnapping would be the source of those funds, that Karl Kottle was the trade-off for enough munitions to blow the lid off Mt. Diablo, enough to make every person of wealth or power in the city lie awake at night wondering if they would be shot the instant they left the house.

But I couldn't go to Charlie Sleet with what I had, or thought I had, because there wasn't any proof at all and because even if there was I couldn't do it without Max

Kottle's approval. All I could do was sit and wonder. One thing for sure, if international terrorists were really behind the kidnapping, then the chances of Karl Kottle being found alive after the ransom was paid were as slim as parchment.

"Why the hoax that Max had died?" I asked after a while, grabbing a question that was floating past.

A grim smile appeared briefly above the set of her jaw. "That was Walter's idea. He said if the kidnappers thought Max was dead, then maybe they would release Karl and try something or someone else. He prepared a press release that stressed how control of Collected Industries had passed to the Executive Committee and that all the current projects were suspended until the committee could convene."

"The SEC won't like Max issuing a statement like that. I'll bet the price of the stock is dropping like crazy."

"Max doesn't care what the SEC thinks. He just wants to see Karl alive. Walter said the Sons and Daughters might not want to deal with a committee. Max thought it was worth a chance."

"Was he right?"

"We don't know. No one's heard from them since the first call."

"The five days won't be up till tomorrow," I pointed out.

"I know that," she said.

I took a deep breath and held it for a minute, trying to clear my head before the last round. "What is it you want me to do, Mrs. Kottle?" I asked softly.

She looked at me for the first time in a while, her eyes shining like sun on snow. "I just . . ." she stammered. "There's no one I can turn to. Max is my only friend, really, and my family is, well, they have nothing to say to me except 'Come home.' I thought you might have some experience in these matters. I thought you might help me, tell me if Max is making a mistake."

"In paying off the kidnappers?"

"Yes."

I shook my head. "I can't say it's right and I can't say it's wrong. Sometimes paying off takes care of it. Other times it doesn't. I don't know what the odds are. No one does, really, since lots of times when the ransom is paid the case never becomes public knowledge. There are probably twice as many kidnappings as the number reported to the police. There's just no way I can tell you what to do."

She nodded as though she had expected that answer, had expected me not to be of help. All of a sudden I found myself wanting to help her more than I had wanted anything in a long while.

"Would you do this, then?" she asked wistfully. "Would you go along when the money's delivered? To see that nothing goes wrong? Walter thinks he can handle it, but I'm not sure."

I thought that one over. Again, there were a lot of reasons not to do it, not to enter a contest where the only prize was guilt if anything went wrong, but there was one big reason to agree and she was sitting right in front of me. "Does your husband want me to?" I asked.

"I don't know. I haven't discussed it with him. I didn't want to get his spirits up if you weren't willing."

"Why did you think I wouldn't be willing?"

"Well, it could be dangerous, couldn't it? I thought you might prefer not to get involved."

The drawl had slipped back into her voice. I smiled and she smiled back. "Where'd you go to college?" I asked.

"LSU," she said. "Why?"

"Whoever taught you psychology did a good job." I met her eyes. She just kept smiling. "I'm on another case now," I explained. "There are things I have to do."

"Please? For Max?"

"Not for Max."

"For me?"

I didn't answer.

She looked inside me then, with those red and black orphan's eyes. I tried to make everything in there invisible but I doubt if I succeeded. "I suppose your motives are unimportant," she concluded finally.

"To Max. To you. But not to me."

She just nodded.

"Okay," I said briskly. "I have to be out for a while tomorrow. Have your husband call me and hire me back. If I'm in on this and things go wrong, I don't want him blaming me."

"He won't."

"He might."

"Perhaps you're right. I guess I don't know him that well."

"No one knows anyone that well."

"I'll talk to him," she said. "But you must be ready. They could even call later tonight."

"I'll be ready. If I'm not in, my service will take the message. I'll check with them every half hour."

Belinda stood up, pressing her skirt to her thighs, patting her hair to her temple. "I appreciate this, Mr. Tanner," she said uneasily. "But you should know, there are certain forms of payment that are not available, not as long as Max is alive. I hope you understand."

"I understand that; you understand this. I'm strictly a capitalist. Cash and carry. No barter involved. Never."

She kissed me lightly and said good-bye.

Twenty-Four

If you make your living as a detective you tend to write off mornings. No matter what's involved in the case—money, sex, love, hate—nothing of significance ever happens before noon. So by the time I found myself strolling down Columbus on the way to the office it was already past lunchtime.

I'd drifted in and out of sleep all night, alternately listening groggily for a telephone call about a kidnapping and dreaming fitfully of sailing to sea on a sloop called *Idiot* with an all-girl crew and a tattered mainsail. As a result, I was hung over and tired. Life had gotten complicated. Two cases were active, two people were dead, two men were missing, and one puzzle was unsolved, which was one more than I felt capable of solving at the moment.

The situation was simple enough. Karl Kottle was still missing, only this time in order to find him I would have to find his kidnappers. Mark Covington was missing also, most likely because he wanted to be, and to find him I was going to have to be a lot luckier than I felt.

As a result of Belinda's visit my attention had shifted almost entirely back to the Kottle case. There seemed to be danger there, as imminent as a winter storm, and on top of that there was a client I wanted badly to please, so I ran the previous week's activity through my mind and picked out some threads that were loose enough to grab onto. At the same time I tried to dilute my guilt over my temporary abandonment of Chet Herk with the thought that the little volume of Howard Renn's poetry I'd found in Mark Covington's files might mean there was a connection of some sort between the two cases. That thought diluted my guilt the way sweat dilutes the sea.

I had one stop to make and I made it. Jerry was wearing the usual smile on his face and the usual apron over his clothes. He knew what I was there for and he ducked into the back room for a moment, then brought them out immediately.

"These are pretty lousy pictures, Marsh," he told me as he emerged from behind the curtain. "Even for an Instamatic. The backlight from the window washes everything out, the subjects were moving, and whoever pressed the shutter must have had third-degree palsy."

"Other than that, how are they?" I joked.

"See for yourself."

Jerry tossed a flat gray packet on the counter and I opened it up. He'd blown them up to five by seven, and they weren't bad, really, but only because Jerry was a wizard with a negative, any negative. The one on top was of Amber, the one I had taken, full face, dimly desperate. "I shot this one," I said, showing it to Jerry.

"Well, it's better than the others, but if I were you I wouldn't count on displacing Avedon."

"I don't count on finding a clean shirt, Jerry."

I leafed quickly through the rest of the pictures, then went through them again, more slowly. About half were individual shots and half groups of two or three. Some were identifiable, but a lot were so blurred or hazy I couldn't tell one form from another. Still, I got a nice surprise: souvenirs of Karl Kottle's appearance at the Encounter with Magic.

Thanks to Jerry I could recognize three different people. One was Amber and one was Howard Renn. One was Rosemary, Karl Kottle's half-sister, the girl I'd trailed from Cicero's. Which meant one must have been Karl. I looked at that one the longest.

Mrs. Renn was right. He had changed a lot since high school. He was slim, almost emaciated, with a receding hairline and an aquiline nose and small, black eyes that tried but failed to look pleased at the frolic the rest of the group was engaged in. The only trace of his boarding school days was in his posture. He was sitting stiffly on the edge of the bed in Amber's room, staring reluctantly and sadly into the camera, Torquemada at a satyrs' reunion.

"Two bucks," Jerry said.

"It should be more, Jerry."

"It should be what I say it is, Marsh. Two."

I gave him the money. "How's your search for the mysterious Madonna coming?"

"Slowly," Jerry said. "Oh, so slowly. I'm positive she shops at the Marina Safeway. One of these days I'll ambush her in the finger food department." Jerry was still nodding happily to himself when I left his shop.

When I got to the office I turned up the heat and put on the coffee and opened the mail, then nestled next to the telephone. My first call was to Gwen Durkin, my companion of Monday night past.

She answered the phone after the first ring. She said she was doing fine, was busy, was tired, and was looking forward to the next week when she would begin working two evenings a week at the Hunter's Point Medical Clinic.

At the first gap in the conversation I told Gwen I wanted to see her again sometime soon. She asked if I had anything specific in mind. When I said that because of a case I was on I couldn't make any time commitments for a while, the smile went out of her words. When I asked if she'd reconsidered her refusal to tell me about why Karl Kottle had been seeing Doctor Hazen on a regular basis, she said she most definitely had not. Her voice hardened with each phrase.

I asked if Doctor Hazen was in. Gwen said he was over at the hospital. Then she said she had better things to do. Then she hung up.

My gut started to swirl a little, the way it does whenever I've hurt someone unnecessarily, but I had to get on with my job.

I dialed again, this time to a stockbroker I'd defended once back in my lawyer days. A semisenile widow whose husband had compiled the biggest portfolio of losers since '29 had been persuaded by a Market Street shyster to sue Clay Oerter, the broker, for churning her account. Clay told me he had just been unloading the losers as advantageously as possible, and we put together a chart that proved it. I got the case tossed out on a summary judgment, but Clay was still out a lot of embarrassment and a lot of business and a lot of money for my fee. Now he's a confirmed member of one of the largest clubs there is: The Lawyer Haters. The club will keep growing as long as any lamebrain can put a person through the agony Clay went through just for the price of a filing fee.

"How you doing, Marsh?" Clay said. His voice popped like bacon frying. "Want me to put you onto a sure thing? Amalgamated Synthetics. Five-and-an-eighth bid. Zero downside risk. Also Milton Mufflers. Sell short against the box."

"No dice, Clay," I interjected before he could go on.

"Why not?"

"No money."

"Don't feel like the Lone Ranger. The only people with money these days are selling drugs or writing horror stories or bought gold at ninety-five. What can I do for you besides pray?"

"How about Collected Industries?" I asked.

"How about it? Max Kottle's dead. Big transition problem. Got to be. I haven't checked our research on it, but off the top I'd recommend staying away."

"I'm not planning to buy, Clay. But do some checking. Find out what's been happening to the stock since the news got out that Kottle is dead. Find out who's been buying, if anyone."

"The first is easy, Marsh. The stock's dropping, I'm sure of it. Kottle put that bundle together all by himself. As far as I know, no one in lower management has anything like his genius. They'll have to bring someone in from outside. It'll take time."

"How about the stock buyers?"

"Not easy. Most shares are bought in a street name, you know. I'll have to get some breaks to have anything for you very soon. When do you need it?"

"Yesterday."

"This afternoon's as good as I can do. I'll have to try to reach the specialist in the stock, and he won't be available till the exchange closes. I'll get back to you."

I thanked Clay in advance and broke the connection and dug another number out of the directory. The line was busy. I gulped down some coffee and tried again. Still busy. I checked my watch. The address was reasonably close to the place I was headed next, so I grabbed a very late lunch at McArthur Park, flirted ridiculously with a waitress who was half my age and twice my sophistication, then got my car out of the lot and drove to an apartment building on Buchanan, in the Western Addition.

I parked behind a Falcon that had been left for dead for at least three months, then climbed the stairs to Apartment 12. The halls smelled of urine and something worse. The walls were streaked with finger marks that could have been dirt or could have been blood. In that neighborhood there's not much difference between the two. The door I wanted didn't open till the sixth knock.

She didn't look much different, except that the stocking cap was gone and the fire in her voice had burned down to coals and ash. The only signs of mourning were her black brows.

"I was sorry to hear about your husband," I began. "I'm the guy you talked to outside his house a week or so ago."

"I remember."

"Do you mind talking with me for a few minutes?"

She glanced at her watch. "I'm moving tomorrow," she explained. "There's a million things to do. Will it take long?"

"It depends on what you know."

She looked at me speculatively, dubiously, then asked me to come in.

She turned and walked into the living room. It was as dreary as you'd imagine it would be, except that the boxes stacked all around the room indicated the dreariness was about to be passed, like seisin, to the next tenant. Over in the corner a little blond girl was stacking blocks. She paid no attention at all to me. I didn't blame her.

"I'm rich all of a sudden," Mrs. Renn declared. "Did you know that? Howard's parents bought a big insurance policy for him when he was small. The fat fool never got around to replacing me as the beneficiary. Too busy mauling eighteen-year-olds. Well, thanks to dear old Howard I may maul a few eighteen-year-olds myself."

"Lucky for you. Lucky for the boys. Lucky for everyone but Howard."

"Oh? Am I supposed to pretend I'm bereaved? Am I crass to speak ill of the dead? Bullshit. He treated me like scum, so good riddance. I just wonder how lily-livered Howard got up guts enough to make someone mad enough to kill him."

"I wonder about that, too. I thought you might be able to help me find the answer."

"Why on earth would you want to do that?"

"Because whoever killed Howard may be involved in a case I'm working on."

"And what case would that be?"

"That would be a confidential case. Like all cases."

She smiled, smug and complacent. "My, my. How mysterious. I'm trying to think of a reason why I should tell you *anything*, but I'm having trouble. Perhaps you can help. If not, perhaps you can leave."

I got a little hot. "Whatever happened between you and Howard at the end, at the beginning you loved each other and had a child together and presumably one or two months of joy. He's dead. You've got his money. You've got your child. What do you have to gain by concealing his killer?"

She didn't say anything, but she was thinking. I threw another stick on the fire, a big stick. "I didn't read anything in the papers about you sitting outside Howard's house all day every day for the past month. The cops will be interested to learn that. The killer will be even more interested."

The flames were back, and she was mad as hell at me, but she was also scared just a little. "What do you want to know?"

"I want to know what you saw while you were sitting out there all those days. Who went in there? What went on that was unusual? Anything?"

She walked over to the couch and wedged herself in between two boxes. One of them tilted as she sat down and something slid out of the box and onto the floor. I picked it up. It was a picture of her husband. He was smiling happily. Beneath his beatific face he'd written a couplet. It was pretty funny and pretty erotic. I handed her the picture. She looked at it and swore.

"I saw a bunch of girls," she said sarcastically, "and the only thing any of them could kill is a marriage. I saw some nut driving around in the dark with his sunglasses on. And I saw the guy who was there the day you were, the one in the lumber jacket. Remember?"

I remembered. Then I remembered something else. "Who's Woody?" I asked.

Mrs. Renn smiled. "Rosemary. Rosemary Woods, you

know? Only this is Rosemary Withers. She's Karl Kottle's half-sister. She leeched around Karl like a groupie."

Another connection. Karl and Rosemary. Rosemary and Cicero's. Cicero's and Renn. Renn and Covington. The links were being forged, but not rapidly enough. The chain was too short for anything but scrap. "Who was the guy in the sunglasses?"

"I don't know. It was just something I noticed one night. It's a pretty stable neighborhood up there, you know. A dog barks and they call in the SWAT team. I only saw him once."

"What else can you remember?"

"Nothing. I don't have time to remember anything else. You'd better leave."

"May I use your phone first?"

She nodded and I called my answering service. No word from Belinda about the kidnappers. I went outside and got in my car and drove over to Steiner Street and parked again.

Twenty-Five

The bottlebrush tree still sprouted out of the sidewalk in front and the lettering on the door still read "*Parkway FArms,*" but this time I wasn't planning to go inside. This time I was just going to wait and watch, employing the most prosaic and the most desperate weapon in the detective's arsenal: the stakeout.

The tactic was even less promising than usual, since it was clear that if Mark Covington was using his hideaway at all these days he was using it sparingly and with caution. The odds that he would show up while I was waiting for him were poor. Which made them as poor as the odds on any other lead I had to go on.

I parked down the street and around the corner from the entrance to Covington's building. I could just see the front door from where I sat, but I couldn't see the window of the apartment itself, so after waiting a few minutes to make sure nothing unusual was afoot I got out of the car and walked to where I could look up at the window. No lights, no opening, no shadows, no nothing.

I stared at the glass a minute, seeing warped reflections

of sky and buildings, then walked around the block to see if anything else of interest was going on. Nothing, unless you counted the woman in the mink coat who was curbing her poodle. I called in and then got back in my car before Eddie Winkles could come out and catch the census man snooping around the neighborhood again.

And I waited. It's what you do more than anything else in this business except swear. I'm pretty good at it, but I'm not great at it, because someone who lives alone tends to use up all the good waiting thoughts in his day-to-day life.

A year ago a friend of a friend's friend wanted to teach me self-hypnosis. He claimed that through the technique of age regression I could spend the time on a stakeout taking myself back to pleasurable, or at least interesting, points in my personal history—ball games played, women loved, entertainments witnessed. Almost everything in your past is accessible through hypnosis, or so they say. It's all there, every bit of it, waiting like a cage of frisky puppies for someone to come along with a key. I didn't take the lessons, though, I guess for the same reason I didn't take LSD when everyone else was and for the same reason I've never consulted a shrink. I have a hunch I'm better off leaving all that right where it is. In the cage.

You can pursue a bit of age regression without the aid of hypnosis, of course, and I was somewhere back around 1950, in a room in the Brown Palace Hotel in Denver with a girl named Sparkle, when someone pulled the door of my car open and got in beside me. It was dark enough by then so I couldn't tell right away who it was, and I was reaching semi-seriously for my gun when my new passenger laughed. "Hold it, big boy. It's only me. Pamela Brown. Girl Reporter."

My hand slipped back to my side the way a smile slips off the face of a stewardess when you make a crack about hijacking. "Fancy meeting you here," I said.

"Ditto."

She eyed me closely. In the dim light of a far-off street lamp she appeared intense, calculating, physically threatening. I pressed against the door beside me, putting as much distance as possible between us. Pamela saw me change position and smiled confidently. "Let's not beat around the bush," she said.

"Let's not."

"Okay. How did you find this place?"

"What place?"

"Fuck you, Tanner. Covington's place. Over there in the Parkway Arms."

"How did *you* find it?" I countered.

"You first."

"No. Me second. If at all. I have a client. You don't have anything more tangible than curiosity. Or do you?"

She paused a minute and chewed on a thumbnail while she thought it over. "No," she muttered finally. "That's all it is. Curiosity." She shrugged. "Once I thought it was something more, but it's not. I guess it never was."

"So how did you find the place?" I repeated.

"How? Mark brought me here one night and fucked my eyes out, that's how."

"How long ago was this?"

"Years."

"How many people do you think know about this apartment?"

"He said I was the only one who'd been there."

"Did you believe him?"

"I did then. I don't now."

"How long since you've seen Covington?"

"Here?"

"Anywhere."

"Weeks. Lots of people saw him after I did."

A man was walking up the street and I watched him. He walked with a limp. And a cane. And a smile. He passed the Parkway Arms and went into the next building. I looked back at Miss Brown. "What are you up to? Why are you here?"

"The same reason you are. I'm trying to find Mark." She was defensive, the way losing coaches are defensive. I asked her why she wanted Covington.

"Like you said. Curiosity. Plus the possibility of a good news story. Plus the chance to make Covington look like the horse's ass he is. Pick any two."

"What do you want from me?"

"Help. Or, if you beat me to him, an exclusive. I want to be the first one you tell."

"What's in it for me?"

"Also help. An extra set of eyes and ears and legs. Someone who's been asking questions of people who didn't want to answer them for the last five years. Someone who's smart as hell. Cute, too."

I didn't say anything.

"Well?"

"I'll think about it. Besides, I thought you had something else on the fire."

"I did, but I decided this was more interesting. I think Covington may have bit off more than he can chew on this one. He needs the cavalry, I'm sure of it. I want to be there when it comes over the hill. And you look like an old cavalry man to me."

"Thanks a lot."

"Don't be so sensitive. Old cavalry men are sexy as hell. All the girls say so."

"How exciting."

Her face twisted with exasperation. "Look, Tanner. Legwork and luck is what most of these disappearances come down to. You know that as well as I do. With me you get twice as many legs and twice as much luck."

"Legs I can use. Luck, I'm not sure."

"Luck? Are you kidding? Hell, Tanner, I'm the luckiest girl you ever met. I believed in the rhythm method till I was twenty-five."

Her laugh filled the car with puffs of confidence and youth. I thought for a moment they might smother me, but then they disappeared.

We sat there for a while, Pamela Brown and I, measuring each other in silence, trying one yardstick and then another, applying the calculus of self-interest, which is the only calculus there is. Miss Brown lit a cigarette and rolled down the window a crack. I straightened my legs as far as I could.

She blew a lungful of smoke out the window and looked at me. I could barely see her, except in the light from passing cars. "Did you check on the Biloxi Corporation?" she asked.

I should have run a bluff but she caught me before I had a chance to try. "Forgot, huh?" she said. "Hard to believe you make a living at this, Tanner. Maybe you got family money."

"Yeah. It's all tied up in sowbelly futures, though. Tough to make ends meet."

"Well, I hear you get some real nice things with food stamps these days."

"Lighten up, Miss Brown. I'll call the Secretary of State tomorrow and see what they have on Biloxi in their files."

"I already did that." The words were round with smugness.

"What did you find out?"

"Just a bunch of names. The only one I could trace was a guy named Quale. Harrison Quale. He's a lawyer."

"I know."

"The address of the corporation is the same as the address of his law office. Did you know that?"

"No. But that's the way they do it, especially when they want to keep things secret. The lawyer who draws up the Articles of Incorporation lists himself and a few of his secretaries as the incorporators and the initial directors. Then the real parties in interest take over after all the filings have been made. Keeps nosy people like you from running them down."

"Where do we go from here?"

"I don't know. I'll think about it."

Actually I did know. Harrison Quale was like most lawyers, he liked to talk, about himself and about his clients. Mostly he liked to talk to other lawyers. I'd been a lawyer once, and I'd served on a committee with Quale a while back, so I might be on his list of confidantes. If I played it right he might tell me something about Biloxi Corporation.

Something caused me to look up just then. It was a dark figure, moving slowly in the distance, coming toward us cautiously, mysteriously, looking for other bodies, other eyes. When it reached the entrance to the Parkway Arms it hesitated, then fumbled with a mailbox until a little door swung open and the figure took something out of the box and closed it back up. There was more fumbling, and the figure opened the main door and disappeared inside the building.

From where we sat there hadn't been much to see— dark slacks, ski jacket, stocking cap, hiking boots—but something about the figure seemed familiar. "Wait here," I ordered, then hopped out of the car and went to where I could see Covington's windows.

The apartment lights went on just as I got into position. A shadow moved through the room behind the blinds, stopping here and there, a dark cloud across a yellow sky. I took two steps toward the front door. The lights suddenly went out.

I hurried to a point across from the entrance and crouched down behind a parked car and watched the door. In another minute it opened and the same dark figure emerged, carrying what looked like file folders and some other papers. I couldn't be certain from where I was, but I thought it was a woman.

She looked up and down the street once, then twice, then began walking east, away from me and away from my car. As soon as I thought I could do it without being heard I scampered back across the street and ran to my car and got in.

"Do you have a car here?" I asked Miss Brown.

She nodded.

I looked at my watch. "Still want to be partners?"

She nodded again.

"Okay. I couldn't get close enough to see for certain, but I think that was someone Covington sent here to pick up his mail and some other things from his office. I think it's a girl. She's down at the end of the block. Go after her. Get your car if you have to. Be smart about it. When she gets to where she's going, call me at this number." I handed her a card. "I'll tell you what to do from there."

"What are *you* going to be doing?" she asked skeptically.

"Talking to a woman about a kidnapping," I said. "Now get going or you'll lose her."

Pamela Brown wanted to stay behind and ask some questions but the scent of Mark Covington was too strong. With one final glance at me she was gone. I started the car and drove home.

Twenty-Six

My apartment absorbed me like a damp sponge. I checked with my answering service but there was nothing from Mrs. Kottle. There was nothing from anyone, except the lingering message from a dead man. I puttered around, pouring a drink, heating some soup, reading the mail, shedding my tie and my coat and my profession.

The soup was hot. I poured it into a cup and put the cup beside my highball and myself beside them both and settled down with a diversion, Le Carré's new George Smiley saga. The blunt and linear progression of my own life soon became diffused by English indirection and within an hour I had my psyche back in a reasonable state of repair.

I fixed another drink and checked with the answering service again. Still nothing.

The second drink went down faster than the first. It always does. Through a frightening exercise in rationalization I convinced myself that if I got too drunk to function, then the universe would order itself so that I wouldn't have to. But something about the way my skin was tingling convinced me that Belinda Kottle would call before daybreak, that the ransom drop would take place somewhere, sometime before I slept again.

I got up and went in the kitchen and poured the dregs of my Scotch down the drain and picked up the telephone.

Once when I was practicing law I had a divorce client who called me up at two A.M. to tell me her estranged husband had just been by to visit her and had gone to the bathroom and refused to flush the toilet. She asked me what I was going to do about it. I told her. She got herself another lawyer. Which is one of the reasons why I hesitate to call professional people after hours. But I make exceptions to everything. Clay Oerter didn't seem to mind.

I asked Clay how many widows and orphans he'd fleeced that day and he asked me how many keyholes I'd peeped into and there was just enough truth in both of the jibes to make each of us pause for half a second. Then I asked Clay if he'd come up with anything on who was buying Collected Industries in significant quantities. He told me that as far as he could tell no one was. The price had dropped three more points that day, and until a new management team was in place and was proving itself on the bottom line of the income statement there seemed no reason for the price not to fall even further, at least to a price-earnings multiple of five or so. I thanked Clay for his time and asked him to keep an eye on the stock for a few more days and hung up. Three seconds later the phone rang, as though by placing the receiver on the cradle I had caused it pain.

I was afraid the caller would be Mrs. Kottle, and even more afraid of what she might need me to do. The phone rang on and on, majestically tolling each of my fears. I picked it up before the tones became one long cry for help.

I was saved. It was Pamela Brown. Girl Reporter.

"What are you doing, Tanner?" she asked loudly.

"Nothing. *Nada.* How's it going with the tail job?"

"You're drunk."

"Not really," I said, remembering she was the second woman to accuse me of the crime within two days.

"You're drunk. Jesus H. Christ. You send me chasing all over hell so you can go home and tie one on. And I thought reporters were bad."

"Reporters *are* bad. Detectives are bad, too. So are the people they try to find, the people who hide from them. It's a bad, bad, bad, bad world. They made a movie about it."

"You're not funny."

"I know."

For some reason Pamela Brown decided not to pillory me further. "Guess where I am," she demanded.

"Where?"

"Guess."

"Come on. Who did you follow from Covington's place? Do you know?"

"I don't know who she is. Some girl."

"Where'd she go?"

"Sausalito," Pamela Brown said.

"Sausalito," I repeated. Then I repeated it again. "Big house. Side of a cliff. Edwards Avenue. Carport. Blond hair, green eyes, round, tan bottom." I laughed. I laughed because suddenly I was working on one case, not two. I laughed because you never know.

Never.

"How the hell did you know all this?" Pamela Brown sputtered, making me glad there was a bridge between where she was and where I was.

"Call me Swami," I said gaily.

"You're still not funny, Tanner," she said. "Were you just getting me out of the way?" There was enough disgust in her words to feed a battalion.

"Where are you now?" I asked seriously.

"Still in Sausalito. For some reason I thought I should call and see what you thought I should do. Which, given your mental state, was the best idea I've had since the day

"Go home, Miss Brown," I urged. "Have a drink. Invite a friend. Make both yourselves happy."
I let Mark Covington buy me a drink after work."

"Are you suggesting yourself as the friend?"

"I don't think so."

"Too bad for you."

"Maybe." I hung up, but not before she did.

I made some coffee and tried to call Harrison Quale so I could take a shot at prying something out of him about the Biloxi Corporation, but he wasn't home and he wasn't at the office. Then I broke the connection and dialed another number, this time the Central Station, San Francisco Police. I asked for Charley Sleet and he came on the line in a hurry. He sounded as though he'd forgotten how to sleep.

"Charley," I said.

"Marsh."

"Howard Renn."

"What?"

"Wake up, Charley. Howard Renn. Poet. Dead. Who done it?"

Charley grumbled something to someone, then someone muttered something back. "Renn?" he repeated finally. "I don't know who done it. Shit, the last time I thought I knew who-done-it the jury gave him a pat on the cheek and told him to go home to mommy."

"When did Renn leave us?"

"Sometime Sunday."

"Could it have been a woman who sent him off?"

Charley thought about it. "Sure. Small-caliber weapon. Body moved but not far. Sure. Why? Who you got in mind?"

"No one. What else? Motive?"

"None that we know of."

I waited for him to say more but he didn't. There are times Charley talks and times he doesn't. We're still friends because I know which is which. "Okay, Charley. Go home and get some sleep."

"Sure. On Saturday I'll sleep. What's your interest in Renn?"

"I liked his poetry. Great imagery. Blinding metaphorical insight. Stunning formal experimentation."

"Bullshit. Do you know anything I should know?"

"Have you talked to his wife?"

"Not yet."

"Do it. Don't tell her I told you to, but talk to her, quick."

"Why?"

"Just do it."

"Thanks, Marsh. You get anything firm, I want to know."

"I know you do."

After I put down the phone I was still feeling silly and unattached, the symptoms of an overdose of solitude. I tried to bring myself out of it by putting on some Mozart, but even that didn't do it. The apartment seemed so tawdry, so small and tacky and irrelevant. I turned out the lamp beside me. That helped. I turned off the overhead in the living room and the one in the kitchen. Then I sat in the dark and waited, trying all the while to avoid figuring out what I was waiting for.

By the time the telephone rang again the air felt grainy and thin, like midnight or after. "Mr. Tanner?" The voice was flat, not fully inflated. I acknowledged it.

"They've called," she said.

"When?" My stomach tightened, then hurt.

"Just now."

"Where's the drop?"

"That's just it. I don't know. They just wanted to make sure the money is ready."

"Is it?"

"Yes. Two million. I can see it from here." She stopped to consider her next words. "It's obscene," she added quietly.

"When will they get back to you?"

"Anytime. Walter's supposed to be ready to travel at a moment's notice."

"What's he drive?"

"A Mercedes. Black."

"Figures," I said involuntarily. "Okay. It's the same deal. I'll be here until nine in the morning. After that try the office first. I'll check with my service every fifteen minutes if I have to go out. Okay?"

"Okay."

"Did you talk with your husband? About me?"

"Yes. No. Not exactly. I started to, but he didn't seem receptive."

"So I'm sub rosa."

"I guess that's what you'd call it."

"I'd call it stupid if I was in a better frame of mind."

Mrs. Kottle inhaled sharply and audibly. "You'll still do

it, won't you, Mr. Tanner? You'll go along and see that nothing happens?"

"I'll try," I said. "But if it looks like my presence is going to screw it all up I'll have to pull out. You understand that?"

"Of course. Nothing must jeopardize Karl's safe return. That seems to be all Max cares about."

The words were mechanical, man-made, but then it was three o'clock in the morning. Nothing natural goes on at that hour of the night. "Is Karl going to be at the drop?" I asked.

"I don't know what you mean."

"I mean is it going to be an exchange, Karl for the money, or do they claim they'll release him later?"

"Later."

"One more thing. What did they say about Max being dead? Supposedly."

She thought it over. "That's funny," she said slowly. "They didn't mention it. It's as if they didn't care."

"Who answered the phone?"

"I did."

"Who did they ask for?"

"Max. They asked for Max. It didn't even occur to me. They knew he was alive."

I spoke rapidly, without giving her time to think. "Keep your fingers crossed, Mrs. Kottle," I said.

"They've been crossed for months."

There was death in her words, death and dread. She hung up and I took off my shoes and climbed onto the bed and lay atop the spread and let my mind drift into whatever backwaters it chose. The next thing I knew someone was pounding on the side of my head with a hammer that rang like a bell every time it hit. By the time I figured out what it was, the sound had become intermittent, a sandwich around a center of pain. I picked up the receiver. "Tanner," I said.

"They called again. It's Ocean Beach. Walter's just leaving. He has one of those CB radio things. They'll tell him what to do when he gets there."

She was whispering, talking faster than I could listen, getting it all out before something happened to cut her off. "I'm on my way," I told her, and stumbled to the floor to fulfill my promise.

Twenty-Seven

I wasn't at all sure I could catch Hedgestone and the Mercedes, and even if I did it would be foolhardy to attempt anything but observation. Karl himself wouldn't be at the drop, and I had to assume that any attempt to interfere would bring harm to him, quite possibly death. I hurried anyway, hopping into the Buick and slipping down Broadway to Gough, then south on Gough to Geary, then west on Geary toward the ocean.

It was a cold night. Steely cold. The car seats were as warm as a bench in an igloo. My hot breath condensed on the windows, creating a private, purplish cocoon.

Dawn was only a prediction. The city seemed broken into pieces, each clump of light separated from all the other clumps of light by black walls of apprehension and disappointment. The few night people I encountered stared at me with the frankness of kittens at the first sight of one of their own. But after the first glance the night people turned away. I had a purpose, so I was out of place in the early morning, a geometric stripe through the splashy formlessness of the predawn city.

Geary Boulevard became Point Lobos Avenue and Point Lobos took me to the Cliff House, a revived relic on the edge of a bluff overlooking Seal Rock and the sea. By day a major tourist attraction, complete with tour buses and foreign dialects and trashy souvenirs, by night it was a looming hulk of indeterminate intent. I pulled next to the curb and parked.

Mist dotted my windshield immediately, skewing my view of the beach below. The Monterey pines across the road to my left seemed to be slipping toward me, an implacable blob of danger. I started the car so the wipers would wipe and the heater would heat, then looked down toward the beach once again.

The Sons and Daughters had picked well. Ocean Beach ran the entire length of the city, from Point Lobos just behind me to Fort Funston and the Olympic Club some four miles to the south. The beach itself was more than twenty yards wide when the tide ran out, flat and gray and uninspiring, separating a seemingly graven expanse of cold and unlovely ocean from an equally bleak seawall.

The Great Highway ran parallel to the sea and the wall, straight and sand-sprayed, dull and unlandscaped and badly misnomered. The highway was well lit just below me, but farther along the glow of the streetlamps became progressively fainter in the mist, dying stars in far-off galaxies.

At the north end of the beach, the end nearest me, the Great Highway broadened into an esplanade that formed the parking area for what used to be a static and dilapidated circus known as Playland-at-the-Beach. But Playland had been sacrificed to a real estate developer who immediately razed the rides and the peep shows and the concession stands and dug a huge hole in their place. Then the developer had in turn been razed by his creditors, so that what was once a place of fun and frolic had become a pit of silence and desolation, a ghostly Alexandria, lost city of time gone wrong.

South of the parking area the highway narrowed again, leading past the stub end of Golden Gate Park before bordering a stretch of breeze-bleached houses and apartment buildings which wore the faded, forlorn faces of seafarers everywhere. Whatever was going to happen was going to happen down there.

I couldn't see very far from where I was, but I was starting to remember more and more about the surroundings, and I wasn't happy with what I remembered. For one thing, the kidnappers could view the entire stretch of beach and highway from any of several points in the vicinity, including the Sutro Heights Park just above me. There was no way I could get close to the drop without being seen.

Then I remembered something else about the beach, and realized they were going to be able to pick up the ransom and get away without the slightest chance of being caught, even if anyone had been there to catch them. I swore under my breath and put the Buick in gear and curled slowly down to the beach.

It was a netherworld of shape and void. In the distance a single car drove slowly south, its taillights flickering like smudge pots in the darkness. Other than that, nothing, except for the two cars in the parking area, lights off, immobile, apparently unoccupied.

I looked them over. One was a '69 Chevrolet with a missing fender and a flat tire. In the light from a street-lamp I could see the ribbon of rot that decorated its rocker panels and wheel wells. The front windshield was a snowflake. It didn't have anything to do with why I was there.

The other car was more interesting—a brown BMW, recent vintage, grazing like Secretariat in the exact center of the lot, equidistant from the nearest lights. Without seeming to, I checked it out as carefully as I could. No one was in sight, but that didn't mean I wasn't being watched.

I drove on my way, looking straight ahead, an uninteresting man driving his uninteresting Buick from one uninteresting place to another. It's the best role I play. Somewhere behind me the BMW seemed to whinny.

By the time I reached the Lincoln Way intersection I'd decided to head back to the Cliff House, where I could at least see what was going on along the beach and the es-planade. I wouldn't be close enough to provide a remedy if things went bad, but if I stayed where I was I would scare everyone off. Or worse. I slowed for the turn, but far down the road ahead of me I saw something that made me keep going straight.

It was a dark shape, another car, pulled off into a small parking square cut into the dunes to the right of the high-way. I drove toward it, slowly but not suspiciously so. On my left the windmill in the park suddenly loomed out of the darkness, nudged toward me by the dawn. I thought of Don Quixote. I thought of me. I laughed silently and shook my head. The windmill didn't have any arms.

My head started to ache. I fumbled in the glove com-partment for a tin of aspirin, squeezed it open and ate two of the tablets. My mouth turned dry and chalky so I fumbled again and brought out a half-empty pint of bour-bon and took a drink. I was better or worse, I wasn't sure which.

I drove on. The sea sighed faintly at my side, warning me in the way it warns everyone who trespasses against it. The ice plant growing in the median between the lanes of traffic was black and puffy, like strips of putrid flesh. I was the only one on the road. The only man alive.

It was Hedgestone and his Mercedes all right, and by the time I realized it I also realized that I had done just what the kidnappers wanted me to do. From where I was there was no place to turn around until I got all the way down to Sloat Boulevard, more than a half mile away. I was stuck—helpless if I kept going, obvious if I did anything else.

I crawled past the Mercedes. There was only one man inside it, sitting in darkness, squarely behind the wheel. I assumed it was Hedgestone, but neither of us acknowledged the other. Once past him I fixed my eye on the rearview mirror to see if Hedgestone did anything. He didn't.

As far as I could tell everything stayed the same until I got to Sloat. I turned left and drove east for a few seconds, in case I was being watched. Then I made a U turn at the Skyline intersection and headed back to the beach.

At the stop sign at the Great Highway I tried to spot the Mercedes but I couldn't do it. It wasn't where it had been, I was sure of it. My pulse shifted gears. It was a shade brighter out now, the morning light beginning to perform its magic act, but I still couldn't see the car.

I looked south. Nothing. I looked in the northbound lane of the Great Highway. And there it was. Hedgestone was driving slowly northward along the highway, his lights off, the big black car as dauntless as the tanks that moved through the Ardennes. I didn't know what else to do so I pulled onto the road and began to follow, a couple of hundred yards behind.

When the Mercedes was halfway back to the esplanade, in the middle of the stretch of road that intersected nothing, a light flashed up ahead of it, just once, small and bright, like a flashlight clicked on and off. I had been expecting something like it.

The brake lights on the Mercedes caught fire, and I could see Hedgestone get out and run to the edge of the road and throw something over it, then run back to the car and get in and drive on north again, faster this time, but still without lights.

I stopped and got out of my car and climbed onto the hood to get a better view, but it wasn't good enough. Nothing moved except the Mercedes. Then an engine started up, a loud one, somewhere off to the right. After a couple of roars it settled into a steady growl, then got progressively faint, retreating. I still couldn't see a thing.

It had happened just the way I'd figured it would. To the right of the Great Highway, running parallel to it but

in a depression some twenty feet below it, was La Playa
Avenue. La Playa intersected with ten or fifteen streets between the park and Sloat, but none of those streets intersected the highway. Hedgestone and I were high and dry
and the kidnappers were somewhere down below us with
the money and Karl Kottle and there was no way to get at
them without a set of wings. A slick operation, almost
foolproof. All hail the Sons and Daughters.

I was about to get back in my car when I heard another
sound, one that forty years ago could have been mistaken
for a backfire but now can't be mistaken for anything but
what it is.

Up ahead the Mercedes was stopped in the esplanade,
right next to the old Chevy, its taillights smoldering. The
brown BMW was parked across its hood, cutting off further progress. Two figures stood beside the car. I was too
far away to tell what was going on, too far away to be
anything but curious. I got in the car and headed for the
men as fast as I could without lights.

When I was halfway there one of the men ran to the
BMW and got in and roared off toward the Cliff House. I
hit the lights and increased my speed and stopped beside
the Mercedes as the BMW disappeared behind the Sutro
Heights bluff.

Hedgestone was leaning against the car door holding his
left arm, breathing heavily. He seemed dazed and incom-
petent, but still immaculate except for the stain beginning
to spread through the fibers of his coat. I pried his fingers
away from his bicep and checked his wound. It wasn't
serious, but gunplay had to be as foreign to Hedgestone as
a callus. "The tweed's hurt worse than you are," I told
him, then asked what had happened.

"Tanner," he observed roundly, as though he'd just realized who it was who was ministering to him. He shook his
head as he absorbed the situation. "I don't know *what* happened. That is, I know what happened but I don't see
how. I did everything I was told. Everything. Parked
where I was supposed to, started out with the first flash of
light, delivered the money at the second. But something
went wrong."

"What?"

Hedgestone shook his head. "It seems impossible, but
apparently I gave the money to the wrong people."

"You what?"

"Unbelievable, isn't it? The man who shot me, the one in the brown car, he said *he* was the one who was supposed to get the money, who was supposed to give the signal to deliver it. But someone beat him to the punch. He accused me of trying some sort of trick. He was furious. He said I'd be sorry."

"You won't be as sorry as Max Kottle will be," I said, a bit cruelly.

Hedgestone shifted position, grimacing at the pain in his arm. "I *know* that," he said. "I feel wretched. But I don't know what else I could have done, do you?"

I told him I didn't, not if he'd followed instructions. He assured me again that he had. I asked if he'd gotten the license number of the brown BMW. He shook his head helplessly. I didn't tell him he wasn't the man for the job he'd been asked to do, but I thought it. Then I asked him about his arm.

"It hurts," he said. "I've never been shot before. Have you?"

"You can't get a P.I. license in this state unless you've been shot at least twice. Regulations."

"You're joking."

I nodded. "But only about the regulations. Do you want me to drive you home?"

"I can manage," Hedgestone said, pleased with his bravery. "But follow me. Max will want to know everything. Perhaps you saw something I didn't."

"I didn't see much, but promise me a cup of coffee and a fried egg and I'll follow you anywhere."

Hedgestone smiled tightly. "Of course," he said. Then he looked at me directly for the first time that evening. "What are you *doing* here, anyway?" he asked.

"First the eggs," I said.

Twenty-Eight

There were three of us sitting around the table in the breakfast nook—Hedgestone, Belinda Kottle and I, snuggled together under a white globe of light like a brood of oversized, oversedated pullets. Max Kottle wasn't with us because he had fallen asleep just before we arrived and Mrs. Kottle didn't want to wake him unless there was

something crucial to be done. There wasn't. It was six A.M.
I hadn't slept since Easter.

Hedgestone had lost a little of his luster during the night
but not nearly all of it. His hair was still as smooth as the
pelt of a gray fox and his tie was still snug at his throat.
Compared to the rest of him the gauze around his bicep
seemed a band of eccentric panache. Despite his wound,
or maybe because of it, he was more awake than I was.

We both had our eyes on Mrs. Kottle. She was impos-
sibly lovely, given the hour and the event that had
preceded it. The shiny satin of her blousy pajamas touched
her in several appropriate places. Her lack of sleep gave
her eyes an almost mystic sheen.

She made both of us breakfast, and a good one, but
now she was listening as Hedgestone began his report on
the night's events. It took him a while. In the meantime I
counted the electric appliances I could see from where I
sat, the blenders and food processors and coffee grinders
and can openers and the like. There were eleven of them.

When Hedgestone was through Mrs. Kottle looked at
me quizzically, as though for assurance that her decision
to engage me had been both correct and productive. I
wanted to give it to her but I couldn't.

"I don't have much to add," I said instead. "I do know
that the money ended up with someone on a motorcycle
who zoomed off into the Sunset District as free as the pro-
verbial bird. I was about to go after him when Hedgestone
got himself in trouble, but I couldn't have caught him anyway. It was a good plan."

"You should have gone on," Hedgestone said valiantly.

"I've found it's not generally a good idea to run away
from gunfire. Not until you know who's shooting and
why."

Hedgestone shrugged. "I'm sorry," he continued. "I
should be grateful, I suppose. He might have harmed me
further if you hadn't come along."

"He might," I said. Absurdly, I glanced at Mrs. Kottle
for some assurance of my own. Her nod made me warm
and cozy. "I've got a question," I said to Hedgestone.

"What?"

"What did he look like? The guy who shot you."

The smooth brow wrinkled. "If you were to ask me
what the gun looked like I could tell you exactly. It was
big and black. The size of a howitzer, it seemed. But the

man. Tall. Black curly hair. Plaid jacket. Handsome, in a vicious sort of way. I don't know. I guess I was too afraid of him to look at him."

A lot of people could fit that description, of course, but one of them was the guy I had seen come out of Howard Renn's house and go with him to Cicero's bar. I tucked the possibility away somewhere behind my desire for a good night's sleep. I rubbed my eyes and made them sting even more. I needed a third cup of coffee. What I got was a question.

"What could have happened?" Mrs. Kottle asked me. "How could anything have gone wrong?"

"Two possibilities," I said. "One, the money didn't go to the wrong people at all, and this is just a ploy to allow them to hit you again. That, or else someone sold out to another bidder and leaked the plan for the drop. Either way, it's going to cost your husband more money if he wants Karl back."

"He'll pay," she said resignedly. "He'll pay *anything*. It's as though finding Karl has become some kind of last rite for him."

"The obsession is typical of the mental aberrations that afflict terminal patients," Hedgestone said heavily. "Obsessive neuroses, possibly of physiological origin. I still believe we should ignore it, and devote our time to making Max's last days as pleasant and as diverting as possible."

"What if it's not neurosis at all?" I said. "What if he just loves his son?"

Hedgestone smiled tolerantly and Mrs. Kottle got up to pour some more coffee. I watched her do it.

From somewhere over the sink a buzzer sounded, low and harsh. "Max is awake," Mrs. Kottle exclaimed, and hurried out of the kitchen through the far door.

"He won't be pleased," Hedgestone predicted needlessly. "It might be better to omit any reference to your presence at the beach this evening, in fact. I could say I consulted you after I returned. It might prevent Belinda from being hurt."

I shook my head. "It's too early in the morning to lie. I don't get good at it till after lunch. And I think Belinda can take care of herself."

Hedgestone shrugged and Belinda came back in the kitchen. "He wants to see you. Both of you," she said. "I told him why you're here, Mr. Tanner. Not the details, but he knows I'm responsible. He wasn't happy about it," she added, echoing Hedgestone.

I got up and followed the group into Max Kottle's bed chamber. It was like a stage set, dark as dirt around the perimeter but white and bright in the center, the lace-white hospital bed lit by a single Tensor lamp that rested on the table beside it.

Max Kottle looked the same or worse, propped up by the inclined bed, pillows billowing behind his head like muffins, his smoking jacket smooth and rich across his chest. He stared at me in silence until I'd taken a chair. "Is my boy dead because of what you've done?" he asked roughly.

I shook my head. "If he wasn't dead before, I don't think he's dead now. They still want money, and since they apparently didn't get any tonight Karl's still their best bet. They can't be certain you won't demand proof of his existence before talking further. In fact, I'd suggest just that, in case anyone's interested in my opinion."

"For the sake of your professional reputation you'd better hope you're right," Kottle said.

"Look," I said. "I'm not Captain Marvel. Something may well have happened to Karl. But neither you nor I can be sure that it was because of something I did or because of something you didn't do, like call in the authorities. We're both playing it by ear. Recriminations are premature and pointless. In my opinion I didn't do anything that had any impact at all on what happened tonight, except maybe prevent your economist over there from having his Gross National Product perforated."

A guilty conscience brings out the worst in me, and a semiguilty one isn't particularly attractive either. Luckily, Kottle ignored my taunt. "If the kidnappers don't have the money, who does?" he asked, to no one in particular.

"As I told your wife," I said, "it's likely that someone who used to be in the gang decided he deserved a larger share, or maybe someone made him a better offer. What I didn't tell her, but what someone in this room should be thinking about, is that the leak of the plans for the drop could have been on this end. Not likely, but a possibility."

"Nonsense." Kottle and Hedgestone spoke simultaneously.

"I'm not saying it happened," I said. "I'm just saying someone should think about it."

Kottle shook his head, as if to expel the possibility from his skull. "What can we do now?" he asked.

"Wait," I said.

"Nothing else?"

"Call the cops. The FBI, specifically. These people don't seem all that sophisticated to me. The group is evidently split by greed already, and who knows what else might be going on. The FBI is pretty good at exploiting that kind of thing, given half a chance. Plus, if you wait much longer, you'll never see the money you dropped tonight, regardless of what happens to Karl."

Kottle looked at Hedgestone. "I don't care about the money. We went over all this before, didn't we, Walter?"

"Yes, sir," Walter said obediently.

"We decided no risk was acceptable, however small, did we not?"

"Yes, sir."

Kottle looked at me. "The money is not important. My son is."

"Okay," I said. "I just wanted my recommendation on record."

"What do you think they'll do?" Hedgestone asked me.

"Ask for more money. Do you have it?"

"I can get it," Kottle said firmly. "It won't be easy. I'll have to sell more stock, and since I'm supposed to be dead it will violate every section of the Securities Act to do so, but I'll do it. The other stockholders will suffer because the stock price will drop even further than it has already, but I'll do it. I have to."

"Do you want me in or out?"

Kottle surveyed his retinue in turn, lingering on his wife, then turned to me. "Belinda assumed a large risk in inviting you to join our dilemma, Mr. Tanner, the risk that I'd be violently angry when I discovered what she'd done. She was completely out of line." Kottle looked at his wife and suddenly smiled. "It was the kind of risk I often used to take when I was younger," he continued. "She evidently saw something in you that merited her trust. I value her concern and her courage. You're in if you want to be."

"I'll do what I can," I said. "But I have another case that's active. I can't promise you my undivided energies. On the other hand, the other case may not be altogether divorced from this one. There seem to be connections."

"What connections?" Kottle asked.

"A couple of things. I've been hired to look for a man who's been missing for several weeks. The man kept a secret apartment under an assumed name. I found the place and checked it out. In one of his files he had a book of poems by a man named Renn. Howard Renn was your son's best friend when they were at Berkeley. I should also tell you that Renn is dead. He got that way quite recently."

"Dead? How?" Kottle's interest in the subject was tempered by fear.

"Murdered."

"By whom?"

"No one knows."

"What else?" Hedgestone interjected. "What other connection is there?"

"A girl came to the apartment while I had it under observation. She was followed when she left. It turned out she was Karl's half-sister. Your first wife's daughter."

"Good Lord," Kottle said. "Rosemary? The last time I saw her she was in rubber panties and red ribbons."

"Not anymore," I said. "Not panties, at least."

"What's that mean?" Hedgestone asked.

"Private joke."

"Who's the man you're looking for?" Mrs. Kottle asked quietly.

I shook my head. "There's no point in going into that now. I haven't put all the pieces together, but there are some leads I want to work on. One of them may turn out to tell me something about Karl. Keep your fingers crossed."

I looked at Mrs. Kottle. She was looking at her hands. There were tensions in the air I couldn't fathom, a solution in which I couldn't remain buoyant.

I stood up. Max Kottle sighed. "The treatments yesterday took a lot out of me," he said. "The pain is getting worse. I don't mean to bore you with my symptoms, Mr. Tanner, but please proceed with all deliberate speed. Do whatever you can, but do not interfere with the process of my son's return. Do whatever they ask. We must conclude this soon. Quite soon."

Kottle's head lay back on the pillow. Belinda stood and beckoned for me to leave the room. I followed her to the elevator. She took my hand in hers and squeezed it. I squeezed back. Neither of us said a word before I left for home.

Twenty-Nine

I crawled into bed at eight and out again at ten without having accomplished my mission; it's been years since I've slept in the daytime. After a bowl of Grape Nuts and a cup of Yuban and a glance at headlines about the new police chief and a kid who survived a jump off the bridge I went to the office.

It was empty, the way it always is in the mornings, a silent repository of the partially recorded past of the small number of people I've been hired to chronicle over the years, a collection of historic fragments of interest only to me and my clients. I read the mail, then wandered around trying to avoid making a decision about what to do next. When I finally got a form around my melted brain I sat down at the desk and made some notes. They didn't amount to a damned thing. I picked up the telephone and called the Encounter with Magic.

The frizzy-haired girl told me Amber wasn't due in for another hour. She said there were other girls available. I said I was sure there were, then hung up. As I was fixing a cup of coffee the phone rang. It was Clay Oerter.

"I got something for you, Marsh. On Collected Industries."

"Shoot."

"The exchange has been open for about three hours now, and guess what? All of a sudden there's a steady market for Collected Industries. In fact, yesterday the exchange had considered suspending trading in CI because there were so many more sellers than buyers, but when they looked at the orders this morning they changed their minds. Steady buy orders all day."

"What's happened to the stock price?" I asked.

"Well, it opened two dollars lower, at twelve, then moved back to fourteen and it's hanging right around that level. Even went up a point over that about an hour ago. Understand, if it wasn't for Max Kottle being dead this wouldn't be any big deal. It's not a major move into the

stock or anything. But in the circumstances, any market at
all is unusual."

"Okay, Clay," I said. "Let's have it. Who's the buyer?"

He laughed. "It cost me a case of Bordeaux to find this
out, Marsh, on top of using up a lot of favors."

"Put it on my tab."

"It's a corporate buyer. A nominee. No one knows
who's behind it, at least that I could get to. Whoever it is
hasn't come on strong enough to call it a takeover move,
but another day like today and that's what it'll be. Sooner
or later they'll have to make a filing under the Williams
Act, though, if they really want the company and are going to make a tender offer for the shares. Hard to tell
what they're up to at this point."

"What's the name of the nominee?"

"The Biloxi Corporation."

I'd known it, somehow, the way you know it's going to
rain after you wash the car, the way you know you're going to dribble all over your silk tie the first day you wear
it. The link to the Covington disappearance, once as flimsy
as Howard Renn's volume of verse, was now as strong as
tempered steel. Covington had been looking into Biloxi,
and Biloxi was moving into Collected Industries, which
put Covington and Kottle in the stands at the same game.
I was there, too, but I didn't know which game it was.
Yet.

"How many shares has Biloxi bought?" I asked.

"As of twenty minutes ago about fifty thousand. And
still buying. At the market."

"That's better than half a million, right?"

"Right."

I thought it over a minute. "Let me ask you something,
Clay, just between you and me. What if it turned out Max
Kottle wasn't dead?"

"What?"

"Just suppose. What if that story got out for some reason that didn't have anything to do with the company or
the stock or anything like that?"

"Well, if that really happened, Max Kottle would be as
good as dead anyway. The SEC would go after him immediately, to enjoin him from having anything to do with a
listed company, and the Justice Department would indict
him for issuing false and misleading statements, and some
New York lawyer would file a class action on behalf of all

the sellers of stock and ask for a few hundred million in damages. And that's just for starters. Kottle would be finished on Wall Street, and he'd probably end up in jail." Clay paused for a moment. "But that just can't be true, about his not being dead. Can it?"

"No comment," I said.

"Jesus, Marsh. That's unbelievable."

"You don't know the half of it."

"Hey, Marsh. If the SEC ever asks, we never had this conversation. Okay?"

"Okay. One more thing. What's the word on Max Kottle's right-hand man? Hedgestone?"

"Walter? A good second banana. Brilliant, particularly on the multinational aspects. Why?"

"How would he be as the head of the company?"

"Collected Industries?"

"Yeah."

"Lousy. Too much a specialist to bring it all together."

"Does he want it? Control of the company, I mean?"

"I don't know," Clay answered. "Probably. You ever meet an intellectual who thought someone else could do a job better than him? Any job? But why don't you ask him?"

"Maybe I will," I said.

Clay told me he had a few more orders to execute and hung up. I dialed Harrison Quale. His secretary told me he wasn't in, wasn't expected back for the rest of the day, could not possibly be reached at home. I thanked her for the noninformation and hung up and tried again. Frizzy-hair told me Amber had just walked in. She also told me to make it snappy. I didn't tell her what came to mind, for fear she wouldn't let me talk to Amber.

Amber's voice was soft as pudding, as uncertain as an immigrant's. I asked her how she was.

"I'm okay, Mr. Tanner," she said. "I'm leaving here at the end of the week. For good. I've got a job at Macy's, selling perfume. It's not much, but it's better than this, I guess, even though the money's a lot less. No more sugar daddies, you know? Now I'll have to put up with their wives." Her laugh was hollow as a gourd.

I told her she'd made the right decision, then asked if she'd heard anything from Karl.

"No. Nothing. Every time the phone rings I jump, but it's never him. Have you found him yet?"

"No. But I think he's in trouble, Amber. If you can remember anything, anything at all, it might save his life. I mean that."

"His life?" Amber exclaimed. "What's happened to him? Is he hurt? Are the cops after him? What?" Concern drove her voice into a higher register, momentarily reestablishing innocence and youth. I calmed her down.

"He's fine as far as I know. Now think. Can you recall anything about Karl that might tell me where he is? Anything about the time he came to see you there at the Encounter?"

She considered what I was saying. "Is he really in trouble? Are you being straight with me?"

"I'm being straight."

"Well, I didn't want to tell you before, but maybe this will help you get a line on him." She paused for effect. "Karl's a junkie."

"What! Are you sure?"

"Sure I'm sure. He shot up right here in this room. It's weird, you know. He spent all that time back when I was his old lady trying to get me off the stuff, and now he's on it himself, worse than I was. I looked around and there he was with a needle in his arm. He's really sick from it, too."

"How sick?"

"I think it's screwed up his nerves or his veins or something. He hurts. He couldn't even hug me without it hurting him. He kept groaning, you know? And he limped, too. Or not so much limped, but didn't walk right. Like he was walking on fire, you know? He's real strung out." Amber's voice bubbled with eagerness. "I think I could help *him*, now, don't you?"

"It sounds that way," I said. "If he calls you, or if anyone calls you about him, get in touch with me right away, will you? It's very important."

"I will, Mr. Tanner. Hey. Don't let anything happen to Karl, okay? I think I'm getting my shit together now. Maybe Karl would want to make it with me again, you know?"

"Good luck with the perfume."

"Thanks. It'll be nice to smell something pretty for a change."

I hung up on her hopes and thought over the possibilities and put on my coat and walked over to Sutter Street.

The entrance to the building I wanted looked like something stolen from the temples at Karnak under cover of night. A golden canopy etched with hieroglyphic designs jutted over the sidewalk, beckoning in triumphant rococo. Inside, the black marble walls were streaked with trails of marshmallow. The lighted building directory stood out from the dark like a tablet of divine origin. I looked over the list of names until I found the one I wanted, then entered the elevator and pushed the button for the fifth floor.

The office was seedy and neglected except for the parakeet chirping in a wooden cage and one other aspect—the pieces of shiny metal sculpture that decorated the room as subtly as a parading Shriner. The forms were abstract and large, great gobs of melted steel, polished and gleaming and looking more like freshly extracted organs than anything else I could think of.

I walked to the closest one and looked it over. Intricate, almost dainty, designs had been welded onto its surface in obsessive bursts of effort. A small white card taped to the base announced the piece was entitled "Essence" and could be purchased for two thousand dollars.

There was a reception desk at the end of the waiting room but there was no one behind it. There was no one waiting, either. I sat down in a wicker chair and thumbed through a six-month-old copy of *Vogue*. The article I turned to was about Herbal Wraps and Loofah Rubs. A door opened somewhere to my right and I looked up into the face of Gwen Durkin.

"It's you," she said stiffly. Her dark skin stretched over her cheekbones like the bark on a maple. She was clearly annoyed, most likely at me.

"It's me," I agreed. "How are you?"

"Busy."

I glanced around the room. "Solitaire?"

"What do you want?" she asked, angered rather than amused.

"I'd like to see Doctor Hazen."

"The doctor isn't taking on any new patients just now."

"Good," I said. "I'm not taking on any new doctors."

"Come to the point, Tanner. What is it you really want?"

"Information."

"That's not our business."

"The information I want could save someone's life. I

mean that literally. Does that sound anything like the business you're in?"

Gwen frowned, started to say something and then stopped, and walked behind the reception desk and sat down and looked at me steadily—detached, scientific, neutral. There was no trace of the woman I'd skipped down the Filbert Steps three days before, but then why should there have been. "I don't think you lie," she said finally. "I assume you mean it when you say the information is important. To you."

"Not just to me."

"Whatever. I can't pretend I didn't enjoy the other morning. I let my hair down in a way I haven't in a long time. I was hurt when you didn't ask me out the next night."

"I explained why I didn't."

She nodded. "It should be enough but it isn't."

I shrugged. I had business to take care of. Gwen was in my way. There was more to it, but not right then.

"I did get a nice dinner out of you," Gwen continued. An artful smile spread gradually across her lips. "So I figure I owe you. Not much, but something. I don't like to owe men, so what I'm going to do is get you in to see Doctor Hazen. Nothing more. Once you're in his office you're on your own. And we're even. Anything between us from now on starts from scratch. Fair enough?"

"Fair enough."

"Wait here a minute."

She went away and left me alone with about three tons of steel, then came back a minute later and said, "Come on." I followed obediently, white manservant after black mistress.

She led me past rooms containing examining tables and medicine cabinets and skeletons and X-ray machines and God knows what else to the office just before the one at the end of the corridor. The door was closed. She knocked and went in. I followed.

The man behind the desk was familiar, but I couldn't remember where I'd seen him. He was short and stout, barrel-chested, with forearms the diameter of goalposts. His wide face was flat with anger; his annoyance seemed to encompass both Gwen and me. I find all doctors a little silly, and Hazen was no exception.

Gwen introduced me quickly and then backed out of

the office and closed the door. Doctor Hazen uttered a single word: "Well?"

I thought about sitting down, then decided against it. "I need some information on one of your patients," I said.

"Who?"

"Karl Kottle."

That seemed to surprise him. I knew because he blinked. "You mean Max," he said mildly.

"I mean Karl."

"Who says Karl is a patient of mine?"

"A little bird."

Hazen nodded once, then reached for the telephone on the desk. He dialed a single number and then spoke. "Miss Durkin? This man has just asked me about Karl Kottle. You are therefore dismissed. Do you understand? Be gone by the end of the day."

Hazen replaced the receiver and looked at me, an arrogant smile curling his puffy lips. "Does that give you an indication of how I feel about the confidentiality of my records?"

"You made a mistake," I said. "She didn't tell me."

"Of course she did," Hazen replied. "I am not a fool, Mr. Tanner. You, on the other hand, apparently are one if you expect me to disclose information about my patients on the basis of a whim. I once defied a court order requiring me to give up certain records. I was sustained on appeal, but not before spending some time in our disgusting County Jail. I have no intention of telling you anything."

With guys like Hazen you have to take your best shot right off the bat, because one is all you get—usually. I took mine. "Max Kottle won't be very happy to learn that his long-lost son has been consulting you regularly over the past several years and that you never even mentioned it to him."

"Is that a threat to tell Max what you know? Or what you think you know?"

"Maybe."

"Consider it ineffective. Even if you had proof of your contentions, which you don't, my position is sound, both medically and ethically. You may tell Max what you wish."

I took another tack. "Is Karl Kottle a junkie?"

"What makes you think that he is?"

"That same birdie."

"Well, your birdie is mistaken."

"I don't think so."

"Suit yourself."

"Look," I said. "I'm not really as interested in Karl's medical condition as I am in his whereabouts. Medical ethics don't prevent you from telling me that."

Hazen shook his head. "I construe the physician-patient privilege in its broadest possible scope, to include the fact of the relationship itself. I will tell you nothing."

"Does Karl need continuing treatment?"

"Why?"

"Because he may be in a position where he can't seek it if he needs it. He may not be able to get medication, to move about freely for any purpose."

Hazen seemed puzzled. "I don't know what you mean."

"I mean Karl is likely a prisoner, which means he could be dying if he needs regular medication or regular treatment by a physician. If he does, surely you have an obligation to see that he gets it. The only way is to tell me where I can find him, what address he listed in your files."

Hazen looked at me squarely, the smile finally off his face. "You sound as though he's been kidnapped."

I didn't say anything more. Hazen leaned back in his swivel chair and looked at the window to his left. In front of it was another piece of sculpture, this one shaped like a pancreas. Hazen seemed to feel there was an answer somewhere inside the metal, that the alloy included a dash of enlightenment that could be extracted by an act of will. I waited.

"I have no way to know whether you're telling me the truth," Hazen said finally as he swiveled toward me. "With confirmation I might change my position. Without it, I'm afraid I can tell you nothing."

"What kind of confirmation do you need?"

"A call from Max Kottle. Telling me his son's in danger. Telling me to disclose whatever information I may have to you. Telling me everything. Can you get that for me?" Hazen smiled tolerantly.

I thought about it. "Not now," I said.

"I thought not. Now, you'll have to excuse me. I must insist."

The doctor picked up a file and began to leaf through it slowly. I left him without a word and went back to the reception area hoping to find Gwen. She wasn't there. The only thing she'd left behind were some empty drawers and a whiff of rose petals in the air.

Thirty

She'd changed the tune. The tones were still slightly flat, the source still deep within the house, but it was no longer Rachmaninoff. The new phrase was vaguely familiar, but uncommon and unidentifiable. Villa-Lobos, perhaps. I pressed the button a second time, just so I could hear it again. The rich can do anything.

Randy opened the door. He was still frowning and still dressed like a Beverly Hills shoe salesman. "You didn't call first," he challenged, after he put together who I was.

"How do you know?"

It put Randy on edge. The possibility that things were going on inside that house that he wasn't aware of clearly upset him. For the next few seconds he tried to convince himself I was bluffing. He didn't quite succeed. "You didn't call," he repeated. "Shelley doesn't see *anyone* without an appointment."

"Great," I said. "If I was here to see Shelley I'd feel real frustrated."

"You talk too wise, buster. Now get out of here. You're nobody." He took a step toward me.

"If you spent more time in the gym and less at the hairdresser I'd break out in a sweat, Randy. Now do us both a favor. Put your macho back in your shoulder bag and go tell Rosemary I'd like to talk to her for a minute."

He'd been about to test someone's manhood, his or mine, but my request brought him up short. "Rosemary? Why her?"

"I'll tell that to her. If she decides she wants to tell you, then we'll all know. Maybe we can start a club."

"Get fucked," Randy said darkly. For some reason he was suddenly relaxed. "Rosemary's not here. So get out of here and take your corduroys with you. Jesus. *Nobody* wears corduroy."

I let Randy enjoy his insult for about four seconds, then shouldered my way past him and went on inside the house. Randy muttered something and came after me, but by the time he put his paw on my shoulder we were in the living room and Shelley Withers had an amused eye on both of us.

I had to hand it to her. Despite her age, despite her ridiculous surroundings, despite her Day-Glo lips and her Blush-On cheeks and her Forever Blond hair, she took the fight out of both of us with a single glance, turning us into a pair of footmen awaiting our instructions for the day.

Randy's hand slipped off my shoulder. "He didn't call, Shelley," he pleaded. "He says he wants to see Rosemary. I told him to leave, but he didn't. You want me to throw him out?"

The question was as real as a billboard. Shelley Withers looked at me while she spoke to Randy. "Let's not embarrass Mr. Tanner today, Randy," she said, her eyes twinkling like the top of a sugar cookie. "I'll talk with him briefly, then I'm sure he'll leave peaceably. In the meantime, why don't you finish packing my things?"

"I better stay," Randy groused. "This guy thinks he's tough."

"We both know better, don't we?" she crooned. "Now go on. I'll ring if I need you. My bell's right here."

Sure enough, a little ceramic bell rested merrily on the coffee table, gaily decorated with little blue milkmaids holding even littler yellow milk pails. Somehow I kept from laughing.

Randy started up the steps, then detoured toward the fireplace. There was a blue Wedgewood bowl on top of the mantelpiece. Randy took off its top and reached inside with his thumb and forefinger.

"No." The word was as hard as the eyes of the woman who spoke it.

"Just one line? Please, Shelley?"

"No. Finish your business. Maybe then."

"A snort. A few grains?"

"Leave it. I mean it, Randy."

The little blue bowl and the cocaine inside it went back to the mantelpiece and Randy went out of the room in defeat. At some basic level I felt sorry for him, the way I'd feel sorry for a starving weasel.

I took the two steps down into the conversation pit and joined Shelley Withers on the couch. "Going someplace?" I asked her.

"Barbados," she answered cheerfully. "I haven't been

warm for months." She paused, then turned to face me. Her dressing gown slipped over the satin couch like a canoe over a mountain lake. "Would you like to go along, Mr. Tanner?"

I just smiled.

"My treat, of course," she added.

"What about Randy?"

"I don't believe Randy's going with me this time. He'll be crushed, naturally, but after all, he could hardly expect me to support him forever, could he?"

"Hardly."

"Are you certain you won't join me?"

"Maybe next season."

She lowered her eyes. "Pity," she said. "You have such interesting calves. So large."

I had nothing to say to that so I asked her if Rosemary was home.

Her nose wrinkled, reminding me of cauliflower. I hate cauliflower.

"Rosemary, Mr. Tanner? Somehow I would have doubted you were the type to lust after the young ones. You must be more boring than you look. I withdraw my invitation."

I shook my head. "My interest in your daughter is strictly business, Miss Withers. She knows some things I'd like to know, too. If she cooperates I'll be out of here in five minutes."

She laughed dryly. "If Rosemary's involved, your business is undoubtedly immoral and quite possibly illegal as well. The best day of my life was not the day I married Max, or the day my first novel came out, it was the day Rosemary turned twenty-one and I no longer had any responsibility for her actions."

"The limitation is legal, not biological, Mrs. Withers."

She ignored my comment and stood up and crossed the room and stared into the glass case that contained all of her books. The body beneath her gown had been carefully preserved and carefully camouflaged, but here and there the effort failed to meet the challenge. Through a slit in the side of her gown I could see a crosshatch of blue veins lurking behind her knee, and around it an expanse of flesh the texture of dried beef.

She turned back toward me and I raised my eyes to hers. "You're a man of the world, Mr. Tanner," she said softly, "or at least a man of California. Are all children an albatross around their parents' necks, or only my own?"

"I couldn't say," I said. "I know most kids think it's the other way around."

"I suppose," she said absently. "Well, I haven't the faintest idea where Rosemary is. She came in early last evening and went out again and I haven't seen her since. I'm sure when you do find her she will be very cooperative, as long as you treat her like a cross between Emma Goldman and Linda Ronstadt."

I laughed and she came back and sat down beside me. "I'll be away for two months," she said. "Randy may or may not be here. Shall I leave a note for Rosemary?"

I shook my head. "No, thanks. I'll find her one way or another."

"Would you like a key to the house? So you can wait for her?" It was an offer that needed consideration to be binding. I was the consideration.

I looked around. "Nope," I said. "I try to avoid situations which might get me accustomed to luxury. Generally it's the easiest thing I do. I'd like to keep it that way."

"Suit yourself." Shelley Withers was dismissing me.

I stood up. "Have a nice trip."

"It would be even nicer with some company," she purred.

"I'm sure you'll dig up a beach boy or three," I told her. "They'll take care of you a lot better than I could."

She shook her head. "I know all about beach boys, Mr. Tanner. At my age you become concerned with quality, not quantity. Ah, well. Something will turn up. It always does, generally about the time I wear my diamonds to dinner." She raised her hand to me and I took it. "I'll be home in March. Come see me."

I squeezed her fingers and let them drop, then climbed the two stairs and walked down the hall toward the door. I was just about to open it when Randy appeared from somewhere behind me.

I stiffened and turned to face him, my eye on the soft bulge beneath his sternum, but his hands stayed at his sides. "Hey," he began, "is Rosie in some kind of trouble?"

I shrugged. "Don't know," I said truthfully. "It's possible."

"With the law?"

"Maybe."

"If I was sure it would get her into trouble, and I mean big trouble, I'd tell you where you can find her."

I thought it over. Time was short. Leads were few. "If she's in trouble at all," I said, "it's the biggest kind there is. But I won't know until I find her. Where is she?"

Randy eyed me closely. "What the hell are you, anyway? A cop?"

"Nope."

"What?"

"A leech. A parasite. I live off other people's problems. People want something and I try to give it to them. I charge a fee for the effort. After I finish leeching off one person I start leeching off another as fast as I can. Sound familiar, Randy?"

"Hell no." He didn't want to think about it. "You know Potrero Hill?"

"Sure."

"Well, you drive up there, see, and right at the top, the north side, there's a little bookstore. Carolina Street and Twenty-second, I think. And down a bit from the bookstore, across the street, there's a burned-out house. Tile roof. Spanish, you know? Right on the edge of the hill. Well, Rosie's been messing around with some guy on the QT, you know, and she wouldn't tell me about it, so one night I followed her and that's where she went. Spent the whole night in that dump, don't ask me why. When I asked her about it she clammed up. But I bet that's where she is now. She was out all last night, I know that."

"Did you see anyone else at the place?"

"No. I don't peep in windows. I mean, you have to draw the line somewhere, right?"

"Right. How long did you stick around over there?"

"Not long. That area of town gives me the creeps. I get real nervous every time I go south of Market, you know?"

"They probably get just as nervous when they see you coming. Thanks for the dope."

"Just come down hard on Rosie. She needs straightening out. You talk real tough. Maybe you're the man that can do it."

I waved good-bye and got in my Buick and drove into Sausalito and downed a plate of calamari at the Flying Fish, then called my answering service. No messages. I got back in the Buick and drove across the bridge and across the city and wound my way to the top of Potrero Hill.

I parked just around the corner from the bookstore and waited. When nothing moved but my watch, I started the car and drove past the store and past the burned-out house. It was black as walnuts. I went back around to the place I'd started from and parked again.

The house was so suited to aspiring terrorists it was almost a cliché. I was going to have to find out who and what was in there, no question about it, and I was nervous. Not because of the people, but because of the explosives that come with them. If a little band of saviors was in there, already on edge because their ransom try had gone sour, and they got spooked by something I did, the whole place might go. I'd seen a building like that once, an arms storehouse for a group called the Ethiopian Defense League. It had blown up on the troops one night during a cell meeting, and three seconds later there wasn't enough left of the building or the troops to fill a shot glass.

It was time to think. I thought. I thought some more. The more I thought the more nervous I got. When I heard someone walking up to my car I drew my gun. When the car door opened I was ready to fire.

Thirty-One

"Hey," she yelled. "Put that thing away. Who do you think you are, Eliot Ness? Every time I see you you're pulling a gun."

I exhaled and did what she said and watched as she clambered into the car, head first, looking like a kid entering a culvert. The dome light made her hair seem metallic and brittle, as though it would break if I touched it. Curiously, I felt glad to see her.

"What the hell are *you* doing here?" I asked.

She closed the door and pressed the lock button, then turned to face me. "You didn't think when you told me to go home last night that I actually was going to do it, did you?"

"You followed her over here."

"That's exactly what I did."

"Pamela Brown. Girl Reporter."

"In the flesh."

"Been here all night?"

"Yep."

"All day, too?"

"Yep."

"The girl you followed from Covington's. You know who she is?"

Pamela Brown shook her head.

"Rosemary Withers," I said. "The place in Sausalito belongs to her mother."

"Money."

"Binsful. Her mother is Shelley Withers. Writes women's books. Rape. Incest. Handsome strangers. Helpless virgins."

"Never read them. What's the daughter got to do with Mark Covington?"

"That's what I came over here to find out. Has anything happened since you got here?"

She shook her head again. "Nothing. The girl went into that dump down the block and since then, nothing. No lights. Nothing. I don't even think there's any electricity in there anymore, I couldn't see any lines."

"Did you look inside?"

"I checked it out as well as I could, but it's all boarded up. I couldn't see anything but my breath." She pulled her hands out of her coat pockets and rubbed them together. "What's going on in there, anyway?"

"Skulduggery."

"No, really."

"I'm not sure. Did you watch the place all night?"

She started to say something and then didn't. For an instant the light from the streetlamp struck her face, creating complex and pleasing contours of light and shadow. Then she moved into the blackness.

I asked her if she was cold and she nodded so I started the car. The air from the heater smelled of age and dirt and fossil fuels.

"Did you?" I repeated.

"Did I what?"

"Watch the place all night."

"No, dammit. I fell asleep."

"When?"

"About two. Woke up about five. Real dumb, I know."

"Happens all the time," I said. "Don't worry about it."

"What if they're not there?"

"Then we'll go home and get some sleep and try again tomorrow."

Actually it was what I hoped she would say. It meant that someone could have gone in and out at the time of the kidnapping drop, and that Karl Kottle could just possibly be inside the building. "Did you see any cars around?"

"No. Not any that seemed out of place."

"Motorcycles?"

"No."

"Is there a garage in the house?"

"In the back. Underneath."

"Anything in it?"

"I didn't look."

"Okay. I'm going over and check the place out. You stay here. When I get back we'll decide what to do."

"What to do about what?"

"What to do about rescuing Karl Kottle."

"Who?"

"Tell you later," I said, and got out of the car and closed the door on her next question, feeling stupidly optimistic about what the rest of the night would bring.

The street was dark and empty, the streetlight dull and inadequate. Most of the houses were dark. Those that weren't seemed to hide secrets.

I glanced in the window of the bookstore. A single bulb glowed in the back by the cash register. Volumes were piled all over the floor. The book on top of the stack nearest me was *Ethan Frome*. Overhead, the moon lurked like a landlord behind a screen of gray-black clouds. The air was heavy and cold.

In the distance, far below the hilltop on which I stood, the lights of the city spread northward, golden sequins spilled carelessly over a black shag rug. It seemed impossible that anything wretched could occur amid all that glitter but, like all glitter, it was merely a mask, a diversion from the real; lovely, if at all, only at first glance.

Walking slowly, I moved toward the abandoned house down on the corner. It was lifeless, its windows boarded shut, its front steps broken, its roof crushed in places, missing in others. On the side nearest me someone had painted the words "Free Puerto Rico" with a can of spray paint. Red. Above the words were the dark scars of the fire that had gutted the house.

I crossed the street and kept walking. At a point directly across from the house the street began to drop toward the bay. I walked on, casual, unhurried, an insomniac from the next block. Nothing moved, nothing sounded. I looked at my watch. It was eleven thirty.

I rubbed my hands and took a deep breath and crossed the street and inched my way down the driveway to the garage. There was a small window in either side of the garage door. I looked in one, then wiped it off with my elbow and looked in it again, at a lot of worthless junk and one thing that wasn't: a brown BMW. Secretariat had returned to his stall.

Hunching my shoulders against the cold, I backed away from the garage and looked up. There was a door up there, just above and to the right of the garage, some ten feet off the ground. It was a door with a knob and two hinges and everything else a door should have except one—some steps leading to it. I looked at the door for quite some time. It seemed an artifact, a Dadaist comment on the real and the imagined and the relationship between the two.

There was nothing in the yard to help me get up there, no ladder, no box, no barrel, no rope: the house had been gutted by more than fire. But it was different in the neighbor's yard. At the rear of his lot, right along the back fence, some concrete blocks lay piled one atop the other. They rested patiently beneath a clear plastic sheet, ready for their owner to being some home improvement project or other, a patio or a porch or a porte cochère. The only thing between me and the blocks was a Cyclone fence.

I thought it over. It was the type of neighborhood where the people own dogs and guns, the type of neighborhood where a man who sees something in his backyard after midnight may shoot first and ask questions later. But what the hell. I walked over to the fence.

No dog barked, no gun fired. Somewhere nearby Johnny Carson was running through his monologue in someone's bedroom. The fence creaked and groaned and rattled under me, as loud as a steel band it seemed, but not loud enough to interest anyone that I could see. I went over to the pile of blocks and picked up one in each hand and walked back to the fence and lowered them to the other side. They were heavy as water, and they got heavier as I worked.

Back and forth. Back and forth. If anyone caught me I would just pretend I was stealing, needed a new foundation for my mobile home, can't afford blocks what with prices these days, no hard feelings, I'll put it all back. Sure.

Fifteen trips, then back over the fence. Pile the blocks beneath the door. Rest. Twenty after twelve. Neighbor's lights go out. Silence. Apprehension. Sweat. Time. I climbed to the door.

More by feel than by sight I discovered a slight crack between the door and the jamb. I pressed, and when nothing broke I pressed a little harder. Light came through the crack, faint yellow light like the yolk of a store-bought egg. I took out my knife and cut a notch into the edge of the door, sawing away silently, hoping the rotting wood wouldn't give way with a crash.

With my eye against the notch I could see most of the room inside. In a far corner was a kerosene lamp, an old one, its wick orange with flame, a dandelion in a tar pit. As far as I could tell there was only one other thing in the room besides grit: a mattress with a man on it.

He was lying on his back, eyes closed, wrists crossed on his chest. The wrists were bound. His ankles were bound, too. A white rag gagged his mouth. I pulled away and blinked to clear my vision, then put my eye back to the notch.

It was Karl Kottle, for sure, dressed exactly as he had been in the snapshot of him taken in Amber's room at the Encounter with Magic. I climbed off my blocks and walked back to my car and got in.

Pamela Brown was half asleep. "I need some help," I said. "There's someone in that house. The man named Kottle I told you about. He's been bound and gagged, probably drugged as well. He's a kidnap victim. If I'm going to have a chance to get him out of there I need a diversion."

She yawned sleepily. "And I'm the diversion."

"Right."

"How many people are in there?" she asked.

"I don't know. I don't think I can find out without getting discovered."

"Guns?"

"Guns."

"What's the plan? I'm not agreeing to anything, you understand, but what's the plan?"

"Have you got your car here?" I asked.

She nodded.

"What kind?"

"Toyota."

"New?"

"A junker. Why?"

I reached into the glove compartment and took out the pint of bourbon. "Swill a little of this around in your mouth. Spill the rest of it over your clothes. Get in your car and drive down Carolina Street at about fifteen miles an hour and run right into the light pole across from the house. Then make the horn honk continuously like it's stuck. Scream. Carry on. Act drunk and hurt and angry. Get people outside."

"Anything else? How about reciting the mad scene from Macbeth?"

"That'll do it," I grinned.

She shook her head in disbelief. "I'll probably get arrested, you know."

"Probably. But if you don't drink the bourbon you'll pass the blood test. Reckless driving at most. Plus damage to the light pole. I'll take care of that."

"Plus damage to my car, you bastard."

"I'll take care of that, too."

"That's real big of you," she said heavily. "It pains me to mention it, but why not just bring in the cops?"

"I think it's more likely to work this way."

"You think. Anything more solid than that?"

"Nope. Well? What do you say?"

She looked me over, blatantly estimating the chance of success. From the expression on her face I judged her estimate to be fifty-fifty at best. That's about where I put it, too.

"If it comes off, I get the story," Pamela Brown demanded. "Exclusive!"

"Exclusive."

"And you tell me the whole damned thing, beginning, middle and end."

"If the client agrees, sure."

"Fuck the client. Who is it?"

"No comment."

"Shit. I should tell you to go fly a kite."

I shrugged and stayed silent.

"Kottle," she mused. "There's a Kottle who just died. Big man. Any relation?"

"Father."

"Okay. Now tell me this. How does Karl Kottle connect up with Mark Covington? He's why I'm over here, after all."

"We won't know till we ask him, will we?"

Pamela Brown thought it over, more than once. A car went by, wearing its exhaust fumes like a plume. "Okay," she said finally. "Here goes nothing. Is what we're doing illegal, by the way?"

"Not if it works."

She opened the car door. "Check your watch," I told her. "It's twelve thirty-seven. Time it so you hit the pole at twelve fifty-five exactly. That'll give me time to get ready."

"Got it."

"Hey. Pamela Brown. Thanks."

"Hey. Tanner. You'll get a bill. Believe me."

She got out of my car and walked back toward hers. I gave her a minute, then drove off, circling to a place just below the burned-out house, a place that was all downhill from the room where Karl Kottle was being held. If necessary I could roll him all the way to the car.

At twelve fifty I opened the trunk and took out a tire iron, a screwdriver and some gloves, then checked to be sure my gun was still in my coat. As I hiked back to the house, the tire iron swung heavily against my thigh, the jawbone of a twenty-first-century ass. When I caught my breath I climbed the concrete stairway, teetering clumsily, and checked the boards over the door, feeling for the best place to pry. By twelve fifty-five the tire iron was slipped in behind the upper edge of the plywood and I was ready to apply some force. Thirty seconds later I heard the crash.

It sounded like Spike Jones Meets the Who, a cacophony of glass tinkling, horn honking, metal tearing, woman screaming. Moving as quickly as I could I pried at the plywood and a big hunk came away in my hands. I eased the wood down to the ground and worked away at the second sheet. It came away easily as well, and within two minutes I stepped up off the blocks and into the house. Out front, bedlam still bellowed. I paid silent homage to Pamela Brown.

The room I entered had once been the kitchen. Sometime or other, before the fire or after it, it had been stripped of everything remotely culinary, leaving only dangling electrical conduits and decayed linoleum spots and brown-stained ceilings in the wake of the destruction. The odor of wet wood and ashes tickled my nose. I squeezed it so I wouldn't sneeze. Over in the corner the lamp flickered like a hyped-up firefly.

Karl Kottle was where I had seen him last, unchanged. I walked past him and put my ear against the sliding door that led to the front of the house and listened. A deep voice murmured something and a higher voice answered softly, leery of being overheard. From outside I thought I could hear the garbled voice of a police dispatcher coming over a squad car radio. I looked back out the door I'd just come through. The night air shimmered periodically with flashes of blue light. The cops had arrived.

I went back over to Karl and pressed my finger to his throat. Strong pulse. The airway seemed clear as well, despite the gag. I started to remove the gag, then reconsidered. I put a hand on his shoulder and jostled him, my other hand ready to clamp over his mouth if he began to cry out, but there was no danger. It would take more than a shake to bring him back from wherever they had sent him.

There was only one thing to do, to move and move fast, so I maneuvered Karl onto his side, then squatted in front of him and hoisted him into the fireman's carry. As I struggled to my feet I came close to dropping him, but I hunched him higher and got a firm grip under one arm and one leg and headed for the door. Dirt and glass shards crumbled noisily beneath my shoes, sound effects for a cereal commercial. If anyone came through the door behind me I wouldn't have a chance.

His head bumped on the way out, hard. He moaned once, but the horn was still blaring and the moan was soft, more like a lover's sigh. It scared me anyway. Adrenaline squirted into my system, making me faster and stronger. I squeezed through the door and tottered my way down the makeshift steps with the man who was at once my burden and my prize.

My lower back began to ache. From the feel, it could

go out any minute. I wanted to look back but I didn't. From over the roof of the house I could hear voices arguing, voices cajoling, voices pleading, but over them all was the voice of Pamela Brown—belligerent, intoxicated, profane and wonderful.

My luck was running and I ran with it, down the hill, faster and faster, until I was afraid my momentum would drive me right into the ground. I got back in control, somehow, just before reaching the car. With less care than I should have used, I deposited Karl on the sidewalk and opened the car door, then took his feet and dragged him over to the car and stuck the feet inside, as far in as I could get them. Then I went around behind and took his shoulders and folded the rest of him into the front seat. As I started to close the door he slipped to the floor. I just left him there.

Sweat emerged hot and then turned cold. I was making enough noise to wake the dead or make myself join them. I slammed the door and ran to the other side and got in and unfastened Karl's gag and then drove off. My passenger sat slumped over his knees, wedged beneath the dash, looking more dead than alive.

I made my way to Army Street and then onto the James Lick and took it north to Clay Street, where I exited and made my way toward Nob Hill, where Max Kottle's apartment was. I was going to deliver Karl in person, whether he liked it or not. What happened after that wouldn't be my problem.

At the corner of Clay and Mason Karl started to groan and thrash around. Because I was afraid he might hurt himself I pulled to the curb and cut the ropes around his wrists and ankles and got him up onto the seat. He slumped back against the door and began to rub his head in his hands, up and down, until I was afraid the flesh would tear. Finally he stopped and dropped his hands and looked at me blankly, then past me out the window.

"Where are we?" he asked, the words thick and dry and idiotic.

"About a block away from your father's place, Karl," I said. "I'm going to take you there. Everything's okay."

He didn't seem to have heard me. "Do you understand, Karl? Are you all right? Can you hear me?"

A lot of time went by. I grew more and more concerned

about him. There are drugs these days that change the brain forever once they get to it. I watched him closely.

"Who are you?" he mumbled finally.

"My name's Tanner. Your father hired me, sort of, to get you free. He wants very badly to see you, Karl."

He looked at me for several seconds. I grew more certain that his mind had snapped, that whatever they had given him had made him crazy. He didn't blink, didn't move, didn't seem to breathe. Then he opened his mouth.

"My name's not Karl," he said.

Thirty-Two

"Then who *are* you?"

The question emerged reflexively, an autonomous being, but I knew its answer before it was fully uttered.

"I'm Mark Covington."

I nodded stupidly, the movement aping my self-assessment. Covington eyed me casually, his reporter's instinct apparently unbowed despite the drugs and the bondage. "How do you feel?" I asked, trying to buy time to figure out the things I should have figured out before.

"Lousy," Covington grunted. "I could use some coffee."

"Where do you want me to take you? Home? Hospital?"

Covington considered a moment. "I've got a place down off Union Street, a sort of home-away-from-home. Maybe you could drop me there."

I nodded. "I know where it is," I said.

Covington's head had been lolling against the car seat. Now it floated upright. "You do?"

"I do."

"I think I'd like to know how."

"I think we should talk."

The brightness was back in Covington's eyes; they became beacons in the blackness, in search of unspoken truth. "Maybe we should," he said. "But first, some coffee."

I drove down to Lombard and pulled into the Sambo's parking lot and went inside and ordered six coffees to go, then drove up to Covington's hideaway and parked. "You mind if I come in for a while?" I asked. "There are some things I need to know."

Covington shrugged. The ride had burned off whatever foreign substance was in him. "I don't understand any of this," he said. "I'm glad to be out of there, though. How the hell did you know where I was?"

He paused for a minute. A group of revelers fresh from a big night of drinking their way down Union Street bounced past us on balls of drunken laughter. One of the men cupped a hand around one of the women's buttocks. She laughed and pushed him away. His grin seemed evil and perpetual. Then Covington spoke again. "But you didn't know, did you? You didn't have any idea I was in that place."

"No," I admitted.

For the first time Covington looked at me with interest. "Come on," he said, and got out of the car. We went inside and spent several silent minutes drinking coffee from Styrofoam cups. The coffee tasted thick and oily. After he'd drunk three cupsful Covington slipped off his shoes and climbed onto the bed and propped a limp pillow behind his head and leaned back. "Do you know who I am?" he asked.

"Mark Covington. Reporter for the *Investigator*. Chet Herk and I are good friends." I eyed him squarely. "Three days ago Chet hired me to find you."

Covington's eyes rolled, like slot machine oranges. "He did? Then why did you think I was Karl Kottle?"

"Because a week before that someone else hired me to find Karl. For some reason the two of you came together. Leads that turned up in one case shoved me into the other one. I thought you were Karl because I saw a picture taken at a place called the Encounter with Magic. I assumed it was a picture of Karl, but it was you, because you were there, too."

"Amber's place. Yeah. Karl took most of the pictures that day. But how did you get to Potrero Hill from Amber's room?"

"By following Karl Kottle's half-sister."

Covington nodded. "Woody," he intoned.

"Woody. The question is," I went on, "where's Karl Kottle?"

He didn't respond right away. He was clearly tired, but agitated underneath, a lengthy barge driven by a hidden engine. I was certain he'd either fall asleep or leave, and I needed some questions answered before he did either one. "Where is he?" I repeated.

Covington smiled wearily, then chuckled. "I'd say he's about ten feet from where you found me. Before they gave me my nightly sleep potion, Karl and Woody and Wes were all in the living room, snug as bugs in a rug."

The information didn't make me feel any better. I felt depressed by the thought of tasks undone, of toil to come. "Is Karl all right?"

Covington shook his head. "He's sick as hell."

"Other than that?"

"Sure. He's fine. Why wouldn't he be?"

"Kidnap victims sometimes aren't."

"Victim? Are you kidding? Karl's not a victim of anything, except maybe his own idealism."

"But a ransom demand was made on his father."

"Of course it was. And do you know who thought of it? Karl. A neat little way to raise money for the cause."

"What's the cause?"

Covington blinked several times and rubbed his eyes. "Well, that's where it becomes a little fuzzy. The other guy, Wes, he talks like he wants to blow up every high rise in town and shoot down every guy wearing a three-piece suit just mainly for drill. Sort of a militant anticapitalist, you might say. Karl, he's more idealistic. He wants to open people's eyes to the forces of oppression and the plunder of the planet. He keeps talking about how it was in Berkeley back in the sixties, how the students finally stopped the war, finally woke the country up. He wants to wake it up again, I guess. What he really wants is to bring back the days when he didn't have a doubt in his head. Then Woody, she does whatever Karl says, except when she's sleeping with Wes. Then she wants blood, too."

"Is anyone else involved with this outfit?"

"Only one that I saw. A guy named Renn. But he may be out of it now. I haven't seen him around for a while. And then Karl keeps talking about all these other people who were at Berkeley when he was and are just waiting for someone to tell them to march and what tune to do it to. Apparently they're all over the place."

"Renn's dead," I said.

"Jesus. How?"

"Murdered."

"Wes," Covington said, simply and immediately.

"Are you sure?"

"No, but Renn was flaky. When Karl brought the kidnap ruse up, Renn didn't want any part of it. Wes probably was afraid Renn would talk. That's all it would take for Wes to snuff him."

Covington slid over Renn's death too lightly. I was starting not to like him much once again. "What's this guy Wes look like?"

"Tall. Curly hair. Dresses like a lumberjack. Handsome, I guess, at least Woody thought so. Smart, like a raccoon. A rabid one."

It was the same guy I'd seen in Renn's house and followed to Cicero's, the same guy Randy had described, the same guy Mrs. Renn had seen hanging around Howard's place. Curiously, Wes seemed to be someone Covington envied, a kindred spirit. Whether it was because of Rosemary or because of something else I couldn't be sure. "How did Wes hook up with Kottle and Rosemary?" I asked.

Covington shook his head. "I don't know, really. They were all together by the time I got into the act."

"About the kidnapping. They didn't get the money, did they? At the drop?"

"No. Why? Do you know anything about it?"

"I was there."

"Are you the one who got the dough?"

I shook my head. "Some guy on a motorcycle got it, at least that's the way it looked to me."

"Well, Wes about had a fit. He claimed he shot the old bastard who made the drop. Did he, or was that just more of Wes's act?"

"If Wes drives a BMW, that's just what he did."

"That was Wes. I thought he was all talk. I guess there was something there after all." Covington didn't seem pleased.

"I'm starting to put it together," I said, "but there's one more thing. On Sunday the media reported that Max Kottle had died. Why didn't that put a stop to the ransom demand, or at least slow them down?"

"Because Wes knew it was a lie. Or claimed he did. Wes said Max Kottle was as alive as I was, and that they should just go ahead as planned."

"Where'd Wes get his information?"

"Beats me."

"The source who put you onto the Sons and Daughters. Who was it?"

Covington shook his head. "Sources are confidential. Totally."

I stood up and stretched my legs. Down below I heard some muffled grunts and shouts. I looked at Covington.

"Little guy down there used to be a jockey," he explained. "Reruns his big races every night. Like goddamned Churchill Downs around here."

I smiled at the image of Eddie Winkles riding an imaginary horse to an imaginary winner's circle, an act more rational than anything I'd read about in the morning paper for days.

"Tell me about Karl's illness," I said to Covington. "What exactly is wrong with him?"

"I don't know and he doesn't either. From what he said he's been going to a doctor for it for years, but nothing seems to help."

"What's his problem, though? Is he a junkie?"

"I guess he must be. He shoots up, that's for sure. But the main thing is his hands and feet. They hurt like hell. He can hardly walk; he can't even pick up a toothbrush without pain. You know those pictures taken at Amber's place? Well, I'll bet they're real blurry, because every time Karl pushed the shutter button he grunted like he'd just been shot."

It seemed interesting but unimportant. "Does Karl know his old man's dying?"

"Sure," Covington said. "He calls it justice."

I walked the length of the room and back. "Now let's talk about you for a minute," I said.

Covington shook his head and smiled. "First you. What the hell are you, a private eye or something?"

I bowed. "John Marshall Tanner. Investigator. At your service."

"Jesus. I didn't know they made those anymore."

"The species is endangered, no question about it. I myself am under careful study by the Smithsonian."

Covington chuckled. "So, Mr. Detective, how did you get to that pigsty on Potrero Hill?"

There didn't seem any reason not to tell him the outlines, so I did, editing as I went. "It started when Max Kottle hired me to find his son. Max wants to see Karl before he dies. Then, when I got pulled off that because Max had died, or so I thought, Chet Herk hired me to find you. He wasn't sure you were missing, but he was plenty worried."

"Good old Chet."

"So I went after you, but the two cases started getting mixed up, beginning when I found one of Howard Renn's poetry books in your files, and ending when Rosemary Withers came by here to search your files."

"That's when you tailed her."

I didn't see any reason to mention Pamela Brown's role, so I just nodded.

"How did you find out about this place?"

"Good detective work."

"Bullshit. Some broad squealed. Who was it?"

"Forget it," I said. "Let's talk about something that might save someone's life. How did you end up hog-tied on a mattress on Carolina Street?"

"Why should I tell you?"

"Because half an hour ago you were ass deep in trouble, and now you're not."

Covington didn't buy it right away. He'd traded for tips for so many years it was heresy for him to give anything away for free. "Max Kottle isn't really dead, is he?" he mused carefully. "Wes was right."

"He's not dead," I agreed.

"Big story there."

"Not so big. From the looks of him he'll be dead in a month. Maybe sooner."

"But still."

"But still."

"You know all about that, right?"

"Not all. Most."

Covington devoted a few more seconds to thought. I devoted the same seconds to measuring my obligation to Pamela Brown. "I want the whole story," Covington said. "A promise."

"Promise," I repeated. He hadn't said when and he hadn't said he wanted it first.

Covington looked like he wanted to dicker further but was too exhausted to make the effort. "Okay," he began. "I've got a lot of sources on the street. Better snitches than any cop. About a month ago I started hearing about a new terrorist group that was looking for people and weapons and money, all the things it takes to give this whole town

the blue horrors. My source was a good one, an old radical from the Automobile Row and Palace Hotel days, so I
took it at face value. If it got to be anything like the scale
of the Red Brigades it would be the biggest story of the
decade. So I decided to infiltrate the group. I went under
cover. Took a long time, and I had to listen to an awful
lot of radical bullshit, but they finally let me in."

"And then someone blew your cover."

Covington nodded disgustedly. "I still don't know who,
but just before they pulled the Laguna Oil bombing Wes
marched in and said he knew I was a reporter for the *Investigator*. I've been a captive ever since."

"What were they going to do with you?"

He shrugged, newly heedless. "I think at first Karl
wanted to convert me to the cause. When that didn't work
they decided on extortion. Making the *Investigator* print
their demands, that kind of thing." He laughed. "It might
have been interesting to see what they'd have gotten for
me in trade."

"What's their next move?"

He shrugged. "They're going to make another try for
the Kottle money, I know that. They want weapons, and I
mean big weapons. Rocket launchers, grenades. Hell, Wes
even talked about tactical missiles. Apparently there are
people around who have them to sell if the money's right."

"What do you think happened at the first drop?"

"Well, Wes thinks he gave old man Kottle too much
time to counter their plan, told him where the drop would
be too far in advance. Woody thought Howard Renn
talked to someone before he died. Karl just kept looking
at Wes real funny. I think Karl thought Wes popped off
somewhere or other, to someone smart enough to cut himself in."

"Could Wes have dealt himself in and everyone else
out? That's a lot of money."

Covington frowned. "Possible. Karl was too sick to
move, just about, and Woody was just a piece of ass to
Wes. He didn't need them. But I always felt there was
someone behind Wes, someone pulling strings."

"Who?"

"No idea."

Covington began to rub his face again. His eyes closed
momentarily, then opened slowly, reluctantly. He'd be
asleep before long.

"What does Karl Kottle think about his father?" I
asked.

"Hates him," Covington said. "The old man's just a
source of funds."

"That's kind of strange, isn't it? They haven't seen each
other for years. What's keeping all that hatred alive?"

"Who knows? It's funny you say they haven't seen each
other, though. Karl seems to know a hell of a lot about his
father. Always talking about what he did or didn't do that
proved he was a neofascist. That's Karl's favorite term:
Neofascist." Covington paused. "Funny," he added.

"What is?"

"That I'd link up with Karl Kottle again."

"What do you mean 'again?' "

"The first story I ever covered for the *Investigator* was
the ROTC fire over at Berkeley. A girl died in it. They all
said Karl must have done it, mostly because he'd
threatened to so many times. You know about that?"

"A little. Anything strange about that whole thing?"

"Like what?"

"I don't know. Just fishing."

"Well, I don't know much. They pulled me off the story
right away and stuck me onto something else. Chinatown
gangs, as I recall. The *Investigator* was very big on Chinatown gangs there for a while."

"What's the name of the girl who died?"

Covington shrugged. "Who knows? That was ten years
ago, man. What difference does it make?"

"Who knows?" I said, with truth.

"Well, there's probably a file on it somewhere in there if
you're really interested," he said, pointing to the file cabinets.

I lit a cigarette and tried to stay up where the adrenaline had put me, but I couldn't. I started falling like a
stone. Covington inhaled and let the breath out slowly.
"Hey, Tanner," he said. "I got to get some sleep."

"I'll take off," I assured him. "There's just one more
thing."

"What's that?"

"What's the Biloxi Corporation?"

Covington opened his eyes and frowned. "Biloxi? How'd
you know about that?"

"ESP. What is it?"

"It doesn't have anything to do with this."

"Maybe, maybe not. Who's behind Biloxi?"

Covington sighed. "Hell, I don't know. I was in the office real late one night. No one knew I was there. I picked up a phone at the switchboard to make a call and somehow got hooked into a line that someone else was on. He was asking some guy named Quale all about Biloxi, whether it officially existed yet, when they could start moving with the rest of the plan, that kind of thing. It all sounded fishy to me, so I did some checking but it never came to anything. What do you know about it?" He paused. "No. I take that back. I don't care what you know. I'm going to sleep."

"Whose voice was it on the phone?"

"I don't know. It was too soft. Someone at the paper."

I stood up and walked over to the bed. "Don't do anything about this whole thing without letting me know," I said to him.

"Why?"

"I don't want to see Karl get hurt."

"I'll think about it," Covington said casually, "but as far as I'm concerned we're even. So don't expect any favors. Now get out of here."

"Listen to me, hotshot. If you start babbling about this, or printing it, one of your competitors is going to learn just how snugly you were tied and gagged out there, and how someone had to carry you out like a sick calf. It'll be hell on your image."

"Okay, okay. I get your point. You know, Tanner," Covington added sleepily, "when you were carrying me out of that place I must have come to for a second. I heard a woman yelling, or thought I did. It sounded just like a chick I know at the *Investigator*. She's a real bitch, too. Weird, huh?"

"Weird."

Covington closed his eyes. I walked over to the file cabinets and began to thumb through them. I finally found what I wanted in a file labeled "ROTC." The dead girl's name was Linda Luswell. She'd lived in Berkeley at the time of her death. Dean's list. Music major. Popular, cute and dead.

I put the file back and looked at Covington. He was snoring, his mouth a cavern of bestial sounds. I let myself out. Eddie Winkles was still bringing home a winner.

Thirty-Three

By the time I got to my apartment it was four A.M. and felt like it. I fixed a drink and slipped off my shoes and sat in the living room in the chair facing the window and looked out across the street. The neighbors had left the Christmas tree lights on. There were red, blue, green and yellow lights, gold ornaments, silver tinsel, a tin star on top. Popcorn strings. Paper chains. I had a vision of neat little packages arrayed under the tree, red bows and white paper, and inside the packages all varieties of precious gifts—cocaine, hashish, angel dust, smack. To Debbie from Santa.

I fixed another drink, then sat back in the chair. Tension crawled up and down my back like feasting maggots. My eyelids felt infected—hot and bloated. A dull ache inhabited the nether regions of my skull.

In the midst of these sensations I tried to think about the case. The cases. First one, then two—Kottle, then Covington and Kottle—and now one again. But maybe not. I sensed two strands still, a bifurcation, multiple vectors. Karl Kottle kidnapped, but not really. Ransom money paid, but not received. Max Kottle announced as dead, but still alive. Wes the leader, but someone behind him. Biloxi benefiting, but shareholders behind it. Threads dangling, still unwoven. Tangled.

I finished off my drink and pulled out the telephone book and looked up the number of Zenger, J. P. Mark Covington hadn't been in very good shape when I'd left him, and I wanted to remind him that Wes and the other Sons and Daughters knew where his apartment was and might decide to come and reclaim him. But Covington didn't answer. I hung up after the twelfth ring, hoping he was merely sleeping and not headed back to Potrero Hill in search of the Pulitzer prize.

During the next few minutes I considered whether to call Charley Sleet and tell him where he could collect Karl and Wes and Woody. It was risky, but in the end I decided against it. They didn't have the money and they didn't have a hostage. They had to be more concerned about the breach in their defenses than in staging further

assaults. With any luck their capacity for effective terror
had become severely limited, at least for a while. If
Charley stormed the place someone might get hurt. Thus
fortified with rationale, I called my answering service instead of Charley Sleet.

I hadn't expected a message but there was one. A
sleep-slowed voice told me that Belinda Kottle had called
some forty minutes earlier. She'd left no instructions and
no request to call her back; merely a dilemma.

It was a barbaric hour to be telephoning anyone but an
undertaker. Still, she might need me. I pulled the telephone onto my lap and called the Kottle number.

The phone rang six, seven, eight times. I was about to
put it down when a voice came over the wire. "Yes?" it
inquired, sounding very far away.

"Hedgestone?"

"No. Walter is asleep. Everyone is asleep. This is Max
Kottle."

"Mr. Kottle. I'm sorry to wake you. This is Marsh Tanner."

"Yes, Mr. Tanner. How are you?"

"I'm fine. How are *you*?"

"Alive. Rather amazingly, Doctor Hazen tells me."

"Your wife called me about an hour ago. I was out. My
service took the call. I thought I'd better check with her to
see if everything was all right. I didn't mean to wake you."

"Everything is under control, Mr. Tanner. However, the
kidnappers have called again."

"They have?"

"You sound surprised."

"I am, a bit," I admitted. "What did they say?"

"They want three million this time. I'm to have it ready
by the end of the day. Fortunately, my contact at the
Bank of America has been cooperative. The money will be
available."

"Don't pay it," I said bluntly.

"What?"

"Don't pay it."

"Of course I'll pay. They'll kill Karl if I don't."

"No they won't."

"How can you know that?"

"I just know. Listen, Mr. Kottle. This isn't the time to
go into it, but there have been some new developments.
You shouldn't make a decision about the ransom before

you're aware of them. I have a couple of things to do this morning, then I'll come by your place and tell you all about it. If they call before I get there, stall. Tell them you're having trouble getting the money."

"I won't jeopardize Karl, Mr. Tanner."

"You won't be. Take my word for it. I'll be there by midafternoon at the latest."

Kottle took his time. "I'll see what they say," he announced finally. "I can't promise anything. It's my money, after all. And my son."

"Get some sleep, Mr. Kottle," I said.

He laughed. "I think not. Sleep seems inexcusable, somehow, in my circumstances. Fortunately, my malignant cells have apparently become indefatigable. I'm not at all tired." He paused for breath. "Is Karl alive, Mr. Tanner? Can you tell me that?"

"Yes," I said. "At least he was an hour ago."

"You've seen him?"

"I'll tell you about it later."

"Come as soon as you can. Please."

I told him I would.

After hanging up the phone I went to the kitchen and dug out a fresh pack of cigarettes and lit one. When I reached into my jacket pocket to put the matches back I felt something small and oval and hard, like a pebble shaped by the rush of a stream. I pulled it out. It was a pill, blue and shiny, the capsule I'd picked up off Max Kottle's floor the first time I'd seen him.

I toyed with it for a few minutes, rolling it around in my fingers like a small kernel of truth that would grow into something much bigger if planted in the proper soil. Several minutes later I rounded up some unread *Chronicles* and took them to an all-night restaurant on Columbus and waited for the people I wanted to talk with to wake up.

Five cups of coffee and three hotcakes later I was on the road, a counter-commuter driving in the opposite direction from the rush-hour throng of East Bay businessmen and Christmas shoppers, plunging headlong into the rising sun and into the past of a family who undoubtedly preferred to forget it.

The Luswell house was on Blake Street a couple of blocks below Shattuck, white, square, pert. As I pulled to the curb a white panel truck backed out of the driveway next to the house and drove off toward the bay. The words "World of Plumbing" were painted on its side in red above a globe with a pipe wrench clamped around it. I walked up to the door and rang the bell.

The woman who answered was gray-haired and tiny. I smiled down at her. "Mrs. Luswell?"

"Yes?"

Her hair hadn't been combed yet and it embarrassed her. As she tried to pat it down I apologized for coming by so early. When she finished with her hair she gripped the throat of her housecoat around her more securely. "Are you one of those Moonies?" she asked, with sudden ferocity. "Harold told me not to let any more of those Moonies in here."

"I'm not a Moonie."

She looked me over as though the truth were inscribed somewhere between my forehead and my belt. "You do seem a trifle old for it," she said dubiously. "What is it you want?"

"I'm here about your daughter," I told her.

"Nan? But she doesn't live at home anymore. She was in Albuquerque, last I heard, working with some kind of Indians. Has that boyfriend of hers gotten her in trouble? Is that it? Harold said it would happen sooner or later."

I shook my head to spike both the tide of nerves and Harold's prescience. "Not Nan," I said. "Linda."

"Oh. Linda."

Strangely, her contracted features suddenly relaxed, became smooth and serene, as though Linda had caused all the harm she possibly could, as though no matter why I was there it couldn't be worse than what had gone before. "Linda's dead," Mrs. Luswell declared simply. When I told her I knew it, she seemed disappointed.

"I'd like to ask you some questions about her," I said.

"Whatever for?"

"Because Linda's death may have something to do with some strange things that have been happening to people over in the city. I'd like to find out if there's some connection."

"It's so long ago. How could that be?"

"I won't know until I learn more about Linda."

She looked up at me, suddenly strong and unblinking, assessing my suitability to know more about her dead daughter. "You might as well come in," she said finally.

I followed her into a small living room that was dominated on one side by an upright piano and on the other by a harp. Stacks of sheet music rose in the corners, the top sheets spilling to the floor like leaves. The couch under the front window was draped by a thread-bare blanket with a rim of blue ribbon. The only chair in the room was a recliner, one of the ones you can put right next to the wall. On the small TV screen Phil Donahue was talking to Norman Mailer about a book about a killer.

Mrs. Luswell asked me to sit down. Then she told me her husband had just gone to work. Then she asked if I would like some tea. Lipton's. I said that would be nice, and she went off to fetch it. While she was away I gave in to an impulse and went over and plucked a few harp strings. The sounds seemed naked, overexposed. I retreated to the couch.

When Mrs. Luswell came back she had a smile on her face that said she was prepared to be civil and hoped I was, too. She placed two tea cups on the end table and then walked to the harp and sat behind it and whirled her hands across the strings and made a waterfall, a breaking wave, a flood. Then she stopped and came and sat beside me. I bowed my head to applaud her and took a sip of tea.

"What do you want to know about Linda?" she asked as she got comfortable.

"Do you mind talking about her?"

"Not really. Not now. In a way it's a pleasure to meet someone who's still interested in Linda. Harold hasn't uttered her name since the funeral. He forbids me to mention her. Ever."

"How old was Linda when she died?"

"Twenty. A junior at the university."

"I read a newspaper account of the fire. She seemed to be an exceptional girl."

"Well, it's prideful to say so, but yes. She was. Exceptional."

"And she was just studying in the ROTC building? She didn't have any connection to the radical groups?"

"No. Not at all."

"Are you sure?"

"Don't misunderstand, Mr. Tanner. Linda was not unaware or unconcerned. She was as disturbed about the war and that type of thing as anyone. But protest marches weren't her style."

"What was her style, Mrs. Luswell?"

She beamed. "Music. She took after me in that way. You should have heard her play that piano; Chopin himself would have cheered. The teacher at school said she could have a concert career if she wanted it. I have some tapes, if you're interested."

"Tapes? Sure. That would be nice." I looked at my watch.

Mrs. Luswell started to get up, then sagged back and looked at me sadly. "Of course you're not interested. Why should you be? But thank you for saying you were."

"I'd enjoy hearing them. Really."

"Don't be silly," she sighed. "I shouldn't even have mentioned it. Now go on with your questions."

"Does the name Karl Kottle mean anything to you? He was a student there at that time, too."

"Kottle. No." Her hand went back to her throat, clutching the housecoat. "Wait a minute. He's the one who set the fire, isn't he? He's the one who killed our Linda." The gray eyes blazed, weapons of a fierce defense.

"That could well be what happened, but no one's ever proved it, Mrs. Luswell."

"Are you this Kottle boy's lawyer or something? Have they finally found him after all these years? Are you trying to get him off, is that it? Harold always said something like this would happen."

I shook my head, hoping I would never have to meet Harold. "They haven't found him and I'm not his lawyer. I'm not interested in who set the fire, Mrs. Luswell, I don't want to mislead you. I'm just trying to learn who Linda knew, what she did, where she went, that kind of thing."

She sighed. "I see. I'm sorry. It's just that no one seems to be blamed for anything anymore. Kids can kill other kids, or mug old ladies, or leave their parents and go off to a desert somewhere with a bunch of Indians, and no one does anything to them. You know what I mean?"

I nodded. What I knew was that Mrs. Luswell was like the rest of us, she had a list of grievances she wanted others to be aware of, and to validate.

"I need some more tea. Do you care for another cup?"

I shook my head and she left the room and I went over to the harp and tried to whirl my hands the way Mrs.

Luswell had but it didn't work and it hurt my fingers. I started to go back and sit down when I noticed something back in the corner behind a pile of music. It was a lump of metal, oblong, crevassed and folded, and vaguely anatomical in appearance. I looked it over and then sat down. When Mrs. Luswell came back I asked her what it was.

"Oh. That. Doctor Clifford Hazen gave us that. One of his first works of sculpture. Ugly, isn't it? Harold calls it the Prune."

"How do you know Doctor Hazen?"

"He treated Linda."

"I'm sorry. I thought she died immediately."

"Oh, she did. This was before, when Linda was sick."

"What was her trouble?"

"Cancer. A melanoma. Doctor Hazen is a famous radiologist. Linda was his prize patient."

"I don't understand," I said. "Linda had cancer when she died?"

"No. She had it four years before, and then Doctor Hazen cured her. That's what hurt Harold so, the irony of it all. We thought we had lost her back in sixty-six, then Doctor Hazen came along and performed a miracle when all the other doctors said there was no chance. And then she upped and died in that stupid fire." Mrs. Luswell laughed, briefly and mechanically. "Doctor Hazen used to say that Linda was his ticket to the Nobel prize. I think he was almost as upset as we were when she died. He never seemed the same afterward, at least to me."

Thirty-Four

The office was as cold and empty as an abandoned mine. Peggy had gone on a Christmas trip back East to see her daughter who had been married and divorced all within the past year. In the middle of my desk was a present from her, wrapped in gold foil, the shape and size of a carrot. Taped to the top of the package was a card that read "To the Boss, from his Head Elf." I wanted to open it but I couldn't; it was five days early. Then I wondered if I should have given Peggy something besides money.

I tossed my jacket over the back of a chair and sat down at the desk and put in a call to Harrison Quale.

Quale was one of those lawyers who spends nine-tenths of his time in the halls of the Federal Building because one government agency or another—the SEC, the Justice Department, the NLRB, someone—was always investigating one of his clients. Quale wore high-heeled patent leather boots and suits two sizes too small and white hair that seemed groomed with Super-Glue instead of Brylcream. No one had ever claimed Quale was stupid, and no one had ever claimed he was honest. He'd been charged with jury tampering at least once, and had been divorced and remarried three times. To the same woman.

His secretary put me through to him when I told her I was in big trouble, real big trouble. People didn't call Harrison Quale for any other reason.

"Tanner," Quale said after I told him who I was. "What's the matter? Bureau of Collection and Investigative Services got their beady eyes on you? Someone catch you with your eye in the keyhole?"

"No, Harrison. When I decided to go into this business I decided not to use your methods."

"Results, Tanner. That's what they pay for and that's what I give them. How I get there isn't any business of yours or anyone else."

"That's not what the Bar Association claims."

Quale snorted. "The Bar Association. Bunch of old men who've never been in a criminal courtroom in their lives for fear they'd catch something their dermatologist couldn't identify. The Bar Association thinks the law is contracts and wills, Tanner. The law is war. Me against them. And you know what they say about war."

"All's fair."

"That's what they say. The Marquess of Queensberry never had to defend anybody against a trumped-up tax evasion charge. Now, do you just get off on talking to people who earn twenty times what you do, or you got something on your mind?"

"Biloxi Corporation," I said.

"Biloxi. I see. Yes. Biloxi. Very interesting."

"That's what the man I had lunch with yesterday told me, that it was very interesting. Very profitable, too. The fact that he's the president of the company makes it even more interesting. I asked if I could get in on the action, in a small way, of course. Five thousand or so. He owes me a favor, but he said I should talk to you. How about it, Harrison? Throw some crumbs to the peasants."

The line went unused for a moment, and when Quale spoke I knew I wasn't going to get what I wanted. "This was yesterday, was it, Tanner?" His voice was as smooth as syrup.

"That's what I said. At the Poodle Dog."

"Bullshit. I had lunch with the president of Biloxi yesterday myself. At the Rathskeller. You know it?"

"By the Federal Building. Good sauerbraten."

"That's the one. And guess what?"

"What?"

"The gentleman didn't even mention your name. You're fishing, Tanner. Why, I don't know, but you're fishing. Well, my friend, there are No Trespassing signs up all over and the game warden is real mean. So stay the hell away from the pond. I mean it."

"I should have known better than to try to finesse you, Harrison. And I've got a tip for you, too. The Biloxi thing is fraudulent as hell, and it's going to blow up in the next day or two. If I were you I'd keep clear if I didn't want to spend the next few weeks picking shrapnel out of my ass."

"You're crude, Tanner."

"When in Rome, Harrison. Don't take any wooden nickels."

"Wooden, copper, paper, they're all the same these days. Worthless. My clients pay in gold."

I hung up and thought things over for a while, then picked up the phone and called Max Kottle's number for the second time that day. Belinda answered. I told her that I'd spoken to Max earlier this morning, and that I'd advised him not to pay the ransom. She wanted to know what was going on but I told her it would have to wait for a few more hours. "I've got a question for you, though," I told her.

"What?"

"Where was Walter Hedgestone at noon yesterday?"

"Walter? Why?"

"Just playing a hunch."

"Let me see. Why, he was right here, meeting with some engineers about the oil shale project. The meeting lasted all day." She paused. "You know, they were all close to Max, those big, rough men. The shale project was his pet, and he spent a lot of time out there when it was being set up. All those men think Max is dead, of course. They were talking about him, and Max was in the next room, listening in. What they said was nice. Some of them were even crying. Max was, too. I think Max feels better today than he has in weeks."

"Good. I'm glad for him. And for you."

"Did I tell you what you expected to hear about Walter?"

"No," I said, then said good-bye.

I thought things over once again, for about a half hour. I thought them over very hard, and then I called the *Investigator* and asked to speak to Mr. Greer's secretary. "My name is Quale," I said when she came on the line. It's illegal for a California private investigator to use an alias, but time was short. "I had lunch with Mr. Greer yesterday, perhaps you remember the appointment."

"Lunch? I'm afraid I don't, Mr. Quale." She paused, confused.

"It's not important," I assured her. "The reason I called, I found a cigarette lighter on the floor beneath the table just after Mr. Greer left. I think it must be his. Perhaps you can ask him about it."

"Certainly. One moment."

I enjoyed the hum of silence for a time, then another voice spoke. "Harrison? What the hell's this crap about a lighter? I haven't had a cigarette in two years and you know it. What have *you* been smoking, huh?"

I hung up in the middle of a chuckle, a chuckle from the mouth of Arnold Greer.

My next call wasn't answered for a long time. I was afraid she had already moved, and worse, that she would be out of touch for several days, until her new phone was put in. Then she was there, in the middle of my musings. When I told her who it was she swore.

"I was halfway down the stairs with a box of books. My friend's outside in the van waiting. This is not convenient, Tanner."

I apologized and told her it would only take a minute. "When we talked before you mentioned a man wearing sunglasses in the dark. You said you saw him driving past Howard's house one night."

"Yeah? So?"

"I want you to think back. Picture him in your mind. It's important."

"Okay, but it's no use. I've never seen him before."

"It's not that. What I want to know is, could it have been something else he was wearing, something besides sunglasses?"

"Like what?"

"An eye patch."

She didn't make a sound loud enough to prevent me from hearing my heartbeat. I became suddenly conscious of my hand sweating, of gripping the receiver like a bludgeon.

"Yeah," she said at last. "I guess it could have been that. In fact, that's probably what it was. Yeah. An eye patch. Okay?"

The light in the outer office was pale and weak, diluted by the gray-white ether of the out-of-doors that leaked in through the blinds. I took the cover off of Peggy's typewriter, then pawed through her desk for some legal-sized paper and some correction fluid. Then I began to type, hunt and peck, while composing in my best legalese:

Superior Court of the State of California
For the County of San Francisco
Civil No. 915460

Maximilian Kottle, Plaintiff

   vs

San Francisco Bay University Hospitals and Clinics, et al.,
Defendants

   Notice of Deposition

TO THE DEFENDANTS AND TO THEIR ATTORNEYS OF RECORD HEREIN:

PLEASE TAKE NOTICE *that on Thursday, December 20, 1979, at the hour of two o'clock* P.M., *plaintiff in the above-entitled action, by and through his attorneys of record, will take the deposition of the Custodian of Records of defendant San Francisco Bay University Hospitals and Clinics, on the premises of said defendant, pursuant to Section 2016 et seq. of the California Code of Civil Procedure. Said Custodian is required to produce for inspection and copying, pursuant to the request for production of documents previously served and filed herein, all records, reports, documents, papers, books, accounts, tapes, letters, photographs, or other such material, in whatever form, in the possession, custody or control of said de-*

*fendant which in any way concern or relate to plaintiff
Maximilian Kottle.*
 *Law Offices of Roscoe Pound
 Attorney for Plaintiff*

When I'd finished typing I put the cover back on the
machine and put on my jacket and flipped off the lights
and walked to my car and drove west toward the ocean.

Thanks in large part to the generosity of Max Kottle,
San Francisco Bay University has a reasonably adequate
teaching hospital. In my younger days, when I couldn't afford good medical care, I'd go up to SFBU and let the
dental students scrape my plaque and the medical students
take my pulse and the nursing students weigh my flesh, all
for about a tenth of the cost of having it done by full-
fledged professionals. Of course, there were the usual horror stories about the place—wrong legs amputated, too
much vaccine injected or too little, sponges and clamps
and rings left in postoperative abdomens, undiagnosed tu-
mors, unstemmed viruses—but if it's all you can afford,
you take the risk. Like riding the bus.

The place had changed a lot since then—carpets and in-
direct lights and walnut paneling and recessed communica-
tions equipment and that was just the lobby. Elsewhere, as
in any hospital, were the mind-boggling, ever-gleaming
gadgets foisted onto the health care industry by jobbers
whose chief talent lay in concocting reasons why the old
ones weren't good enough anymore.

The sign I was looking at said "Records." The woman
on the other side of the counter wore a white uniform that
was sufficiently stiff and forbidding to protect everything
from her virginity to her change purse. With a set of lips
as thin as pie crust she asked me what she could do for
me.

I whipped out my freshly typed document. "Records
deposition," I said as officiously as possible. "The micro-
film unit is out in the car. Where do I set up?"

The woman's tag said her name was Miss Daunt. She
took my paper from me without a word or a smile and
read it over and handed it back. "I don't know anything
about this," she announced heavily, as though it were the
only thing on God's earth she could say that about. With a
grump she turned back toward her files.

"You better learn something about it real quick, lady," I

said to her broad back. "I know for a fact that Judge Lassiter ordered this depo to take place today or he'd find you people in contempt."

"Our lawyer always tells me when a deposition is scheduled. He hasn't told me one word about this."

"You better get him on the horn. If I go home without a full set of pictures on my little machine, there's going to be hell to pay."

Miss Daunt just stood there and looked at me, making me shrink. I couldn't afford to give her the luxury of contemplation. "You ever see Judge Lassiter in action, lady? I saw him toss a guy in jail once just 'cause he wandered into the courtroom with his hat on. Real mean guy. He told the lawyers we could get these records today. I saw him do it. If I were you I wouldn't take it on my head to go against him."

"Just a moment." Miss Daunt turned and marched like a Prussian into another room and closed the door behind her.

I was going to have to be plenty lucky to avoid a charge of obtaining property under false pretenses, and I was going to have to be even luckier to get the information I wanted.

Luck. It comes and goes, sails on the winds and swims on the waves, enters through back doors and leaves through windows. As evanescent as smoke or fame. I've had more than my share of it over the years.

When Miss Daunt came back her face was wide with triumph. "I've called our lawyer," she announced grandly. "He wasn't in the office. His secretary didn't know anything about this case."

I shrugged elaborately. "See you in court."

"Just a minute, you," she ordered. Her smile was reptilian. "I didn't talk to the lawyer but I did do some checking. We have no records on your Mr. Kottle. None at all. You're at the wrong hospital."

No I wasn't.

There was one more stop to make before I laid it all out, before I had all the threads I needed to make a rope. This stop was a hospital, too. Children's, on California Street.

A few years ago I'd played a lot of poker in the evenings. The best of the regulars I'd played with was Al Goldsberry, the assistant pathologist at Children's Hospital. Al quit playing about the same time I did, but for a different reason. He was too good at it. Since then he's been playing blackjack at any casino that will let him in the door. Al's a card counter, which means given enough time he can beat any honest blackjack game in the world. Vegas won't let Al play anymore, and neither will the Bahamas. Al doesn't seem to mind, though; Al never seems to mind much of anything. Maybe it's because pathologists so seldom get sued for malpractice.

For some reason they always put the pathologists in the basement, as though those tissue slices and blood samples and virus cultures would recombine into advanced life forms and take over the world if allowed above ground. I found Al in a windowless room, standing at the end of a long counter that was covered with vials and flasks and beakers and burners and that kind of science stuff. He was pouring something red from one test tube into another. There was a smile on his face. There was always a smile on Al's face.

We said hello and I asked Al what he'd been up to.

"Atlantic City," he said simply.

"Big score?"

"About twenty grand. Didn't want to abuse the hospitality."

"Got some time?"

"Sure," he said, then looked at me carefully. "You look a little on edge, Marsh. Problem?"

I shook my head. Then I reached in my pocket and pulled out the little blue capsule. "Can you tell me what this is? What it's for?"

"How soon?"

"Now."

He smiled. "Maybe, but probably not. Is that all you need?"

"One more thing. There's this guy. He's sick. Has intense pains in his hands and feet. Hurts to walk, hurts to touch things. What could that be?"

"Any other symptoms?"

"Not that I know of. Except he's also a junkie."

Al shook his head. "Could be several things, Marsh. Arthritis. Circulatory problems. Gout. How old's the guy?"

"Early thirties."

"He should see a doctor."

"How about poisons? Any of them produce symptoms like that?"

Al's smile faded for an instant. "Poison, huh? Foul play?"

"Maybe. Maybe most foul." I wanted to make it a joke but it wouldn't become one.

Al reached out his hand for the pill and left without a word. I gazed idly at the tools of a trade that was as foreign to me as Pluto and more than a little suspect. Some very intelligent people say that modern medicine invariably makes people worse, not better, and that except for certain chemical triumphs like vaccines and certain mechanical aids like respirators we're all better off putting our fate in the hands of Mother Nature than Hippocrates' descendants. But it's like everything else. None of us plain folks can tell which expert to believe.

Al came back in the room nodding his head. "If you were as lucky at poker as you have been just now, you'd be a rich man," he said. "I think I've got your answers."

Thirty-Five

The door to his office opened easily but the waiting room was as vacant as a balloon. There were no lights burning, no Muzak playing, no birds chirping. The desk drawers were still open and empty, abjectly entreating Gwen Durkin to return. Nothing bid me to enter, but nothing kept me out.

I walked through the waiting room toward the back offices, and when I heard some sounds coming from the direction I was headed I walked faster. The examining rooms were as empty as the waiting area. My guarded footfalls sounded like stakes being driven into a craven heart.

The office I had been in the last time was empty, but the door to the room at the end of the hall was closed and suspicious. I stopped next to it and listened. From the other side came a hissing noise, the sound of a polecat, the sound of an adder, a fearsome sound. I turned the knob slowly and pulled. The door came toward me smoothly and silently, as though afloat. I moved to the side, out of range of whatever might be in there, but no shot was fired, no cry was uttered. I peered around the edge of the door-way and looked inside the room.

Doctor Hazen was there all right, but if it weren't for his small size and his balding head I might not have known it was him. He wore a rubber apron that stretched from his neck to his knees, a pair of round goggles tinted the color of beets, a polka-dot trainman's cap and heavy leather gloves with gauntlets that reached halfway to his elbows. In his right hand was the golden nozzle of a welder's torch, in his left a small, thin rod. His attention was concentrated on the piece of metal on the workbench in front of him and on the flame he was applying to it.

I stood quietly and watched him work. The gases in the tanks behind him were set at a hot mixture of oxygen and acetylene. The flame they produced was white-hot, the metal they touched orange and puddled. Hazen was melting the steel into one of his standard forms—this one resembled something more properly lodged in the cranium of an ox. From time to time a shower of sparks cascaded to the floor, in celebration of the artistic process.

Nearest to me were a couple of finished pieces whose polished glow contrasted sharply with the grimy dullness of the raw materials of the craft. As with the other pieces of Hazen's they were awesome but not admirable. Else-where, the studio was a mess, a swirl of tools and materi-als, hunks of dull, unworked metal, discarded pressure tanks looking enough like bombs to make me nervous, wooden casting forms, tongs, hoists, anvils, cast-iron buck-ets, rags. The Village Smithy, one century hence.

I stepped into the room, my shoes scraping heavily over the metal shavings and sawdust that covered the floor. The sounds I made seemed as loud as sin, but Hazen didn't hear them. I approached to within five feet of him, until I could feel the heat from the molten metal and the flaming gases, could smell the smoke of combustion and the stench of chemical rebounding. "Doctor Hazen?" I said.

Neither the torch nor the doctor moved, so I repeated his name, louder. When he still didn't respond, I reached out and touched his shoulder.

He jumped. The flame from the torch flashed up off the metal and, no longer blunted, shot into space like the tail of a streaking comet. Hazen turned his head and looked at me. At least I assumed he was looking at me; he was eye-less behind the dark lenses of his welder's goggles.

After a few seconds he placed his rod on the table and raised the goggles to the top of his head and left them there, two amber eggs in a newly built nest. "The office is closed," Hazen said grimly.

"For repairs?" I said, gazing around the studio in a burlesque take.

"I told you before. My records are confidential. They are protected by law, but even if they weren't I would refuse to disclose anything about my patients."

"Oh, I've got all the information I need about your patients, Doctor," I said. "It's you I need to know more about."

"Me?" he exclaimed. "If you want to know *me*, look there. And there. And in the waiting room. My work is me and I am my work. We are fungible. One."

I followed the direction of his finger as he pointed from one piece to the next, my eyes absorbing the twisted metals as my ears absorbed the increasingly insistent rumblings of Hazen's voice. When I looked back at him he was holding the torch with both hands, gripping it tightly, wielding it like a weapon. The light in his eyes made it seem that the goggles had shielded the steel from them and not the other way around.

"Why are you here?" Hazen demanded suddenly. The expression on his face had altered enough to tell me where I had first seen him. He was the little man with the triumphant smile I had seen coming out of Max Kottle's apartment one rainy night a long time ago.

"I'll give you a hint," I said, my eyes locked firmly on the torch. "Several, in fact. I started the morning by driving to Berkeley for a talk with Mrs. Luswell about her deceased daughter Linda. Then I had a brief conversation with the Records Custodian at Bay University Hospital about what records they might or might not have on Max Kottle. Then I talked with a pathologist friend of mine about little blue pills and about an illness that causes pain in the extremities and about the effects of prolonged exposure to cobalt radiation. End of hints."

It probably wasn't as still as I imagined it was, probably not as silent. "You've been busy," Hazen remarked calmly, his lips barely moving. The accusation was sarcastic and ridiculous.

"What do you want from me?"

"I want to know why. And more than that I want to know if I can stop it, if I can save them. If anyone can."

His smile was thin and disdainful. "Why should I tell you?"

"Because it's over. Because there's no reason not to now. Because if they die you'll be in Folsom till you join them."

Time passed as though it were on his side instead of mine. The whole world seemed lit by the torch Hazen carried, and in peril from it. My neck started to ache from lack of movement.

"Who else knows?" Hazen asked, suddenly animated.

"Everyone who needs to."

"No," he countered. "No." His wrist moved. "Only you."

A yellow-white flame shot out at me like a spear, the lance of the Lord. I jumped back but it seemed to keep coming, to be fueled by the atmosphere, by the universe itself. I jumped again, and when I landed it wasn't on the floor but on something round, something slick, something that rolled and took my feet with it.

I stumbled backward, my hands thrust blindly into the space at my back. I was afraid to look at anything but the flame.

Then the flame receded as I slipped, falling. The back of my head hit something hard and I lost it, thinking in the final second that I heard the sound of gongs.

Thirty-Six

By the time I knew where I was it was black inside the studio and even blacker inside my head. Something seemed loose that shouldn't have been loose and something else seemed larger than it had been before I fell. My heart had traveled magically to my skull, where it throbbed and stopped, only to throb again.

The first time I tried to stand I didn't make it. But I did stir the huge mobile that had knocked me cold. The next time I tried to get up, I wished I hadn't. As soon as I could, I felt my way out of the studio and into the hallway, where a dim light shined down on my predicament and on my pain.

I checked my watch. I'd been out for two hours. Probing gingerly, I felt my head. It was cut, but the blood had dried into a crusty, hairy mat. The lump beneath it seemed as large as Oakland. I stumbled down the hall.

The first door on my left was open. I went through it slowly, my hands on the nearest surface for support. The examining table beckoned as seductively as Loren, but I passed it up and went to the medicine cabinet. After what seemed like hours I found a bottle of Empirin compound and swallowed four tablets, washing them down with water in a paper cup the size of a thimble. As best I could I poured some alcohol over my cut. The pain almost put me back on the floor. I wanted more than anything to take my head off and put it to bed till it got well.

There was a telephone on the small desk in the corner and I picked it up and placed a call. She answered immediately.

"Is Doctor Hazen there?" I asked.

"No. He isn't."

"Is everything all right?"

"Yes. Everything is fine."

"If Hazen comes, keep him away from your husband. Seduce him if you have to. I'll be there in ten minutes."

Dizzily erratic, I made my way outside into the darkness of the city. The streets were tiled with rumbling cars. The fumes they eliminated soured my stomach even further. If I regurgitated it would eat its way to Shanghai.

The chances of finding a place to park on Nob Hill were so poor I decided to walk. Halfway up the hill I decided I'd made a mistake. My head was getting worse instead of better, my brain bouncing with every step as though dribbled with a porcelain hand.

I stopped to rest, leaning against a building, looking drunk or sick or crazed or all of them. It didn't get any better but it didn't get any worse so I moved on, step by step, walking the way I used to walk during forced marches back in basic training almost three decades ago. I'd hated it then and I hated it now.

Somehow, the next time I thought about anything but putting one foot in front of the other I was at the entrance to the Phoenix. The elevator whisked me to the top. After my stomach caught up to me I pressed the bell until my thumb hurt.

When the door finally opened I almost fell into the

apartment. Fortunately, Belinda Kottle didn't seem to notice how I looked or how I smelled. She was wearing a floor-length robe of blue velour on her body and nothing, not even an expression, on her face. She turned without a word and I followed her into the breakfast nook and sat down at the table. There was nothing there with us except a half-empty cup of coffee. I asked if Hedgestone was around and she shook her head, then lowered it to her hands. The irregularity of the butcher-block slats she was leaning on made me dizzier than I was before.

"Okay," I said. "I'm not sure I'm thinking straight yet, but here goes. I'll tell it to you first, then you can decide what to do from here."

She nodded wearily. She seemed blithe and superficial, but then she didn't know what I was going to say.

"I'm not one hundred percent certain about all this," I began, "but most of it can be checked easily enough. The worst part has to do with Hazen. Max's old buddy. Hazen's been on a vendetta against both Karl and your husband. He's been killing them, Belinda, murdering them, slowly but surely, year after psychotic year. Those letters were from Hazen, not Karl.

"I don't think Max even has cancer, but if he does it was brought on by Hazen and his cobalt machine. I don't know much about radiation, but I know it can kill as well as cure, and either way it's torturous. Hazen has been using it to inflict pain, and possibly prolonged physical debilitation as well. He's slipped Max in and out of that hospital in secret, the way they used to do with Howard Hughes. There are no records of his treatment, no evidence he's ever been in the place. As head of radiation Hazen could probably treat the facility as his private toy. That new wing Max paid for might have had something to do with it, too; Hazen probably blackmailed the staff and the administration to let him treat Max in secret or he'd have the money cut off. To top it off, Max's pain medication is all placebos. Sugar pills. He had no help at all for the pain, except for the pot Gwen Durkin slipped him when it got real bad. What I don't know is whether anyone can do anything about it. Understand? It may have gone too far. If Hazen aimed his machine at the spinal cord the damage might be irreversible. The same with the kidneys, with any other organ. If the exposure was high enough he might have induced leukemia, or even a tumor.

There's no way to tell until we get Max to another doctor. But I have to warn you. Max may die anyway. It may be too late."

I looked at Belinda as I caught my breath, to see if I should stop or go on, but I couldn't read her. She took a sip of coffee, coffee that must have been as cold as a creek, but there were no tears, no sobs, no questions, no nothing. I didn't want to go on, but I had to, impelled by the magnitude of Hazen's private pogrom.

"He got Karl, too. He probably started with him, in fact, since it was Karl's killing of Hazen's patient back in Berkeley that unhinged Hazen to begin with. He's been poisoning Karl, regularly, for three or four years. Not enough to kill him, just enough to maximize the symptoms—pain in the extremities. My friend says it's excruciating, indescribable. Karl must have been in hell for the past three years. I'd be surprised if he hasn't lost his mind. Karl's in on the kidnapping, by the way. He's in no danger. That's why I advised Max not to pay. Karl hates Max; I think Hazen has kept the hatred alive over the years, supplying Karl with manufactured instances of his father's evil. My advice is to put the money back in the bank and let things slide. Bring in the cops and let them handle it. There doesn't seem any reason not to anymore. See?"

"Yes. I see," she said, nodding. "Karl's one of them."

"There's another thread to this thing," I continued. "It has to do with the money. The kidnappers didn't get it, and the reason is the kidnappers are being used for purposes that don't have anything to do with revolutionary politics. I thought at first someone was using your husband's own money to take his company away from him, but that's not exactly it. I think someone's gambling that CI is going to make the oil shale thing work, and that if they can get a block of stock now, at a good enough price, there's going to be big money to be made, and quickly. I doubt if the money people had anything to do with Hazen's little plan, but I do think they took advantage of the situation Hazen created to depress the price of CI shares as far as possible. Then they came up with the kidnapping ploy and used Max's own money to buy into CI. Tell me. Do you know a guy named Arnold Greer?"

"What?"

"Arnold Greer. Do you know him? He's publisher of

the Bay Area *Investigator*. Has a private army at his disposal."

She shrugged casually. "No. I don't think so." We could have been discussing crumpets.

"Ever see a guy around here with a patch over one eye?"

"A patch?"

"Yes. Like Dayan. Long John Silver. The Hathaway shirt man. That kind of patch."

"Long John Silver. I loved that story."

"Come on, Belinda. How about Greer?"

"I'm sorry. I'm very tired. I did see a man with a patch not long ago. He looked funny."

"Where?"

"Downstairs. I was just leaving the building. He was driving a car. He dropped Walter off over by the Pacific Union Club."

"Walter Hedgestone?"

"Yes."

"Well, it'll take some more checking, but I think Greer and Hedgestone are the ones behind the CI move. Biloxi Corporation is the nominee they used. The DA can smoke them out. If he can't, the SEC can. There may well be a murder involved also, a man named Renn. I don't particularly want to get into it. I don't particularly want to do much of anything right now. So. What do we tell Max about all this?"

"Max?"

"Your husband. The man in the next room. Are you all right? Have you been taking drugs? Booze? What?"

"I'm fine. I'm just fine. Several people called, but I didn't let them come over. You're the only one."

"What are you talking about? Why did they want to come over?"

"Why, to express their condolences. Mother. She must have called everyone in town after I told her."

"Why condolences?"

"Because of Max, silly. That's what you do when someone dies. Send condolences."

Sure. If I hadn't been so beat up I'd have known it a half hour ago, the minute I heard Belinda's voice on the phone. "Jesus Christ," I muttered. "How long ago?"

"An hour. Two. It seems like a long time, but maybe that's because I don't have anything to do anymore."

"Where's the body?"

"They took it."

"Who?"

She shrugged. "Some men in white coats. Doctor Hazen made the arrangements."

"Hazen. Was he here?"

She nodded wearily. "He was with Max when he died. I was napping. I feel terrible that I wasn't there, but Clifford told me it was quick and peaceful."

"It was quick, you can be sure of that," I said roughly. "Where did Hazen go?"

"I don't believe he said. He did tell me Max's last words were about me, though. Wasn't that nice?"

"Lovely." I stood up and walked around her once, looking down at her, trying to figure it out. "Have you heard anything I've said in the past half hour?" I asked.

"Well, some. My mind keeps wandering, though. Doctor Hazen gave me some pills. My eyes aren't working right."

I pounded my fist on the table, a surrogate for myself. "I'm going to have to take you out of here. Can you leave right now?"

She frowned. "Where are we going?"

"To a hospital."

"Whatever for?"

"Because Hazen may have tried for you, too. I can't be sure what he gave you. You should be under observation."

She seemed to find my concern amusing. "Oh, it was just Valium, Mr. Tanner. The bottle's right over there. I've had it for a long time, ever since Max got real bad."

I looked it over. There didn't seem to be more than a few pills missing, and the date on the prescription was six months old. I decided to let it go. I had other things to do, things like finding a killer and the evidence of his crime.

"I have to go out for a while," I told her. "Is there anyone who can come stay with you? Just for a few hours?"

"Where are you going?"

"To see Doctor Hazen."

"Are you sick?"

"Very. Who should I call?"

"There's no one. But I'll be fine. Don't worry. Everything's fine."

She wasn't fine at all. I excused myself and went to the living room and called a couple of doctors I knew. One

was in surgery, one was in Acapulco. Then I tried someone else. Luckily she was home.

"Gwen? Marsh Tanner. Please don't hang up. I need a
favor. Do you have the key to the Kottle penthouse?"

"Yes." She was tentative, suspicious. I didn't blame her.

"There isn't time to explain. Max Kottle has just died.
He wasn't dead before, but he is now. Mrs. Kottle is all
alone. I think she may be in shock. She's been given some
medication, probably Valium, but I can't verify it. There's
an outside chance she's been poisoned. She should be under observation. I can't stay with her. Could you come
over for a few hours?"

"Just for Mrs. Kottle?"

"Yes. She says there's no one else I can call."

I gave her time to think and she took it. I guessed she
was trying to separate her professional instincts from her
personal qualms about me. She must have managed it. "I'll
come," she said.

"One more thing. Where does Hazen live?"

"Why?"

"I need to see him. He was with Kottle when he died."

"He has a place in Seacliff. Twenty-fifth and Scenic."

"Is there anyplace else he might be, if he's hiding out?
Someplace besides his office?"

"Why would he be hiding out?"

"He killed Kottle."

Her gasp was as sharp as a splinter. "I'll tell you about
it when I get back," I went on. "Where else might he be?"

"I'm not sure. He does have a workroom above his garage. A studio. He spends most of his time in there instead
of the main house. Poor Clifford."

"Poor Max. Are you free a week from Monday?"

"What?"

I repeated it.

"That's New Year's Eve."

"I know."

"I . . . yes. I can be."

"Would you like to go somewhere? With me?"

"Where?"

"I don't know. Someplace."

"Okay."

"Okay."

I asked Gwen to hurry, then called the biggest mortuary
in town. They'd never heard of Max Kottle or Clifford

Hazen. Then I tried the hospital. They paged Hazen and
said he didn't respond and suggested I try his office. When
I asked if Hazen had requested the services of any order-
lies in the past hour or so they told me there was no way
to check. I dropped the phone back in its cradle. It rang
before I could get out of the room. I was afraid Gwen had
changed her mind so I picked it up.

The voice on the other end was tense and crisp. "Is the
money ready?"

"Yes," I said, without thought.

"Here are the instructions for delivery. Get a pencil. No
screw-ups this time."

"Wes?"

"No, this is . . . Who are you? What's going on?"

"Listen to me, Karl. One minute. Your father is dead.
For real this time. He was murdered by Doctor Hazen, the
same guy who's been poisoning you for years. The pain in
your hands and feet. It's symptomatic of a certain kind of
poison. Every time you've gone to see Hazen to get better
he's given you another dose. Do you hear me, Karl? You
can check it. Go to another doctor. Give up the kidnapping. The money will never get to you, anyway. It's going
to buy shares of Collected Industries for a man who needs
to make a killing in the market to refinance his newspaper.
Ask Wes if he knows Arnold Greer. Ask him about
Biafra. Watch his face. Greer got the first two million and
he'll get these, too. Get out of it, Karl. Take Rosemary
with you. Get out and get well."

I'd run out of words, I'd run out of energy, I'd run out
out of interest. For several seconds there was nothing at
the other end of the line but a silent query. Then there
was a click. I went back to see Belinda.

She was exactly as I had left her, mentally and physically. "I've got to leave," I said. "I'm going to see Hazen.
Then I'll be back. I called your husband's nurse. She'll
come stay with you."

"It's Christmas."

"I know."

"I haven't got a tree."

"We'll go get a tree. Right when I get back."

"I haven't seen Gump's windows, either. I always see
Gump's at Christmas."

"We'll go there first. Then we'll get a tree. I know a guy
out in the Avenues, has the best trees in town."

"He has? Does he have Douglas fir?"

"You bet. Now go get in bed. Get some sleep. I'll be back in a couple of hours. Then we'll get that tree."

"And Gump's?"

"And Gump's."

"Promise?"

"Promise."

Thirty-Seven

The house was light blue and forbidding, but more from neglect than from grandeur. There were too many windows and too many doors in the facade, and too many broken slates in the roof. The yard was unclipped and patchy, the fur of an alley cat that has to share the alley. I could almost hear the neighbors complaining. Somewhere behind and below the house the ocean punched at the base of the cliff.

The front door stood ajar, a breach of security more pathetic than threatening, given the condition of the house. I pushed my way inside, sensing I was the first visitor in months.

The smell struck me first, the smell of disuse, the smell of old air. It seemed to rise from every surface, like steam off warm water. Someone had stripped the place of value; in the foyer alone three picture hooks protruded from the walls like naked claws. In the living room there were dents in the carpet where furniture had been but wasn't. Somewhere a toilet made the sound of distant cheers.

I went into the kitchen and flipped on the light. A roach stopped in mid-journey, hoping to be mistaken for linoleum. There were scratching sounds from behind cupboard doors. I shivered from more than cold.

I moved quckly through the rest of the rooms, expecting nothing and finding it. There had been a woman in the place once, but not for years; she hadn't left anything but memories behind. There had been a cat once, too. What it had left behind was detectable best with the nose. There were drawers and closets and other secret places as well, but they could be left for later, for anyone who wanted to know why. I yielded the house to darkness and went outside and followed the driveway to the back.

The garage was blue, too, its door appropriately un-tracked and askew. A white wood stairway led up the side of the garage to a red door in the second story. The light over the door was burning. I climbed toward it, the white steps creaking beneath my weight. The paint on the step faces was chipped and faded and marred with black streaks. Three steps from the top I pulled my gun.

When I reached the door I stopped and listened, but heard nothing but my own body and, seemingly from directly beneath me, the froth and fury of an angered sea. I opened the door for me and my gun.

It was bright as day inside. The room was a studio, as Gwen had said, almost a duplicate of the one at Hazen's office except this one had a bed and dresser and wardrobe as well, along with an efficiency kitchen in the far corner. Hazen was there, standing with his back to me. From the smell of the place he had recently been welding yet an-other piece of captive metal. In light of what he had done in the past hour it made me all the more certain he was nuts.

When he heard me coming Hazen turned to face me, his eyes wide and feverish, his breathing labored—tubercu-loid. He started to move and I raised my gun, the memory of the welding torch hot in my brain. But all he did was walk over and sit on a gigantic steamer trunk, an antique from the look of it, and dangle his short legs down the side like a kid on the edge of a pool. One of his hands was red, badly burned. From the dance in his eyes it seemed possible he would no longer notice anything the rest of us could see. A half-full suitcase lay open on the floor beneath his feet.

"Going somewhere?" I asked pleasantly.

"Going?"

"The suitcase. The trunk."

"Yes. That's right. I'm going away."

"I'm going to have to stop you, you know. I'm going to have to call the police."

"Are there prowlers?"

"No. A murderer."

His eyes widened. "Who's been killed?"

"Max Kottle."

"Max. I know Max. He was my patient. Do you want to know something about Max?"

"What?"

"He's very wealthy. Millions and millions. Everything he touches turns to gold. Some men are like that."

"Yes."

"Everything I touch turns to mud. Do you know something else about Max Kottle?"

"What?"

"He's a bastard."

"Why?"

"Simple. With all that money he has, all those millions, he never once bought one of my sculptures. Not a one. What do you make of that?"

"It's terrible."

"It is, isn't it? Max deserves to die."

"He has died, Doctor Hazen."

"He has?"

"You killed him."

"I did?"

I took a deep breath and exhaled slowly and put my gun back in my pocket. Hazen's legs began to swing again, back and forth, back and forth, slamming heavily against the canvas sides of the trunk. His eyes seemed no longer linked to his brain. The song he was humming sounded like "Ramona."

There was a telephone over by the work table and I went to it and called the Central Station. Charley Sleet came on the line with a grunt. I told him where I was and who he would find when he got there and what he should do with him and why I wouldn't be around when he arrived. I assured Charley I'd be in his office first thing in the morning to explain it all. Charley grumped and growled and said he hàd a couple of stops to make first, but that he'd be there in a half hour. I told him that would be fine. Then I made another call.

I talked a little, then she talked a lot, then I talked a little more. She had a million questions and I only answered half of them. She wanted a lot more than I gave but I told her what she had was enough for the first installment. The Girl Reporter didn't like it, but I cut her off anyway and went back to Hazen.

He was sitting where I'd left him, apparently regressed even further into the misfortunes of his past. I took off my tie and fashioned a slipknot and put one end around his left wrist and knotted the other around his right, leaving six inches of the tie stretched in between. When I tugged,

Hazen obediently hopped down off the trunk and followed me over to the workbench. He sat down where I told him to and raised his hands when I told him to do that. After guiding the six inches of slack between the clamps of the vise I wound the screw as tight as I could. As though he were a boy with a bruise I patted his head and told him someone would be along soon to set him loose. I didn't tell him that same someone would also take him to jail. When I asked him about his burned hand he didn't seem to know what I was talking about.

I turned toward the door, then stopped. There was someone in it. He was as thin as straw, his face livid with barely governed rage and stiff with pain, his eyes sinking slowly into bone. His clothes were loose-fitting and comical, but there was nothing comical about what he carried in his hand. It was an M16, that slick piece of weaponry that seems so much like a toy—light and plastic, with an easy-to-carry handle—until you pull the trigger and in the next second it spits fifteen rounds of 5.56 millimeter ammunition at you with a muzzle velocity of three thousand feet per second. Then somebody dies or wishes he had.

Karl Kottle had his rifle trained somewhere between Hazen and me. He looked ready and able to use it. I yawned, from nerves.

Karl looked over the room, then did the same with me. "Who are you?" His voice was soft as down.

"Tanner."

"The man on the phone?"

"Yes."

"Is it true?"

"Yes."

"Even about my father?"

"Yes."

"Why? Why did he do it?"

"The fire. The girl who died was Hazen's patient. He'd cured her of cancer, using a new technique. Nixon was just cranking up his war on cancer, throwing money at everyone who had anything remotely promising going for him. The Luswell girl's death took Hazen out of the game; without money for further research he didn't have a chance. He was a man determined to make a big splash. He blamed you for draining the pool. You must have gone to see him for treatment sometime after that."

He nodded soberly. "I had a virus. I thought Doctor

Hazen would help me and still keep my whereabouts
secret, perhaps not from my father but from the authorities. He'd always seemed like a nice man. A concerned
physician."

"Hazen used that visit to begin inflicting punishment for
what you'd done. He gave you rat poison, Karl. One particular brand. It turned you into a diabetic. After that he
gave you enough insulin to keep you alive, along with
enough poison to keep the pain at maximum levels. Year
after year."

"He said I was getting better."

"All you were getting was tortured."

Karl let the gun muzzle drop toward the floor and it became a toy again and I could look elsewhere. Karl was
clearly struggling to grasp what had happened, to believe
that the agony he had endured was inflicted by the little
man on the floor by the workbench. He kept glowering at
Hazen, but Hazen was oblivious. "You know what?" Karl
asked finally.

"What?"

"I didn't even set that fire. I didn't have anything to do
with it."

"Who did?"

"It's not important, he's dead now. A few people used
the movement as an outlet for their own aggression. They
were only in it for the violence, just like the cops on the
other side of the barricades."

"Not all of them."

"A lot. Too many."

Karl looked down at his weapon as though surprised to
find it there, as though aware of how it undermined his
nonviolent stance. Then he looked over at Hazen again.
"Did he poison my father, too?"

There was a long answer to that and a short one. I gave
him the short one.

"Max was sick anyway, wasn't he? Cancer?"

"That's what Hazen said."

"If it was cancer, then maybe it was a favor. Maybe it
was an easier way to die."

"Maybe."

Karl couldn't take his eyes of Hazen. He was rapt, as
though entranced by a conjurer's indirection. "It's not the
pain I mind so much, you know," Karl remarked, almost
casually. "It's the time. He stole nearly five years from me.

Redirected my energies, my concerns. There was so much else I could have been doing."

"It's been a lost decade for all of us, Karl. No one did anything right in the seventies. In two weeks we get a new chance. Go away and get well. Come back and start again. You've got plenty of time. A lifetime."

"What about him?" He gestured to Hazen.

I shrugged. "Since he's a doctor his lawyer will be able to find lots of prestigious experts to say he's insane. Then after he's found not guilty by reason of insanity other experts will say he's been miraculously cured. But he'll spend a lot of time at Vacaville no matter what, in the wing for the criminally insane. You ever been to Vacaville?"

"No."

"Those poor bastards go to hell for a vacation."

"Can anything else be done?"

"One thing. I've already done it."

"What?"

"Called a reporter. The whole story will come out in the *Investigator*—Hazen, Greer, the kidnap, all of it. Hazen won't be able to put together a life no matter what happens in court."

Karl smiled sadly. "They've unsurped everything, haven't they?"

"Who?"

"The media. Even the system of justice has become irrelevant. The only thing that matters is what's printed in the papers or shown on TV. There's the real revolution. The media used to be for imagination—religion, myth, Howdy Doody. Now no one believes anything until they see it on the tube. Truth, morality, legality—they're all determined by people who don't have any obligation to anything but their own ambition."

"We've always been in the hands of people like that, Karl. The faces change, but they're the same people."

"No, they're not. Not all of them. I think maybe my father wasn't always like that."

"Maybe he wasn't," I said.

"Where is my father? His body?"

"I don't know."

"Why did Hazen kill him, too? Because of me?"

"I think it started that way. But it changed. Hazen came to resent your father's money, his success. Most of all, he couldn't stand having his artistic creations ignored by

someone who could do so much to make him a success.
I've seen it before. A man creates something and suddenly
his friends are reevaluated on the basis of how they like it.
It's not nice, but it's true."

No one said anything for a minute. The only sound was
the beat of Hazen's palm upon his thigh—regular, percus-
sive, mindless. Karl looked earnest and harmless, despite
the rifle.

"You know what your father took when the nausea got
too bad?"

"What?"

"Marijuana."

"You're kidding."

"Nope."

Karl smiled. "That's nice. That's really nice."

"You've got to get out of here, Karl. The cops are on
their way. If you stick around you'll be hauled in on a fel-
ony-murder charge for the Berkeley killing. Take off. Get
yourself well, then turn yourself in. They don't have much
of a case. A good lawyer will get the charge dumped, especially if you give him a crack at your father's will."

"What about my father? I should do something for him,
if only a gesture."

"Just do what I said. It's all he'd want."

Karl began to pace. "I need to think," he said. "I need
to decide what's right."

"Sure. Just do it somewhere else. If you don't leave now
you'll do your thinking in a cell."

Karl turned toward the door, then looked back at me.
"Would you do one thing? Would you ask the reporter at
the *Investigator* to print the manifesto I wrote? As long as
the whole story is coming out? It's an important statement.
The perspective is unique. I worked very hard on it. It
says things that need to be said."

"I'll do what I can. Sure."

I glanced over at Hazen to see if he was still secure. He
was staring at one of his sculptures and then at the trunk,
back and forth. The smile on his face was the smile he
was wearing the first time I'd seen him.

I looked at the trunk. It was a beauty. Leather, iron,
canvas, brass. There was something funny about it,
though. The locks and hasps were welded shut with shiny
new beads of metal. When I looked around at Karl he was
gone.

Suddenly I knew what was in the trunk. Worse, I knew that it wouldn't have been in there if I hadn't spooked Dr. Hazen, hadn't tried to take him alone. And then, God help me, I knew, or at least I needed very badly to believe, that there was a chance that what was in the trunk *was still alive.*

I hunted up a hammer and a sixteen common nail and drove the nail into the side of the trunk, then pried it out and drove it in again, and then again. I found a piece of paper and wrote Charley Sleet a note. I taped the note to the trunk and gave Hazen another pat on the head.

Then I went out to buy a tree.

About the Author

Stephen Greenleaf, formerly a lawyer from San Francisco, is now writing mysteries full-time. DEATH BED, Mr. Greenleaf's second book, was a Dual Main Selection of the Playboy Book Club, and GRAVE ERROR, his first novel, was a Mystery Guild Alternate Selection. Mr. Greenleaf now lives in Ashland, Oregon, with his wife, Ann, and his son, Aaron.

MURDER...
MAYHEM...
MYSTERY...

From Ballantine

Available at your bookstore or use this coupon.

____**DEATH IN A TENURED POSITION, Amanda Cross** 30215 2.25
The country's most prestigious university faces a scandal guaranteed to mar its
perfect reputation.

____**THE JAMES JOYCE MURDER, Amanda Cross** 30214 2.50
Mary Bradford had many enemies indeed, and one of them hated her enough to shoot
her...but who?

____**GRAVE ERROR, Stephen Greenleaf** 30188 2.50
The wife of a leading consumer activist is afraid her husband may be killed or blackmailed.

____**DEATH BED, Stephen Greenleaf** 30189 2.50
A typical missing persons case becomes woven with murder, kidnapping, disappearances and ends with a final gruesome twist.

____**THE OUTSIDE MAN, Richard North Patterson** 30020 2.25
The hot and steamy South inhabited by genteel wealthy people who sometimes have to
murder to protect what is theirs.

BB **BALLANTINE MAIL SALES**
Dept. TA, 201 E. 50th St., New York, N.Y. 10022

Please send me the BALLANTINE or DEL REY BOOKS I have
checked above. I am enclosing $ . . . . (add 50¢ per copy to
cover postage and handling). Send check or money order — no
cash or C.O.D.'s please. Prices and numbers are subject to change
without notice.

Name_____

Address_____

City_____State_____Zip Code_____
Allow at least 4 weeks for delivery.

TA-43